THE
FIRST
LOVE
MYTH

Casey Dembowski

The First Love Myth
Red Adept Publishing, LLC
104 Bugenfield Court
Garner, NC 27529
https://RedAdeptPublishing.com/

For my readers, who gave me the courage to take this one back out of the drawer

Chapter 1

Liz

Not Pregnant. Well, that's direct. Digital pee sticks give no fucks when it comes to a woman's emotions. There's no agonizing over whether that second line is there or not, whether the fact that it's your fifth instead of first pee of the day makes a difference. It's simple. Pregnant. Or Not.

I drop the test into the garbage pail and turn my back on it before slowly washing my hands. Now is not the best time to be pregnant. I know that. My husband fired his top account manager almost four months ago, and since then, his occasional business trips have turned into monthly outings. Julian hasn't traveled so much since our post-grad days. With film festival season coming up, it's exhausting. I can't imagine dealing with this while hormonal. What a disaster that would be. And yet disappointment weighs on me. I can't deny it. Will there ever be a right time for me and Julian? I bury the answer that's crawling its way to the surface. Just because we haven't found the right time yet doesn't mean it will never present itself. And maybe a surprise baby is exactly what we need to find the time—to put our family and our future above work and passions and every other thing we use to keep us from really trying.

Because sometimes, I want a baby so desperately it hurts. There was that miscarriage in our first year of marriage, and honestly, we weren't ready. But new birth control and poor timing and bad luck had other ideas, at least for a few weeks. After that, trying again didn't seem appealing. I wanted to bask in the honeymoon stage. Five years later, my biological clock is all but screaming at me. Not that I'm old at thirty-four by anyone's definition except my obstetrician's, but I can't shake the nagging feeling that maybe it isn't meant to be. Not me and Julian—the baby part.

Or maybe it's time to be a bit more proactive. I search for ovulation trackers on my phone. We agreed not to go overboard, to let this foray into family planning be casual—let's have a lot of sex and see what happens. It works for Julian, and I am by no means complaining. Our sex life hasn't been this good since the first months of our engagement. But it can't hurt to pay more attention to my cycle. It has never been normal. The negative test and my week-late period proves that. My doctor said I most likely don't ovulate when I'm supposed to, so knowing when I do could be quite beneficial. And it's not like I have to pee on sticks every day like my sister-in-law. I can plug in some data from my last periods and see when it's time to turn up the charm. No harm done.

Before I can even open the app store, Julian's photo pops up on my screen. I let it ring so I can stare at his photo for an extra second. It's my favorite shot of him. We're on our honeymoon, and he's happy and relaxed and sun-kissed. He's *my* Julian.

"Hey, babe," I say. He's supposed to be flying home today from a conference in St. Louis. The weather forecast was clear as of a few hours ago, but it's possible something cropped up.

"Are you home?" He sounds distracted, and the bustle of the airport crowds the line.

"I am."

"Perfect." The clatter around him quiets, and I know he's walked into a private area or lounge. "I need you to mail something for me today."

"Sure. Flight delayed?"

"Yeah, there's a gnarly thunderstorm happening right now." He pauses, and I hear a few key clicks from his laptop. "I got a day pass to one of the lounges while I wait."

"Your boss will love that." I walk out of the bathroom without another glance at the test. Tomorrow, I will go back to the tried-and-true pink lines. At least the anxiety comes with hope. I debate telling Julian about the test, but aside from the sex part, he's not particularly interested in the intricacies of conception. Sometimes I wonder how long it would take him to notice if I didn't get my period, if the lack of the tampon box would be a glaring admission or an oversight. "Long delay?" I ask when he doesn't respond to my quip about his employer.

"A few hours, maybe."

That's not too bad, considering. I stopped planning anything for Julian's homecomings after his first few trips since we inevitably fall into bed and miss our reservation.

I flip on the light in Julian's office. The room is familiar but distinct. This is his space. It smells like him and looks every bit the creative genius lair that it is. I can't remember the last time I came in here. Julian needs this space to shut out the rest of the world and delve into his fictional ones. It's a trait I learned to accept long ago.

"What am I looking for?"

Papers litter the surface, sticking out at weird angles in one section and neatly stacked in another. It isn't like Julian to be messy with his work or forget to drop something in the mail. An inkling of worry gnaws at me. I swallow it.

"It's an entry form for the Norfolk Screenplay Contest," he says, his voice perfectly normal.

Maybe the mess is just a mess, a consequence of his new schedule. Not everything means something deeper, I remind myself. I shuffle through the papers, finding only manuscript and screenplay pages, a few bills I hope he paid or we're about to be in big trouble, and a calendar.

"There should be a check clipped to it and a pre-labeled envelope."

My eyes hit on it as soon as he finishes his sentence. "Got it. I'll make sure it goes out today. Anything else?" I scan the calendar. It's small and not the notebook he uses to keep his travel schedule aligned with contest deadlines and festivals. There are only a few Xs in the last week of the month—almost a week's worth—and then an outlined star on one day and a colored star a few days later. I recognize the date that has the colored star but can't place it.

"Actually, if you don't mind, could you send me a few files while you're in there?"

I perk up at the request. Julian is so tightly wound he never lets anyone touch his work. He almost never works on his films outside of this office. It's his weird creative tic, and while it can be annoying, most of the time I love him even more for his passion.

A garbled voice sounds across the line, and Julian sighs loudly. I know I'm destined for a solo dinner now. Maybe I'll try that new place on Wilton Avenue or see if I can get a facial and pedicure at the spa. It's been ages since I treated myself, and something must be done about my cuticles before flip-flop season.

"Sure." I turn my attention to the computer. "Which ones?"

"Umm... The *Eternity* dailies for April 5?"

The folder for that film and date is huge. It was a full-day-and-night shoot. "All of them?"

"Nah, maybe the first twenty?"

I pull them into the file-transfer program I know he prefers. For a modern, tech-savvy marketer, Julian is oddly wary of the cloud.

"Oh," he says, his voice taking on a sheepish tone. "There's also an entry form on my desktop for submission to a festival. Can you email that to me?"

I scan the few files on the screen before I find it and pull it into an email. "What are you submitting this time?"

"*Cruises Are for Teenage Lovers*," he says, and he's obviously grinning on the other side of the line.

A blush creeps up my cheeks, taking the rest of my worries with it. *Cruises Are for Teenage Lovers* is the beginning of our story, literally. Julian used his skills to make a series of short films, each one highlighting a part of our life together. *Cruises* is the first film—my wedding gift—and tells the story of our first kiss on the deck of a ship. Nothing but ocean and stars and the wind surrounded us. I knew, even then, that my life would never be the same. Not in that teenage, awestruck, every-kiss-is-life-altering way but deep in my soul. He kissed me that night, and in that moment, I saw the future laid out in front of me, and even if I wanted to, I knew there was no going back. Julian Madden stole my heart with a single kiss.

I never knew how that night and that kiss felt to Julian. Not really. But *Cruises* told the story from Julian's perspective. And in his eyes, I was beautiful.

"Did you get the files?" I ask after refreshing his inbox for the second time. It's definitely in the sent folder. My eyes scan the page, narrowing at the email address—Madden.Julian@hotmail.com. Not his normal email address. Or his work email. Or any email I've ever seen before in my life.

"Yes." His answer comes slowly, too slowly. "Thanks, babe. I'll let you know when I board."

I hang up, and though I know it's wrong, I scan the contents of the sent folder. Every nerve in my body is on edge. My shoulders slump in on themselves, and I lean closer to the screen, as if he's going to walk through the door and accuse me of spying on him. This is all sorts of wrong. I don't snoop on my husband. *But he's never had an email address you didn't know about before,* the devil on my shoulder remarks. I shush her. Maybe he wanted to keep his professional and personal personas separate. Maybe he got tired of being confused for a woman with his Jules.Madden email. It is probably nothing. My head throbs a denial.

I click back to his inbox. There's an appointment reminder for Dr. Montague, our old marriage counselor. We haven't seen her in years. Counseling was my condition when Julian proposed. He had bailed on our relationship twice, more than that if you counted micro-breakups, and then after a year of silence, he showed up at my door with a ring.

The sessions weren't romantic, and at the beginning, I thought maybe they were showing us that we weren't meant to be together. But eventually, after a lot of honesty and tears, they brought us to a good place. Of course, no one knew we were in counseling. So our long engagement garnered a lot of attention and complaints. Our families and friends wanted to know when we were going to set a date after a month, three, six—it was unbearable. To everyone else, we have that movie love story, the fairytale, the rom-com. But a kiss and a doorway proposal don't fix a relationship. They don't atone for the betrayal of leaving in the first place. I smiled and nodded, and eventually, I started believing in the romance of it all too. Maybe we *were* fated. Maybe it was destiny. Didn't I know from that first kiss that there was no going back?

And now here I am clicking through every single email from this address. There are no promotional emails, the first giveaway that this is not a work or personal email replacement. The only emails are from Dr. Montague's office and someone named Sheila Sampson. My teeth spear my bottom lip, and an awful thought assaults my brain. Julian uses this address for emails he doesn't want me to see. *Fuck.*

I move the cursor to x out the window. I don't want to see this. If I close the window now, I can go about my day, and none of this is real. If I close the window now, we can go back to being the happily married couple trying to make another life.

But no. I can't close the window. I have to know. The most recent email is dated only three days ago. All the fucking fucks. Subject: *Going to ASMR?* That's where he is now, with a convenient flight delay. Email body: *Had a great time at SRC. Would love to see you in St. Louis.* I scroll to his reply. *Drinks Thursday night?*

I massage my temples. How is this happening? What is even happening? The emails might be a smoking gun, but they are hardly conclusive evidence. Before I can overthink it, I open the Weather Channel site and type in St. Louis—thunderstorms all day. My shoulders relax about a centimeter, but at least he isn't lying about the rain.

The search bar goads me now that I'm already prying into my husband's secret email. It begs me to find out how long Madden.Julian and ssampson123—that's really her email address—have been communicating. My fingers linger on the keys. Type. Delete. Type. Delete. Type. I hit Enter. A dozen or so—*fourteen*, my mind screams—pop up. They're spaced out over the last several months and cover almost all of Julian's trips. Their schedules aren't completely in sync, and they don't email outside of arrangements, which is really smart if you're having an affair. No paper trail, digital or otherwise. Disappointment washes over me. I want definitive proof either way. This sad collection of emails proves nothing and makes me feel like the bad guy.

I pull out the calendar I found earlier from its hiding spot. Why not? I'm already in too deep. The longer I look at it, the more the pattern emerges. I almost have it—all the dates seem familiar—but I can't touch the answer.

My phone rings, and I flail at the unexpected sound. Pete. My manager. *Oh, fuck.* Did I seriously lose an hour peeping on my husband and miss my most important meeting of the day? The meeting I'm supposed to be running.

I palm my face and hit the answer button. "Pete, I'm so sorry. Signing on now."

Chapter 2

Liz

The punching bag is hard beneath my knuckles. I should be wearing hand wraps, but at this moment I don't care. The longer I sat with the knowledge of Julian's *whatever*, the more I wanted to punch something. My hands are going to hurt in the morning, but if I don't hit the bag, I might punch Julian whenever he gets here. Sheila Sampson. Another account director. Yes, I LinkedIn'd the crap out of her. And not on private mode. Let her see her lover's wife perusing her profile. Let her feel the worry and unease that I've felt since I discovered my husband's secret email address.

I attack the bag with a jab and then an uppercut. I know enough boxing to get me through a Jillian Michaels workout and not break my wrist. Julian took it up shortly after we got married, at the suggestion of Dr. Montague. She felt he needed an outlet for his doubts. Of course, she probably meant biking, running, or an ultimate Frisbee club, but Julian picked boxing. I kick the bag, and a small scream escapes. All I ever did was love him. I kick again and follow it up with a one-two punch. Why isn't my love ever enough?

"Babe?" Julian's voice is loud over the sound of my very angry playlist.

I level another punch at the bag before turning to face him. Sweat drips down my face, and my breathing is ragged. A chill sweeps over me that isn't because of the arctic-quality air conditioner we keep down here. "Welcome home." I don't try to hide the rage simmering beneath those words.

"Are you okay?" He takes a step toward me and then, at the fire that must be seeping out of my eye sockets, seems to rethink it and falls back on his heels.

"Who is Sheila Sampson?"

His eyes widen before narrowing to slits. He crosses his arms and looks somewhere over my shoulder. His tell. What an idiot. "You read my emails?"

I don't flinch under his accusation. "Yes, Jules, I did. *Who is she?*" I repeat because he's clearly concerned about the wrong thing.

He steps back even farther at the change in my tone, his eyes staying glued to the floor. I resist the urge to wave a hand in front of his face and shout, "Hello!" I want to give him the benefit of the doubt, but I know my husband. I know him better than he knows himself. My anger is completely warranted. Because even if sex isn't involved, Dr. Montague is. And if Julian is talking to Dr. Montague, it means he's getting antsy. Again. Were his feet warm at any point in the last seventeen years?

"She's a friend," he says in a practiced, measured tone I've heard too many times before.

"A friend who has you contacting Dr. Montague? Who you created a new email to contact? Who drove you back to boxing?" That last part is an assumption, but the dead expression on his face speaks volumes. He's been boxing. He kept all those scheduled appointments. Julian has a business-travel lover. And it's killing him.

"It's not what you think." He runs a hand through his hair.

I bristle at the cliché and grasp the back of the couch, jaw clenched. "What am I thinking, Julian?"

"Fuck, Liz! Would you sit down and let me explain?"

I do not move an inch. My eyes bore holes into him.

He palms his face. "I will explain if you sit down."

I walk around the couch, feigning casualness, and turn at the end farthest away from him. I burrow into the arm of the couch. My heart races. I can feel it hammering in my chest, and yet, I'm weirdly calm. All the frustrations and worries and doubts of the last few hours evaporate. One way or another, I'll have my answer in the next minute.

"Let me start by saying this isn't some torrid affair," he says. When I glare at him, he coughs and holds his hands up. "Yes, we've met for drinks more than once, but until today, nothing physical happened."

"Until today." I clench my hands together. The feel of my nails biting into my skin alleviates some of the pressure building up inside me. *Today? Why the hell today, Julian? Before or after you realized I saw your secret email?* My stomach roils, and I will it to steady.

"She kissed me at the airport."

"Did you kiss her back?" A part of me still wants to know exactly when this happened, but that's not really the important piece of information here. And I can see in Julian's expression that he is already trying to figure out how to spin the story. *We're not having illicit sex, honey. We just like to stay up late and talk.* And true, a kiss is not sex, but it is most definitely still something, especially when you've been married for five years. How does one even go about getting into a situation that involves kissing while married?

"Do you remember what it was like when we were first engaged and I was traveling all the time? You would come with me whenever you could, and our whole life was a vacation? We were young and happy and hungry."

His words fall short of an apology or explanation. There's truth in them—we were all those things—but the angle is off. The period of time after we got back together and engaged in the same second was messy. We were trying to fix what Julian had so callously broken. Those trips were a blur. But the nights on the couch in *my* apartment—not ours, not yet—sharing popcorn and watching a movie, the entire day we spent moving Julian's stuff into the apartment, the hours of love we made afterward, all of that is as clear in my memory as if it happened yesterday. How is it that the trips were what mattered most to him? And how did I not know this?

"And then you got your promotion," he continues, "and the wedding was getting closer, and John told me he could move me into a more stable position in Parsippany. We found the house, and you were so excited to start our life together."

I remember saying those words. I remember the feeling of calm that washed over me as we drove past the sold sign in the yard. Quintessential suburbia seemed like such a big and necessary step.

"You were excited too," I say, my voice barely a whisper.

"Yes, I was. I still am. It's... I didn't even realize there was a problem until I started traveling again."

He continues to ramble, but I can't hear him anymore. *Problem.* The word hits hard. Yes, Julian entertaining thoughts of screwing someone else is a problem. A problem I thought lay with him—not with us, not with me. Why am I so fucking naive? This is the problem with marrying your first love. A part of you, no matter how small, still loves like a teenager.

"I didn't realize how boring—complacent—I'd become. Then the traveling started, and it was like... seeing clearly for the first time."

Wow. Julian only rolls out clichés like that when he's in a bad way. We may have a storybook romance, but he makes sure nothing in any of his films reads as cliché, sometimes painstakingly so. *Oh my god.* He's in love with Sheila.

"Because of Sheila?" I ask, my voice even despite the hurricane ripping apart my chest.

He looks at me, holding my gaze. "Because of me, and yeah, I guess, a little bit of Sheila."

I don't pull away when he grabs my hand, but I want to. His touch is like toxic sludge.

"My whole life I've never loved anyone but you. The times we spent apart... I always came back because it was you. You were the only woman I loved, no matter how hard my youthful rebelliousness tried to convince me otherwise. I'm not saying I'm in love with Sheila, because I'm not."

"But you felt something when she kissed you." I can barely get the end of the sentence out. Julian kissed another woman.

"Yes. And it scared the hell out of me."

I mentally compare the dates in the emails with other dates in our lives. "That's why you wanted to have a baby? Because you met Sheila?"

"Dr. Montague said it was an awful idea. That I'd only grow to resent you. But I had to do something, and I felt good about it at first. And then your period was late that one month, and I was scared in a completely different way."

The calendar from this afternoon flashes into my mind, the pattern finally coming together. Bile rises in my throat. My hands twitch in anger, and I yank them from his. Julian tracked my period. If I overlaid the new calendar with his travel schedule... he planned it. He kept us from getting pregnant on purpose. *Holy shit.* I have to confront him, but I can't. Not yet. I'm stunned into silence. The longer I stare at him, the more his face works. How many more truths will he unwittingly admit to? *Dig your hole deeper, husband.*

"I'm sorry, Liz," he says with feeling. "I don't know what else to say."

I love you would be a start, but I know, somehow, that it's not coming. I stand and walk back to the punching bag. I hit Play on the stereo and slip my hand guards on. At no point do I look at my cheating husband.

"You can sleep in the guest room," I say and then throw my first punch.

Chapter 3

Liz

Our bed hasn't felt as empty as it does now in all the time Julian was away. It's too cold without the comforter but stifling under it. My emotions boomerang between fury and melancholy and uncertainty. His absence weighs heavy in the air, and an unbearable ennui suffocates me. Both my options seem wrong—leave Julian or make it work. We've been here before, and I know deep in my soul that we will be here again. Julian will break us and fix us and break us until we're unfixable. But to him, we'll never be unfixable.

I toss off the comforter again. The chill from the air conditioner cools the burning in my cheeks. I swipe away a few tears and sigh as my eyes land on Julian's book and reading glasses. Every night for exactly twenty-five minutes, Julian reads. But tonight—the first night I've ever banished him to the guest room—the book sits unopened. An hour ago, the washer buzzed, so at least I know he's not sleeping in his travel clothes. Not that it would matter. I don't care if he's comfortable. He deserves much worse than the guest bed.

Standing up before I can decide otherwise, I grab his book and glasses and walk across the hall. The door is partially open, but I knock before entering. Julian lies across the bed, one hand cocked behind his hand, the other holding his phone. He squints up at it, trying to read, I assume. He hates reading on his phone. He must have finished whatever book he brought to St. Louis. The thought brightens my mood marginally. If he had time to finish a book, he didn't spend all his free time with Sheila.

"I brought your things."

He stares at me from his prone position, his body tense and rigid. "Thank you."

I hold the book against my chest like a shield. Tears dance under my eyelids. Even at our worst, we've always been comfortable with each other. The second the thought crosses my mind, I know it's not the truth, but there's never been a moment like this. Mainly because Julian never stayed around to have one. He leaves, and I pick up the pieces. He comes back, and I welcome him with wary-but-open arms. *Don't cry, don't cry.* For once, my body obeys.

Julian comes around the bed to stand in front of me. He stops a few feet away, his eyes downcast, arms crossed protectively across his chest. "Can I... Can we talk?"

I shake my head. "I don't think we can."

"Can you listen, at least? Please?" He says it in a pleading sort of way, and even though I'm tired of listening to him, I nod and sit at the edge of the bed. Nothing he says will make a difference. Not really. Julian will leave. If not right now, eventually. It's a truth I haven't considered in years. After the wedding and the miscarriage, he never wavered. *Until now.*

He takes the book and glasses from me and tosses them back toward his pillow. The glasses clink against the headboard, and I cringe at the sound.

"Those are new."

"They're fine." He links his fingers through mine.

The familiar tingle that accompanies his touch is still there. A shiver passes through me, and my insides rumble. My heart hiccups. All I've wanted for the last three days is his hands on me, his lips on mine... *Absolutely not.*

"I should go, Jules," I say, pulling my hand from his.

"I love you, Liz." It's a shout into the void that keeps me rooted in place. Finally, the words he should've said all night. "Those words don't even properly convey what I feel for you, but they're the best I have."

Untrue. There are at least seven films about our love on his computer. But I'll take the words. For now.

His eyes search mine. "That's why nothing happened with Sheila. Not because I was scared or because there wasn't the opportunity because, well, honestly there was. But I love you, and I vowed to love you forever. And I meant it."

He takes my hand again, and I allow it. Desire ripples through my body again, but it's different. It's not the ache of days alone but the overwhelming need to be intimate with my husband. To feel the connection he's desperately trying to save. It would be easy to jump into his lap and smother the rest of his speech with my lips, but I refuse to move. He deserves to grovel.

"I have no intention of breaking our wedding vows—any more than I know I did today—not tomorrow or next year or thirty years down the line. Everything I told you on that rooftop before our wedding still stands."

An odd memory to recall in this moment. He means it in a good way, and of course, our wedding is a marvelous blur of a memory. But that moment on the roof of the hotel where we had the wedding, when I was uncertain if Julian was planning on making the ceremony or slinking out into the night again, was awful. He's always claimed that he wasn't running or even thinking about it. That he simply needed a moment—several long moments—away from the cameras and the pressures and all of it. I chose to believe him then. I want to continue to believe him now.

"I choose you, Elizabeth Grace Madden. Always."

He kisses me then. It's not soft or slow or repentant. It's possessive and desperate and so hard that my entire body spikes to life, as if I've touched a live fuse. My fingers curl into his hair, and when he nudges me back onto the bed, I let him. I should stop this. It's a mistake. His lips touched someone else's only hours ago. But I can't. I love him. I've always loved him.

He hovers above me, eyes darkened with passion and his desire obvious where our bodies touch. "God, Liz. I love you so freaking much."

I freeze at his words. They aren't helping. No, if he talks, I'll remember why we're making up. If we're even making up. This isn't like any make-up sex we've had before. It's better, which leads me to believe that things are much worse than they've ever been.

I hold a finger to his lips and pull him down to me. "No more talking."

As I watch the sky darken, all the emotions of the past several hours crash down on me. Having sex made everything worse. I knew it would, but I hoped that maybe we would come out of it reconnected. Instead, desperation wafts off me, left behind from every touch and kiss. Julian clung to me, pulling me closer and deeper, moving our bodies as one until we exploded together. Desperation that deep isn't connection—it's goodbye. Julian is again fighting whatever part of himself refuses to let him stay with me. He lost the battle at eighteen and again at twenty-four. We were kids then, playing at love, and I overlooked the flaw. I demanded he make recompense, fully knowing that I would always take him back. But we're not kids anymore. The stakes are higher, the break more complicated. That's why it's taken so long for him to succumb, but he will succumb. This time, I will be the one to go.

My hands shake as I grip the doorknob. Julian is the love of my life. And tonight, I will leave him so that he can't leave me again. I'll break my own heart to save it. Sitting around and waiting to be left isn't an option, not now after all these years and all we've been through. Not when he kissed another woman and lied to me and hid things and plotted. A resolve builds in me. This is about much more than Sheila Sampson and an airport kiss.

Ten minutes later, I'm still sitting in the driveway. My resolve hasn't wavered, but I've spent too long in a storybook romance, and this is exactly when the sign appears. The small or big thing that makes me stay—Julian running out of the house, a meaningful and relevant song coming on the radio, a perfectly timed phone call that makes my troubles seem trivial. But nothing presents itself. With a last look at our house, I pull out of our driveway and say goodbye to the last seventeen years of my life.

Chapter 4
Liz

Things look just as murky in the morning, the truth more glaring in the sunlight streaming into my hotel room. I left my husband. Based on the ten missed calls on my cell phone, he noticed. As has his twin sister and my best friend, Jane. Jane and I met on the same cruise where I met Julian. And like Julian and me, we haven't looked back since. We were college roommates, sorority sisters, and traveled together after graduation. Our friendship has more than survived my relationship and its breaks. Jane was the one who always put me back together. Except this time, she can't. Jane was there for all the heartbreak Julian caused, but when he slid that ring on my finger, she made her allegiance clear. If I ever broke her brother's heart, and not the other way around, she would pick Julian. In the same breath, she told me *not to marry him*. Julian has no idea about any of this, so it's not surprising that he would assume the first person I would turn to would be my best friend and that, of course, Jane would give me refuge.

I lift the lid on the room service that I ordered for much too early in the morning. The pancakes look divine, and I'm glad my pitying self won out over sensible me when I ordered last night. The last thing I can stomach right now is egg whites. I barely slept, my mind is reeling, and the tears are flowing. The knowledge that I don't know where to go is sinking in. My West Dover friends are an option, but too many of them are joint friends—our couple friends—and they don't know the history, not really. I am not ready to tell my mother, and my older sister, Cecilia, lives halfway across the country. Jane is obviously out of the question, leaving me with one option. I really don't want that to be my only option.

I scroll through my contacts until I find my father's number. I haven't called him in months. Daughter guilt sets in. We're not particularly close, but we generally keep in touch on a somewhat regular basis. We aren't at the perfunctory calls on birthdays and holidays stage or anything. But with my younger half sister, Zoey, away at college, the reasons to call have been fewer and far between. And my dad is not good on upkeep either. He probably hasn't realized it's been a few months. And even if he has, he won't hold it against me.

My dad answers on the first ring. "Lizzie?"

I bristle at the name. He is the only one allowed to call me that, and even then, I don't like it.

"Hi, Dad."

"Everything okay?" he asks, using that preternatural sense he's always had. My whole life he would walk into my room the moment I was about to lose it. He'd lean against my door jamb, an innocent look on his face. *Everything okay, Lizzie?*

"Well," I say, feeling a bit more confident in my decision, "I need someplace to stay for a few... for a while."

"Trouble in paradise, honey?" His tone is casual, but there's an undertone of concern there. There always is when we're talking about Julian. I've often wondered what my dad thinks of him, what he saw when he looked at Julian throughout the years. I've always been too afraid to ask.

"*Dad.*"

"You can stay for however long you need. You still have your key?"

Two hours and a sick day request later, I stand in front of unit 509 in Ardena Gardens. It's one of those townhouse communities, the ones my mother helped take over Ardena and all the surrounding towns over the last twenty years, making affordable bedroom communities even more affordable. My dad moved to Ardena early in my senior year of high school after it came to light that he had a two-year-old daughter with his TA. Zoey—said illegitimate daughter and my half sister—was left with dear old Dad to his complete and utter shock when her mother decided to join the Peace Corps. For real. Zoey's arrival threw all our lives into chaos, to say the least. To my mother's credit, she did try to get past the cheating and the child—Zoey *was* adorable—but in the end, it was too much. My dad moved into a townhouse thirty minutes east with Zoey, and they've been there ever since.

The townhouse is quaint, and while the space never felt like home to me, it's better than if he lived alone in a dingy apartment on the other side of town. The situation might not have been ideal, but seeing both my parents thrive in their new lives made the transition better. It helped that Julian lived in the next town over. My dad's place became a sort of haven for us that first year after they separated. My mom didn't say much about it, which as an adult, makes me wonder exactly what she thought about it. But my sister Cecilia was vocal enough for both of them. She cut our father out of her life after the divorce and thought I should as well. Cecilia refused to get to know our sister, a sad truth that extends through today.

I fish around inside my purse for the Rutgers lanyard I've kept the house key on since high school. My dad will be on campus for several more hours. He spends every summer doing research and writing papers, often traveling to other schools in-country and out. Sometimes Zoey goes with him. Other times, she spends the summer with her mother, who returned from the Peace Corps and promptly moved three states away. How Zoey ever forgave her for leaving in the first place is beyond me. But I know she has.

Inside, the townhouse looks like it always does. The living room is fairly clean, considering, but evidence of research papers and stacks of books are littered around the space. Zoey's running shoes sit by the door. Her keys are in the tray. She isn't supposed to be here. My dad said something about work orientation, but he must have been wrong. I follow the low tones of Wilderness Weekend—Zoey's favorite band—to her room. The door is mostly closed, but I use the sliver as an invitation to enter with only a perfunctory knock.

Halfway through the door, I come to a screeching halt. I shield my eyes, but the sight is burned into my retinas. Zoey and her boyfriend—ex-boyfriend, last I'd heard—covered by a sheet but clearly entangled and naked. I peek through the space between my fingers. Zoey stares at me with practiced annoyance. Andrew is detached like the asshat he is.

"You remember Andrew?" Zoey asks in a tone much too calm for this situation.

Remember him? Yes, I remember him. I also remember how they broke up because Zoey walked in on him sleeping with one of her best friends—except they weren't *sleeping*.

Anger rises in me. Who does this boy think he is? I feel righteously angry for all the teenaged girls who believe in the power of first love, who can't let the boy go. For the girls like me. Where would I be if I had let Julian go?

I pull myself to my full height—all five feet six inches of me—and give them my best imitation of a stern parent. "I expect you both downstairs in less than five minutes." I step back toward the door, pausing on the way out. "Do not make me come back here."

Chapter 5
Zoey

I watch my sister pace the length of our living room as I pull my hair back into a ponytail. Andrew practically ran out the door after Liz's interruption, so I'm well within her five-minute deadline. From this vantage point, with worry lines etched onto her face, Liz looks like Dad, which is not something that happens often given how much she takes after her mother. I should go to her, but there's something off about Liz. The first thing being that she's in my house. Sister or not, Liz hasn't been in this house in a year. The second thing is that, sure, this situation is awkward, but does it really warrant pacing? I mean, it's not like she caught us in the middle of the act or even saw anything uncouth. We were completely covered.

I clear my throat and step fully into the room. "Here I am as you demanded."

Liz stops midstep and turns to me. She's pale and not wearing any makeup. Her hair is in a messy bun. And her eyes, usually the same vibrant hazel as mine, are dark, and wide, and frantic. I swallow the rest of the sass I intended to give her. There might be more than a dozen years between us, years that can feel like an uncrossable chasm full of triggers and land mines and other people's opinions, but I know my sister. I spent a lifetime studying her, sometimes wanting to be her and sometimes wishing she'd walk away and leave me be. Something is wrong. Something more than the shock of finding me in bed with my ex-boyfriend.

Her eyes find mine, and when she speaks, her voice is barely above a whisper. "You got back together with him?"

I flinch at the question, at the implication that I have any choice in the status of my relationship with Andrew. As if I'm the one who is keeping us apart. I wish I could say yes. Yes, I took back my cheating boyfriend because he is repentant and he loves me. Despite the tone of her inquiry, Liz wouldn't judge me for that choice. She of all people might be the only one who could possibly understand why I would go back to Andrew. She's been here. Not exactly here, no, but close enough. Liz and Julian were on-again, off-again for so long until they tied the knot. And every time he came back, she accepted him. I want to be able to say yes, but I'm not ready to follow through on that lie, to deal with the emotional torture it would bring.

I shake my head. "We're not back together."

"Jesus." Liz rubs her temple. "How long has this been going on?"

My mind goes back to the night a month ago when it all started. Becca dragged me to a party, declaring that there was no way I was hiding out all summer. Andrew and Claire would not win. So I went to the party, and in true friend fashion, they handed me from person to person until the party started to wind down and those left were paired off.

Andrew found me sitting by the edge of the pool, my feet dangling in the cool water. He sat down too close for our lack of relationship. Andrew knocked his shoulder into mine and then leaned down and kissed the bare skin there. His smile was lazy but real. This was the boy I loved, not the cold stranger he'd been since I found him in bed with one of my best friends weeks earlier. He whispered words of reconciliation and regret, and my heart, still bleeding out, accepted them. My brain knew he didn't mean them, not really. Maybe he did miss me and wish I didn't hate him. In the morning light, sober, he wouldn't feel that way. But my brain stopped being in charge the moment his scent hit my senses. When he brushed my hair behind my ear and cupped my cheek, I let him. And when his lips grazed mine, I leaned in. And when I saw Claire watching us, an awful idea took shape, and I knew, no matter how stupid it was, I was going to go through with it. Because, like Becca said, Claire didn't get to win.

"How long, Zoey?"

Liz's voice pulls me back to reality, and I shake off the memory and the pain. I try not to think about that night or any of the nights that led to it. The only way to get through this *affair*, or whatever the hell it is we're doing, is to not examine it too closely. Sleeping with Andrew is stupid and risky, but having any part of him is better than being without him. Acid rises in my throat at my own thoughts. *Pathetic.*

Frustration, pity, and anger war in my veins as a flush creeps up my body. This is none of her business. "Why does it matter?"

Liz opens her mouth as if she's about to protest but throws her hands up in frustration and sits down in a huff in Dad's favorite chair. She hugs her knees, her eyes locked on mine. "How can you even look at him?"

I sit down across from her on the couch and clasp my hands in front of me. *Because I still love him.* The answer comes automatically, as if her question isn't rhetorical. *I don't know how to be without him.* These are such unhealthy answers. Ones I should be sharing with my therapist. But I can't say those words out loud. I can barely think them without wanting to melt into a puddle of tears on the floor. Because *I* still love him, but *he* doesn't love me. I know that rationally. But when he texts me to come over, when he says my name the way he always has, when his lips touch mine and the world feels right again, the rational part of me falls quiet. The overly emotional, lovesick part claims that if nothing else, I'm winning. If Andrew is sleeping with me, he's not sleeping with Claire. That is my only rule, and despite what happened this spring, I believe he won't break it.

"I have to get ready for orientation." I tear my eyes away from Liz's gaze. I don't want to know why she looks frazzled or why I'm almost certain her question wasn't rhetorical. The reasons might tear apart the fragile belief I still have in first love. That Andrew and I will get through this and find our way back. I know it can happen. The proof is sitting in front of me. Except right now, Liz doesn't look like proof. She looks like a rebuttal.

Liz blinks, and her face pulls itself back together. Her eyes return to normal size, and the creases in her forehead smooth. She unclasps her hands and fiddles with her phone. If she smiled, she would be the big sister that I know and love. But she doesn't smile.

"Are you going to tell Dad?" I ask, getting my priorities straight. Dad and I have a good thing going, mutual respect of a father and his almost-adult daughter living together for the summer. Andrew in my bed as opposed to any other guy will most certainly destroy that comfort.

Liz eyes me, as if taking my measure. She seems more herself each second, the shock of my situation with Andrew having worn off. After an extra second, she shakes her head. "No, I'm not going to tell Dad."

Chapter 6
Zoey

As I sit parked outside the high school, halfway between the building and the track, a million memories come back to me. All good, mostly happy, but no longer rose-colored. Too many feature Andrew, even more Claire. I try to separate how it ended from the rest because I was happy in high school. The Zoey Reid I was at Ardena High had it all figured out. She'd found her place and her people. She had plans and dreams and hopes. That's what I miss most, what I thought my life would be. The Zoey Reid I am now is treading water, if only to keep from drowning. My legs are getting tired.

Would it be this hard if I was still at Bellewood University rather than in this small town? Andrew and I going to college together was a natural decision. And when Claire's top-choice school was across town from Bellewood, college life was looking up. I would have my boyfriend with me and my best friend close enough. Security and room to grow. It was more than I could've hoped for. Except now, there isn't a single place in my life that doesn't have an attachment to Andrew. Memories of him are everywhere, big and small and in between. A ripple of fear rips through me. What will happen when we go back at the end of summer? There's no way I'm leaving Bellewood. It's my favorite place to be, and I have friends and sorority sisters and a life there outside of Andrew. I won't be alone. I'll have all the support I need. But I'll also never be truly free of him—or her. Will our summer activities extend into the semester? Or will all the reasons that led Andrew to stray push him further away than ever?

I stare at the track, pushing back the panic. I know better than to spiral like this, particularly before work. I blink back a few tears and survey the small-but-growing crowd. Ardena Heat Summer Camp is where you hone your skills, and once they are honed, it's where you work for the summer, training the next batch of Ardena Eagles. Volleyball, football, track, field hockey, swim—whatever you're good at, we'll make you better, whether you're ten years old and hoping to get into a sport before modified teams start in middle school or sixteen and vying for an early call-up to varsity.

As I get closer to the field, my eyes take in this summer's staff. It's a good bunch, though I'm the only graduate among the group. I spot the guy with the clipboard. He's young and athletic and immensely good-looking. *Interesting.* I hadn't expected Coach Evans to be in charge. He started my senior year as the assistant varsity football coach. He also taught a freshman course, but I'm not sure what. His arrival was the talk of the school. We didn't often get teachers fresh out of college and not ones who had jawlines to rival Ryan Gosling's.

"Hi, Coach Evans." I push my sunglasses on top of my head. He might not recognize me either way. We didn't interact much before I graduated.

He eyes me for a moment but does not consult his list. "Reid, right? Singer's girlfriend?"

Correction. We didn't interact much outside of football events. I force a smile to my lips. "Ex, now."

"Ah, sorry."

I shrug. It's not the first time that has happened, and in a town like Ardena, it won't be the last. "It's fine, Coach."

"Just Max now." He smiles, and his beautiful face becomes even more beautiful.

I blink a few times, and I feel the corners of my lips quirk up though I made no conscious decision to smile. A buzz runs through my body, and I want to shake it out, but that would be weird.

"Okay, Max," I say, still off-kilter.

Max definitely notices. He drops the smile and focuses on the clipboard. He points toward the far end of the field. "Track and field is over on the ten-yard line. I'll be there once I check in the rest of the staff."

I do a double take and stop midstride, literally snapping back out of motion. "You're heading up track and field?"

He looks up, and whatever passed through me is already quelled. I'm not sure if I'm happy about that or immensely disappointed. Maybe both.

"Yes," he says. "It made the most sense after Coach McCloughan went over to Mansfield."

"He did not!" I can't help the louder-than-necessary volume or the shock and betrayal in my voice. Some things are ingrained in you when you go to Ardena, and a hearty dislike of Mansfield Prep, the private school on the other side of town, is one of them. Not to mention I'm completely aghast that this piece of AHS athletics gossip hasn't found its way to me. It totally trumps my triangle with Andrew and Claire.

Max laughs, and an inkling of the attraction returns. He's never had this effect on me before. I mean, I noticed him—I was off the market, not dead—but not in a legs-quaking sort of way.

"I can't say I mind too much," he says.

"Oh?"

Before he can answer, he's hailed by the group of new arrivals—the junior football staff and his former team. They bellow his name and crowd us, pulling him in for those man-hug things. I step back. I know these guys. They were sophomores when I graduated, all vying to replace Andrew as quarterback, but I'm not part of this moment. They barely notice me.

With a last look at Max, I slip away to the quiet side of the field and the junior staffers who were my campers only the summer before.

No one tells stories about the thirty-yard line. The end zone, the fifty, sure, but the thirty is any other marker. Close enough for a good kicker to score but far enough away that nothing is guaranteed. No one tells stories about the thirty-yard line except me.

I lie there now, my knees bent, my arm slung across my face shielding the sun. Orientation ended a while ago, but several staffers are still on the other side of the field. I remember being one of them last summer—loitering in the parking lot, goofing off, making plans. There are girls I know over there, but I'm not sure I can handle any more side-eye and whispers. The sound of feet on the track calms me. Coach Evans—Max—and some of the football guys are running laps. I'm tempted to join in, if only because I'm faster than all of them, but the thirty-yard line is undeniable. I'm pulled from the hot June day to the brisk chill of an October night. Homecoming confetti dots the length of the cleat-torn field, and the smell of concession-stand cookies mingles with the salty scent of sweat. Andrew and I walk the yard markers like balance beams until we round the corner on the far-side thirty-yard line, and then he kisses me for the very first time.

The memory is so vivid I can almost smell the cookies and sweat, feel the brisk air on my arms. But it's not that night. We're not at the beginning. We're well past the end. I pull out my phone as a distraction. I know what awaits me—a missed call from Becca, a bucket of texts from Haley begging me to save her from the tedium of Ohio, and zero communication from Andrew. He's all sweet words and naked rendezvous and then deafening silence until his libido kicks back in. I'm such an idiot.

I open Haley's novel of messages and read through the texts, her distress and humor brightening my mood. Thank god for roommates who understand. I'm about to respond to one of her many pleas when a shadow falls over me.

Max stands above me, an amused smile playing across his face. "Comfortable down there, Reid?"

I roll my eyes even though they're covered by sunglasses. It helps me vanquish the uncontrollable urge that cuts across my body whenever Max graces me with a smile, which happens a lot. Because apparently, he's a happy guy.

"Quite, actually." I'm pleased to find my voice sounds normal.

He reaches a hand down to help me up. I really don't want to get up, but I grab his hand and let him pull me to my feet.

"What's up, Coach?"

"Max," he says firmly.

"Right. How can I help you, Max?" It's still weird, but there could be benefits to being on a first-name basis with the hottest guy in town.

He shifts his weight and runs a hand through his hair. Is he nervous? Do I make him nervous? Or am I misreading this and I'm about to be fired? No, that can't be. I'm literally the only senior staff for all of track and field.

"Do you want to get lunch?" His voice is steady but tentative.

Did he... No, he couldn't be asking me out on a date. Not directly after Camp Director Larry spent ten minutes talking about the no-dating "suggestion" that no one enforces, specifically because half the staff is already dating. Not to mention Max mistakenly identified me as Andrew's girlfriend only an hour ago. And he has yet to use my actual name.

"To talk strategy and such," he adds quickly, and I wonder what my face is doing.

"Strategy," I repeat wryly.

He nods. "You're the only senior coach for track. I'm going to need you, Reid."

Reid. So not a date. A weird feeling washes over me. I'm disappointed. It might've been nice to give Andrew some competition. But more than that, I'm overwhelmingly relieved it's not a date. I really don't want to explain the Andrew situation. *Sorry, I'm currently in a sex-ship with my ex—your former player—so my treacherous best friend can't get back into his bed, and maybe he'll realize he does indeed love me. So while I'm single, I'm really not available.* How is this my life?

"Can we do this tomorrow?" I ask, thinking of the missed call from Becca. "Or the next day? Or in, like, the thirty minutes before the campers arrive on the first day?"

"Heading out of town until right before camp starts," he says with a shrug.

"The thirty minutes before the campers arrive on the first day, then?"

He laughs. "Come on. Pizza's on me."

Well, that makes it a simple choice. To a poor college student, time is pizza.

"Fine," I say, starting across the field. "But we're going to Nonna's."

Max stops in front of an older-model, two-door Audi. It's in impeccable condition and bright red.

"Didn't see you as a red person," I tease. It's clear that what I really mean is *how is this your car?*

"It was my dad's midlife crisis car," he says, getting in. When I'm secured in the seat next to him, he faces me. "He gave it to me when he knocked up his new wife with twins."

Can you knock up your wife? I refrain from asking but barely. "His loss is your gain."

"That it is, Reid."

"Zoey," I say. "If I have to call you Max, then you have to call me Zoey."

"That's fair," he says, and I think, though I can't be sure considering we've been outside for over an hour, that his cheeks turn a brighter shade of red. "I'm excited to work with you this summer, *Zoey*. I really couldn't believe it when I saw your name on the list."

My cheeks burn. Why is he excited to work with me?

"Wasn't aware you knew who I was. Outside of Andrew's girlfriend, I mean," I deadpan.

"I *am* sorry about that," he says. "Your reputation precedes you."

"Come again?" I cut him a look, my brow crinkling in confusion.

He laughs, but it's a laugh like *of course you have no idea what I'm talking about when it is perfectly obvious.*

"It's not often you get to have your team train with a three-time state record holder."

"Oh." That. Right. I sink back in my seat and watch the scenery change from suburban developments to shore bungalows. Max turns up a song on the radio and sings along. He's calm and collected. This is a work lunch with a talented colleague. No big deal. And, of course, that's what this is. Max is being friendly. He needs me to help him cultivate a winning track team. And yet, there's still something there in flashes and moments. It's not only because he's hot. Though he is. So. Hot. And for the briefest moment back on that field, I felt something I hadn't felt in months—possibility. Maybe there's still a chance for me.

My phone buzzes in my hand. I sneak a glance at Max before looking down at the screen. Andrew Singer.

Chapter 7

Liz

Seven. Eight. Nine. Ten. Downward dog extended into pigeon. *Ouch.* I readjust my front leg, and the stretch feels less like death. I lean forward, but my hip protests, and I straighten. When did I get so old?

"That is the worst pigeon I've ever seen." Zoey stands in front of me, her arms crossed. She examines the pose with the careful eye of someone who knows what she's talking about when it comes to yoga. "It *is* supposed to be pigeon, right?"

"Yes." I narrow my eyes at her. "You do yoga?"

Why does everyone in my life do yoga? It's not even fun. And it hurts. But both my mother and Cecilia go to classes at least once a week. Jane goes three times a week. Even Julian does a short flow each morning.

Zoey sits down in front of me, her eyes still critical. She stacks her legs in a pose called fire log, her knees resting flat against her feet. "I'm a runner. Of course I practice yoga."

I stare at her, the resemblance to Cecilia in both appearance and word choice making me momentarily forget the tangled knot I'm in. Wistfulness slams into me. I wish I wasn't the only connection between the two. I want to capture this moment, send it to Cecilia, post it with some cheesy hashtag and a picture of both of them doing the same thing. But Cecilia will not appreciate any mention of Zoey.

And to do that to Zoey is cruel. It's not her fault our sister has held this grudge her whole life.

Zoey's face relaxes, and the resemblance fades. "Do you need help getting out of that?"

I glare at her before lifting up and uncurling my leg from under me. I pray to all the gods that I do not fall before I make it back to downward dog and stand up. But no such luck. I roll onto my back, my hands flat at my sides.

"This is definitely more my style," I say, staring at the ceiling. Out of the corner of my eye, I see Zoey smile and switch her left leg to the top, her knees still easily sitting on top of her ankles. "Show-off."

She grins. "You're supposed to close your eyes."

I grumble but close them regardless. I take stock of my body, and my hips do feel better, so bad or not, the yoga worked. Hopefully, it keeps working if I'm going to be spending my days in the office again. It's been years since I had to regularly visit the office. I don't even have an assigned cubicle. When I do go in, I generally squat in a conference room for the day. But this morning, my skin literally itched with anxiety. I had to get out after too many days sitting in my father's house, worrying over my life decisions, including the one that led me to even be staying with my dad.

For the last seventeen years, there's been a divide in my family—in my life, really—between Reid Family A and Reid Family B. Family A is my mom and Cecilia, my core unit, the family that survived after my dad's affair. Family B is my dad and Zoey. The lines only blur at *my* life events. And even though I'm part of both families, I've never felt fully part of my dad and Zoey's unit. A fact that becomes more glaring after an extended period of time with them. They understand each other, their whims and tics and nuances. Zoey doesn't push his buttons. Our dad allows her to grow with only gentle oversight. His oversight was far more heavy-handed when Cecilia and I were teens—the arguments over boys and curfews reaching ear-bursting levels in Cecilia's case. I wonder if that would've been the case for me had he not screwed up so monumentally. Zoey and Dad seem to glide past each other, and in doing so these last few days, they've glided past me.

"Do you need something?" I ask with my eyes still closed. "Or are you here to mock me? Because you are seriously killing my flow."

"You can't flow in savasana," she mutters. "And you are the one sprawled out on the living room floor."

I laugh at the affronted tone of her voice. "This is the only room besides the kitchen with enough space."

The *guest room* I currently inhabit is a cluttered office space where I can barely find the floor.

"Dad called," Zoey says, as if it's natural to mention this. As if we cohabitate all the time. "He's going to be holed up in the library most of the night."

"So, like normal," I say.

Zoey doesn't smile at the joke. Apparently, our teasing doesn't extend to our dad. "I was going to get takeout," she says, her jaw still tight. "Do you want anything?"

I force myself not to roll my eyes. The two of them are awful about cooking. Zoey is capable of making the basics. She and Becca were cooking grilled-cheese sandwiches on Saturday night, well after midnight. They both smelled like beer, but at least she wasn't with Andrew. I took it as a win.

"I cooked, actually." I pull myself up into a seated position. "It's simple Crock-Pot chicken tacos, but it should last a few days."

Zoey lights up—I have seriously never seen her not hungry—and makes for the kitchen. She glances at the old and flowery Crock-Pot, straight out of a grandma's house. "So that's what that is."

I roll my eyes. *Teenager.*

"I used to hide bad report cards there."

"They were still there." I motion toward the yellowed stack of papers in the corner. "On what level do those count as bad report cards?"

If she hears me, she doesn't respond. Her head is practically in the slow cooker.

We sit down to a dinner of tacos, instant rice, and fresh avocado. Zoey chatters the whole time about her day, her friends, her freshman year—always skirting around Andrew and Claire. I've always felt like I knew Zoey well. While we aren't the closest of sisters, that's not unexpected with the age gap and family drama, but we have our own type of bond. I make a point to be around and to include her in all my life events, which isn't always easy, but Zoey is my sister. My dad claimed her, kept her, loved her. So I did too, without question. But listening to her talk now, I realize how distant I've been since she went to college.

Zoey is reaching for her third taco when her phone buzzes on the table next to her. Her eyes narrow at the text. *Andrew.* It's obvious. Zoey reacts hyperbolically to most texts from her friends. When it's her mom or our dad, she often answers out loud in sarcastic tones—much more with her mom. She leaves her phone lying around. She texts openly. But sometimes, like now, she goes quiet. Her phone stays angled toward her, her face goes all hard, and she worries at her bottom lip.

"Becca wants me to meet her for coffee." She lies so easily that it makes me wonder what else she's lying about. "She probably wants to talk about Ben. Again." She rolls her eyes. "They need to do it already."

I laugh loudly, her honesty catching me off guard. Adults don't talk about virginity and sex lives much, at least not the married variety.

"If you need a save," I say after her face scrunches at another message, "you can tell Becca I'm forcing you to spend time with me."

Please don't go to him, I send silently and hope she hears me anyway. "We could watch Jules's latest movie?"

The offer slips out before I even think about it. I've barely said Julian's name since arriving. But the night feels so normal, like this is some summer vacation and not my life falling apart. Neither Zoey nor my dad even know why I'm here, not fully. But saying Julian's name didn't elicit the awful ache in my chest I expected. I'm not apathetic, but I should feel something beyond weariness that my sister might now inquire why I'm really staying at her house.

Zoey smiles, though her eyes remain on her phone. "That actually sounds really fun. Can we do that tomorrow night? If I don't talk Becca through the losing-her-virginity panic, she might explode."

"Right, well, have fun," I say, a bit disappointed to lose my companion for the evening. "Be safe and all that."

"Yes, there's sure to be lots of danger at Ardena Café," she says with an eye roll before bringing her plate to the sink. "Can you tell Dad I'll be home late and that I'll text him if I decide to sleep over?"

I haven't even finished cleaning the table before Zoey's slipping on sneakers and rummaging through her tote bag for her keys. My eyes stay trained on the task at hand. If I stop moving, I might be tempted to tie her to a chair until she listens to some sense. But I know girls like Zoey—I *was* a girl like Zoey—and she isn't ready for sense. When she is, I hope it's not too late for her heart.

Slipping a plate for my dad into the fridge, I retreat to the living room. What does late mean to my dad now? When I was young, he could get lost for days working on a paper. I would steal downstairs to wheedle a late-night snack out of him when I was a kid, get him to help me with social studies homework in middle school, and join him working until all hours in high school. His dedication is impressive, but it's also always worried me. Everyone needs sleep. My mother is ambitious, but my dad is passionate. By twenty-five, he'd graduated law school, passed the bar, and been hired as an associate. After five years, he stepped into academia and never looked back, not even when he had to raise a third child on his own. Maintaining this house and raising Zoey couldn't have been easy on a professor's salary.

Sometimes, I wonder if that's what drew me to Julian. Julian is as passionate about filmmaking as my dad is about law and as frenetic. I'm drawn to that energy, maybe because I don't have a passion of my own. I love my job as a creative project manager at a marketing firm. I'm good at it. But it's not a passion or a craft. Yes, I come home some days flush with excitement at an ad slogan I nailed or a client meeting I rocked, but nothing at my job has ever captivated me the way a folder of film dailies captivates Julian. Nothing has motivated me to train the way Zoey did to become the most formidable track star Ardena had seen in a decade. Nothing has inspired me to regularly stay late at work the way my father does. He still isn't home despite the darkening summer sky.

Against my better judgment, I open my laptop and navigate to Julian's website, where our whole life is laid out in short vignettes. Will this summer be here one day? Will his shorts paint a bigger story that eventually becomes a movie? Could I be forced to watch myself fall in and out of love with Julian Madden alongside a global audience? *Who sits next to me in that future?*

My phone buzzes, and I know without even looking it's another text from Julian. I haven't told him where I am, only that I'm fine. He has yet to contact my mom or sister, thankfully. I haven't shared the news with either of them yet. He must realize he's truly on thin ice, though I can't imagine he'll wait much longer if I don't answer at least one of his recent messages. I'm not ready to see him or even talk to him yet. He'll rush over here and try to declare his undying love for me. And he'll mean it. If anything, I believe that he loves me. But I also know that despite that love, I'm not enough for him. He'll always be on the lookout for the next thing, the better thing—at work, with friends, and yes, with me. But I deserve to be enough, and I'm done pretending otherwise.

I'm still in the living room when my dad comes home. His sounds are familiar—his briefcase hitting the ground, his keys clanging in the bowl, his feet shuffling across the floor in only socks—even though it's been so long since we've shared space.

I glance back at my dad, who leans against the couch with a tired-but-genuine smile. He ruffles my hair like I'm ten. "Fancy meeting you here."

A million memories come back to me. Cecilia and me eating breakfast, Dad strolling in in his bathrobe and slippers, me at the dining room table, doing homework long after everyone else is in bed. How many times has he said those words to me?

"There's a plate for you in the fridge," I say.

A yawn overtakes him, and he slides down onto the couch next to me. "It's nice having you here, Lizzie."

"I like being here." The words come out before I can consider them. Consider how I would never be here for a long period of time if I wasn't avoiding my husband.

My dad gives me a smile so full of melancholy that I feel the depth of his pain as if it's my own. His eyes search mine. "What's going on, honey?"

"It's Jules," I say and immediately feel stupid, because of course, it's Julian.

He puts his hand over mine. "It's not usually you who leaves."

Ouch.

Even with his clear invitation to unburden myself, the words elude me. How many chances does Julian get? From me? From my family? It's what has kept me from telling my mother or Cecilia. But my dad... My dad had an extramarital affair. Will he sympathize with

Julian? Try to explain how you can do such a thing and still love your family? The answers can break everything.

"Lizzie?" he prods when I don't respond.

"He was talking to another woman." My stomach roils. "They kissed."

Saying the words out loud is like heaving a boulder off my chest, except that boulder had already shattered my sternum. I'm heartbroken and raw. It's real now. Very, very real. And it hurts. Everywhere. Worst of all, it's not the first time Julian has caused this pain, the kind that shatters your soul and makes you feel as if you are being torn apart bit by bit until the only thing left is a shell of who you used to be.

I swipe at my eyes, banishing the tears threatening to fall. "And it seems so fucking inevitable."

"I'm sorry, honey."

What he doesn't say echoes in the space between us. That my family hoped that Julian had grown out of this phase, that they all held their words and their breath for my sake. Because I wanted Julian despite everything. There was no talking me out of loving him. Not then. And now... I'm not even sure they'll try.

Chapter 8
Zoey

The chances that Liz believes I'm out with Becca are dismal. My sister has no poker face. She thinks she does, but every little reaction Liz has is broadcast in her expressions. She knows about Andrew, and she wants to tell someone. Whether it's half-sister solidarity, Liz's overcompensation for Cecilia's rejection, or something else making her keep my secret I can't be sure. But the window before the truth bursts out of my sister is growing smaller, which is why I stopped at Ardena Café before heading to Andrew's. If I come home with proof of whereabouts, maybe she'll think she was wrong or be placated for another day. Because if Liz spills my secret, my dad is sure to lock me down for the summer. Worse yet, he might ship me off to my mother. This wouldn't be different than most summers, except for the fact that this summer my mother not so subtly informed me that her family—my mom, her husband, and their two kids—was road-tripping to Disney World and that I wasn't invited. What's a few more months on top of a few more months when I barely see my mom as it is?

I roll the Ardena Café bag to preserve the freshness and look up at the expanse of Andrew's house. He and his mother live in one of the mansions in what is called North Ardena. It isn't actually its own town, only a few uptight old men who didn't want to be associated with the "riffraff," as my dad put it when I was old enough to ask about such things. He left out that "riffraff" technically included him and me. Andrew's house is impressive, if not a little formulaic on the outside, but inside it always feels empty. His dad moved out during freshman year of high school, before we met. His mom got Andrew and the house, but they've never been able to fill the space left by Mr. Singer. I'm not even sure they tried.

The house is dark, but that doesn't mean anything. Andrew's room is on the far side, and I know his mom is out for the night. My phone buzzes, and I drop the car door handle. If he is canceling on me now, I'm going to use the spare key they keep under the potted plant and smear this alibi pastry all over his bed. Not really, but he would deserve nothing less.

I scan the notification on my phone. *Hi, it's Max.* What? My fingers can barely swipe the passcode fast enough. He's supposed to be out of town for five more days. Why is he texting me? It's not particularly late at night, but still. Questions swirl through my mind. Did I forget a form? Does he want to talk to me? I should be asking why I'm sweating bullets over those three innocuous words, but not going there.

My phone buzzes again, and I scan the stack of messages.

Back in town early.

Want to train together this week?

Say, tomorrow at the school around 8?

Not exactly worth the jolt that went through my body. And yet... he wants to train with me. What normal human wants to spend their last week of freedom before summer camp training at eight in the morning? I glance back at Andrew's house. Whatever Max's intent, nothing in these messages will keep me from walking into that house. I pause, my hand on the door handle again. Do I want a reason not to walk into Andrew's house?

A knock sounds at the driver's-side window, and I jump back, reaching for the lock, though I know it's already locked. Andrew's laugh sounds outside the car. I glance up to see him smirking as he motions for me to roll down the window.

I do so while glaring at him. He can be such a jackass. "Scaring me half to death isn't good foreplay."

"You're the one lurking in my driveway with your lights off." He opens my door and offers his hand after I roll up the window and unlock the doors. His hands are cold despite the warm night. Goose bumps rise on my arms. I let myself believe it's because of his touch alone. He can still do that to me. I remember his hand on my cheek that night by the pool at that awful party. My whole body felt like it would break apart at his touch. I missed it so much. It hasn't been like that since then, but there's still something. Will there always be? Is that the aftereffect of loving someone?

"I was reading a text message."

He doesn't take the bait. And why would he? Andrew has me, and he knows it. I'm so fucked.

He drops my hand but pulls me against his side, moving his hand to the small of my back as we walk. Like he always did. For the briefest moment, I step back from this night and what I'm about to do and whom I'm about to do it with. I forget my reasons. I forget the ache of losing him. I focus on him. Aside from easy sex, what is Andrew getting out of our arrangement? He made his feelings on our relationship clear before and after his cheating. During our last argument, he told me we weren't good for each other anymore. That we were holding each other back. Don't ask me from what because, for me, Bellewood is the definition of living my best life. The next morning, he rescinded all his comments with kisses and sweet words and promises of giving me a lavaliere one day. And I wanted to wear his Greek letters so badly. I wanted that privilege. But two weeks later, I found him in bed with Claire. Since that moment, his actions and words haven't aligned. When we're together, he is the boy I love. The second we're apart, we're exes through and through. Sometimes

I wonder if he would acknowledge my presence beyond a nod of welcome. That situation has not occurred yet, thank god. Anytime we're at the same place at the same time, we leave together. But beyond that, we aren't putting on a show. No one would mistake us for friends and definitely not for lovers.

Andrew's voice pulls me back from my spiraling thoughts. And I'm grateful. If I go too far down, I'm not sure I'll walk through the door. And if I don't walk through the door, who will?

"Mom's out with Gary." He leads me through his house, as if I don't remember the way to his bedroom.

I try not to look around. I haven't been here since Christmas break. If Andrew remembers that, he doesn't let on. His voice is calm and collected and normal, as if we still do this every day. And we did this so many days. Memories wash over me despite my protests. Dinners and movie nights, double dates with Rob and Claire, hours cuddling and whispering and being in love. *No.* I push everything away. I cannot do this now. If Andrew sees a hint of weakness, he'll stop texting. There's no "I love you" in this arrangement. He's said it more than once in the moment, but I know better. The first time I say those words is when this ends.

Andrew pushes open the door to his room and fixes me with a sardonic look. "She doesn't even try to hide the fact that she's spending the night there anymore."

I turn my gaze from him. His room has not changed. Literally not at all. The picture of us with all our friends on prom is still on his desk, the one of us from graduation on his nightstand. My face stares back at me from amongst his things, and yet we've been home for over a month. There was more than enough time to discard all of this. I did it before I unpacked. But here, our memory remains alive and well. I sit down on the bed and stare at my hands in my lap. My heart thumps a broken beat. Whatever any of this means, I can't think about it now. Or ever.

"Seriously, Zo, it's like I left for college, and she forgot how to be a mother." He hits a few keys on his laptop, and music fills the space. "I told her you were coming over tonight, in case she came home or whatever, and she said, 'Thank god,' and told me it was about time I got my head out of my ass."

I smile, and it's natural. Ms. Singer loves me. Everyone knows that. And I'm a little glad that she sees her son for what he is. That she knows we're better together. Maybe this move from the back of the car and motel rooms and other clandestine spots does mean something, considering he told his mom.

A little ball of hope snakes its way into my heart, and I let it stay.

"I knew that would win me a smile." He crosses the room, lies down on the bed, and then pulls me on top of him. "I miss that smile."

Damn, he's good. Andrew knows exactly what to say to keep me coming back. Tonight, though, maybe because I let myself dig into the truth of what we're doing or because his bedroom offers the comfort of nostalgia, I want to ask the question that trots through my mind every time he rolls out a line: If you feel that way, why did you sleep with my best friend? I'll never ask it. The answer might kill me. But tonight, I want to grab his shoulders and shake him and scream, *Why? Why did you destroy us only to come back to me?*

I don't do this because of course I don't. I'm not an idiot, and I want to have sex tonight. I toy with the buttons on his shirt and then run my hand across the skin I uncovered. His heart beats the same steady rhythm as always.

"You saw my smile last week." I keep my eyes from his, instead kissing his neck and removing his shirt.

"Not that one." He kisses me, long and deep. It's full of want and possessiveness and something else I can't place. Something I haven't felt in the last month from him. "I haven't seen that one in ages."

That's your fault. Another thing I don't say. Instead, I unclasp his belt and align our bodies. Desire rockets through me. He explores my body in the ways I like because he knows every way I like. We pull and tug at each other's clothes until there's little between us. Lust and desire replace love and need. This moment is urgent and fierce and our new normal. This is going to hurt tomorrow, more than any other time because of where we are, because of the softness of his smile, and the three words he whispers as we come together. But tonight, I can't think of that because tonight, it's only me and Andrew and the unerring truth that we fit—always.

Chapter 9
Zoey

The next morning comes too soon and with it all the regrets I pushed away the night before. I am bleary-eyed and grouchy as I walk onto the track despite the cloudless blue sky. Lap by lap, Max draws me out of my bad mood, finally kicking it to the curb with his offer for breakfast at Ardena Café. We sit across from each other, making small talk, as we doctor our coffees. A few minutes later, the waitress drops off our plates. I stare down at my veggie egg-white omelet, wheat toast, and fruit salad. Max is eating bacon. Seriously, he ordered four sides of bacon to go with his eggs and didn't even look bashful about it. I was perfectly happy with my order until Max's Ardena Café Special arrived in all its bacon and pancake glory. Now, I want all the carbs and fats and sugar this place has to offer.

"You can have some bacon." Max pushes the plate slightly in my direction.

I point at him with my perfectly healthy wheat toast. "I think the bacon kind of negates the workout."

"Don't food shame me, Reid." He slides two pieces of bacon onto my plate with the butt of his knife. "I'm wallowing."

I wasn't aware that guys wallowed, but here we are drowning in bacon.

"Zoey," I remind him and pull a third piece of bacon onto my plate and then a fourth. Because why not? "And why are you wallowing?"

"Well, *Zoey...*"

My name in his mouth is sinful. Goose bumps sprout on my arms. How did he make my name sound sexy and scandalous and teasing all at once? I don't dare look up at him. Whatever his face is doing right now will not quell the feelings those two syllables caused. I focus so hard on my bacon, I expect it to start sizzling on my plate.

After a too-long pause that makes me thinks he knows exactly what he's doing to me, he continues. "I spent the last four days moving my girlfriend into her new apartment in Wilmington, North Carolina, ahead of the start of her two-year graduate program."

"That sucks, Max," I say and mean it. "Long distance... I never even considered it... with Andrew—" A laugh cuts off the rest of my thought. *My* laugh, I realize a second too late. Of all the things I was worried about, and it happened right under my nose.

I chance a look at Max, and his gaze is focused on me, his eyes intent and understanding and sympathetic. Uh-oh.

"I heard about Claire."

I'm not surprised by this fact. I am surprised he's sharing it with me.

"How?"

"Teachers are surprisingly tuned in to the gossip train. We need to be, you know, in case something is truly wrong. And something like what happened with the three of you... Well, it doesn't stay quiet for long."

Had he specifically asked about me though? And whom had he asked? I can't imagine teachers sitting around on summer break gossiping about students' love lives. Not that it matters. If Max had asked me what happened, I would've told him. I'm not the one who should be ashamed. At least he isn't giving me the look of pity I see from everyone else, as if my life begins and ends with Andrew Singer. As if Claire was my one and only friend. Sympathy and empathy are fine. People have been here. They have advice and sob stories and soap boxes. All fine. But pity is inexcusable.

"When will you see your girlfriend again?" I take a bite of bacon, as if that denotes my complete nonchalance at Max's revelation.

"Well, that's why I'm wallowing," he says, not quite looking at me. "Turns out she didn't want a long-distance boyfriend, only the help of one to move her belongings six hundred miles down the East Coast."

"Wait, what? You aren't serious," I say, angry on his behalf.

"As the plague." He forks some eggs and a slice of bacon onto one of his pancakes and folds it into a taco. "Broke up with me about ninety seconds after I brought the last box inside."

What a bitch. What a long return trip that must have been. I push the plate of bacon toward him. "Eat the bacon."

The roads are quiet. Everyone has descended on the shore or fled to avoid the tourists. I'm usually one of the runners, heading down to North Carolina for my annual visit with the family. I'm honestly not too heartbroken that I'm not going this year. It would be nice to have some forced distance from Andrew, to meet a cute boy at a different beach in a different state, but then I would miss this time with Liz. And as the days go by, I find that I don't want that.

Summer starts at the end of May in New Jersey, but right now, in my car with the windows down and Wilderness Weekend blasting, it finally officially feels like summer. If Becca wasn't holing up with Ben in Rehoboth all weekend, I would drag her to the beach, Independence Day tourists be damned. Maybe I'll ask Liz to go, or perhaps Max and I can move one of our training sessions to the sand. That could be... interesting.

I'm not thinking about Max shirtless on the beach when I almost hit the car blocking my driveway. I study the silver sedan. Julian sits in the driver seat, and he's talking to himself. I've seen him in a creative thrall before, but this seems different. Apprehension slithers up my spine.

By the time I park the car down the street and walk back to the house, Julian is standing outside his car. He's a mess. There's always this sort of disheveled look about Julian, but this is different. He has days' worth of stubble, and his eyes are huge and almost frantic. It's an overreaction even for him. I know Liz told him she was fine. I watched her send the text. I survey my house and the empty driveway. Julian must not be certain anyone is here. It's midmorning on a weekday, and though Liz has a key, Julian does not. I know Liz is home, though. I talked to her right before I left the café.

"I know she's here, Zoey." Julian somehow sounds pissed off and heartbroken all at once.

I stare at him with my arms crossed. Liz hasn't been forthcoming with details, but I don't like the look of Julian or his tone. And I haven't forgotten the questions that Liz asked me after finding me in bed with Andrew.

"Whatever she's told you, it's not the whole story, Zoey."

Something clicks then, and my heart clenches in an unfamiliar way. Maybe the way Liz's and Cecilia's had when my arrival blew up their lives all those years ago.

"If she wanted to see you, she would've answered the phone." My voice is scratchy, my words weighted oddly as I process this new reality. *Julian cheated on Liz.* I know this deep in my bones. Andrew cheated on me. My dad cheated on his wife. How is this the natural progression of the relationships in my life? Anger and disgust flood my system, and I can hardly look at Julian. He's my brother almost as much as Liz is my sister. They've been the pinnacle of love persevering, of overcoming the odds. How could he? The irony that I feel none of these feelings about Andrew and what he did to me is not lost on me.

Julian steps closer. "You know how she is."

Seriously? I glare at him. Liz is steadfast and the opposite of melodramatic, and we both know it. I may have found Julian on the roof of the venue on the day of their wedding, but it was Liz who got him to the altar. Liz has forgiven him for every misstep, married him despite his cold feet. But this time, whatever Julian did finally broke her. Because Liz is never the one who leaves. The thought sends a ripple of panic through me because if seeing my boyfriend naked and writhing on top of my best friend isn't enough to break the hold Andrew has on me, I don't know what can and how I will survive it.

"Go home, Julian." I move so that I'm standing between him and my house. He stares at me for a moment, a glint of something like amusement behind the frustration.

"Liz!" he screams at the top of his lungs.

He can't be serious. Did he forget we're not in a movie? "She doesn't want to see you."

"I don't care." He squares his shoulders, as if he plans to force his way through me if he must. "This is between me and my wife."

"Jul—"

"It's fine, Zoey."

I spin around at Liz's words. She stands at the top of the driveway, dressed for our yoga session, a cardigan on her shoulders. Her hands are clasped, and her hair falls in messy waves. For a split second, I see it—the sisters in us. It's the slant of her eyes and the tightness of her jaw. It's the way she clasps her hands and the pain etched into every part of her. Her pain reflects mine, and my heart breaks in a new and awful way.

"Come inside," she says, straightening. "Both of you."

Chapter 10
Liz

"**W**as that really necessary?" I ask, turning on Julian, who is hovering by the front door, nervousness wafting off him. Zoey retreated to her room, but the lack of a slamming door proves that she's listening in. Good. Maybe she'll learn something.

"Considering I didn't know where you were for the last several days, yes, it was completely necessary." Okay, maybe he's not nervous per se. Julian perches on the back of the couch and fixes me with a glare. "I guess I could've reported you missing instead."

I roll my eyes. So much hyperbole. "As you called neither my mother, sisters, or father, and I texted you that I was perfectly fine, I think that would've been an overreaction."

"Maybe." He shrugs. "Maybe not."

Oh, I do not like this mood he's in, as if he has the upper hand because I walked out the door. "Tell me what you want, Jules."

"What I want?" He stares at me as if I asked the stupidest of stupid questions. "I want my wife to come home. It was one kiss. How could you leave in the middle of the night and essentially ghost me?"

"I think I earned the right." Ice coats my tone, and resentment rips through the wall I keep it shoved behind. And it feels right. Through all the pain and questioning and forgiveness in our life together, I never stopped to wonder if I resented my husband for his emotional warfare—intentional or not. But it's rising in my gut and spilling over into my heart and mind and words.

"Wow," he says, his tone acerbic. "You're going to hold *that* over my head?"

"Which *that*, Jules?" It's a challenge, one I badly want him to meet. We don't fight like this, but maybe we should. Maybe if we fought more, we wouldn't be here.

He holds up his hands in supplication. "This isn't why I came here."

"Isn't it?"

"No. I didn't. I mean, yeah, I'm pissed, but..." His face softens, and he has the gall to reach for me. "Come on, Liz. This is us."

Dammit. Same old Julian. *Yell. Be mad. Be anything.* I want to say those things, but I don't. Instead, I ask the one question I was too scared to ask before. I know the answer, but to hear it from Julian's mouth will be the deal-breaker.

"Were you tracking my cycle and purposely making sure we never got pregnant?"

Julian drops his head into his hands, giving me all the answer I need, but then he speaks. "I was scared, Liz."

"Of what?" I hiss.

"Of being a father? Of losing another baby? Of letting you down?"

My body trembles in frustration and truth and finality. *He* was scared? "Did you even stop to think what all those months of negative tests would do to me?"

He looks up now, and his face is a portrait of sorrow. Of course he knew. He held me while I cried myself sick after that first miscarriage. He stood next to me while I asked my doctor question after question about the possibilities of another failed pregnancy.

"I... Our marriage is easy, and I didn't want to lose that."

"You lost it, Jules. It's gone."

He sighs and takes a step toward me. "It doesn't have to be."

He's pleading, but for once in my life, it has no effect. I inch backward until the coffee table is between us. Of all the ways he's broken my heart, this is the worst. This is the one I don't know how to get past.

"Yes, it does." I run a hand across my forehead, rubbing the ache away but also stalling and steeling myself for what I'm about to say. "I'm not coming home yet. You left me over and over again, and every time I took you back. I've been understanding when, really, I didn't have to be. And right now, I need a break from you and me to figure out..."

His eyes cloud over, and I know he's filling in a million different endings to that sentence. *Figure out what I want, if I can forgive you, if I can be your wife, if I still love you.*

"For how long?" he asks when I don't continue.

"I don't know," I say, and it's the truth.

Julian white knuckles the couch. "Don't do this. It was a moment of weakness."

"Which part?" I clasp my hands behind my back so that he doesn't see them shaking. "The lying, the cheating, or the scheming?"

He sucks in a shaky breath. "I can't do this without you."

My resolve wavers, but I shove any doubts down deep, in the same place I used to keep the resentment. Julian has survived without me, and he will again. I cross the living room and take his hand in mine. "I need some time to see if I can get past any of this."

"Do you think you can?" he asks, his eyelids brimming with tears.

"I don't know, Jules. This is... a lot."

He kisses my forehead, and it's so heartbreakingly tender that my own tears start to spill over without warning. "Then do what you need to do."

And then he's gone. The front door clicks shut, and the rest of my world crashes at my feet. A shudder rocks my body. I collapse into a heap of tears right there on the living room floor. And then Zoey is there, her arms holding me up, holding me together. She doesn't let go. She doesn't ask questions. She holds me as I hope someone held her all those weeks ago. Zoey murmurs words of sympathy that barely make sense yet soothe the raw edges of the hole I punched through my own heart.

Chapter 11
Cecilia

I wave to the couple walking to their car. They look so young. It was the first thought I had when they walked up the drive of the mansion I had intended to sell today. They were my third visit, and all of them—from the yuppie hoping to move out of the city to the millennial couple who spent the whole time playacting what their kids would say about each room—were wrong for this house. Today, more than most days, felt like an episode of *Property Brothers*. This is the dream, but let me show you what you can really afford. Sometimes, HGTV makes my job a lot harder.

The couple is not the problem though. Not really. It's, well, me and this house. I want to sell it, need to sell it, but also I relish each showing that isn't *the one*. Because I love this house. A two-story luxury colonial in a good neighborhood with good schools. With neighbors who stop and chat through open car windows, kids biking, and couples walking hand in hand, it is a suburban dream. It's only been on the market for a few weeks. Longer than I expected, to be honest, but inflation has buyers hesitant. People were buying above their means, but now they are clutching their purse strings. I could buy it. Sometimes I imagine what it would feel like to have the key handed to me, like I do every time I sell a house. The realization that this beauty is mine. But despite having lived in and outside of Chicago for nearly two decades, I'm reluctant to saddle myself with property. Not to mention, what would I do with all those rooms?

The furniture from my River North loft would cover two and a half rooms. How would I fill the silence that settled in once the thrill of the purchase faded?

I asked my mother that once, as the number of people in our house dwindled from four to three to two and eventually only her. She wouldn't sell even though she knew the value she held in her palm. I might be a good Realtor, but my mother is a mogul, having opened her own ultra-successful agency when I was still in diapers. She shrugged and told me that she simply went room by room and made them hers—a library here, a new office there. The shrug and her nonchalant attitude were the tells that she was not lying but sugarcoating her answer. I knew that she had remodeled her castle of familial bliss into a fortress.

Back inside, I do a quick walk-through of the rooms. I adjust the throw pillows in the formal living room and wipe a spot of dust off the mantel. This room, with its vaulted ceiling, begs for built-in bookcases. It was made to be a library, sliding ladder and all. That's the first thing I would do. I flip off the light and head out into the humid night. I don't look back. This house is not my path. Maybe it might have been once, but that girl hasn't been me in a long time. Not since I watched my mother's world shatter, and mine with it, when my father's affair came out, and I had to watch the pain etched into her face every time he showed up to pick up my sister with another woman's baby in his arms.

So no, I'm not buying this house, and I'm not settling down, as much as I might crave the normalcy of shared nights and spaces with my girlfriend. I can't. I won't.

The sound of my phone buzzing inside my purse brings me back to myself. I shuffle through the mess inside, secretly hoping it's Evie trying again to persuade me to come over for Thai. Even though I woke up with Evie curled around me this morning, I miss her, which is why I turned down her invitation to join her for dinner this morning. All these hours later, I would cave. But when I pull out my phone, my sister's number flashes. "You are alive," I say by way of greeting.

"Cee..."

The teasing evaporates from my tone at the tears in Liz's voice. "What happened?"

The parking lot at Evie's garden apartment complex is busy this time of evening. The traditional workday ended a short while ago, and the usual ebb and flow of people getting home for the day makes it hard to notice Evie's car. Finally, I spot the muted-green sedan a few spots down from the building next to hers, and relief calms the tempest roaring in my mind. Julian and Liz separated. That by itself would've been a sad truth, one I hoped would never come for my sister, but the whole story is infinitely harder to swallow.

My sister left her husband. My brother-in-law had, at the very least, an emotional affair that ended in a kiss, all while purposely planning his work travel to avoid Liz getting pregnant. I feel sick to my stomach thinking about it.

I get out of the car, shouldering my bag, and stare up at Evie's building. I haven't been here in weeks, and even I can admit that makes me an awful girlfriend. But the news rattled something inside me, and the only person I want to see right now is my girlfriend, my rules and boundaries be damned.

I knock on the door of Evie's apartment, equally hoping she's out and praying that she opens the door and pulls me into her arms. I can't carry this new reality myself yet. Liz's revelation hurts in a way I didn't expect and could not have anticipated. Something like heartbreak churns in my chest.

The door opens after my second knock. Evie stands there in yoga pants and a tank top, her auburn hair pulled back in a ponytail. *She's so fucking beautiful.* Her eyes narrow, and she crosses her arms. She's not happy to see me, and I can't blame her. I was tactless this morning when I turned her down.

Her gaze lingers on my face for a moment, and then she steps aside to let me in. When she speaks, her tone is soft. "What's wrong?"

I reach for her, and she lets me pull her closer. "I'm sorry about this morning."

"It's fine." She looks up at me, her eyes wide. It wouldn't have been fine, but Evie's a psychologist, and she has always been able to read me like a book. "I ordered extra, so you can stay and tell me why you're really at my door."

I kiss her then. Because I love her, even if I won't say it. Even if it doesn't matter in the long run. It'll never be more than this, especially not now.

She pulls away first and cups my cheek. "Cee, what is it?"

"It's Liz," I say. "She left Julian."

Chapter 12
Zoey

I toss the volleyball into the air and then tap it back up in a sad imitation of a set. It's a good thing I don't have anything to do with the volleyball sessions at work. Liz retreated to her bedroom after dinner, when she'd put on a pretty good show in front of Dad. With the thin walls between us, I could hear her on the phone with Cecilia, so I felt okay about leaving when Becca texted. Becca, who had returned from her trip with her virginity intact. My best friend's willpower is unmatched, and Ben, hell, Ben is a saint or maybe a martyr.

Spending time with Becca should've made me feel better about Andrew, or Liz and Julian, or both. And it had for a while. I love seeing my best friend head over heels in love, but it hurts too. We were meant to share these moments together, to compare stories and styles and gossip and giggle. But every story I have is an Andrew story, and each of those moments is now viewed without the rose-colored glasses of love.

Now, only two hours after I left, I'm back. Liz is still locked in her room. As far as I can tell, she hasn't even come out to pee. The only proof I have that she's in there is the occasional shuffle of movement behind the door. I'm tempted to put on the emo-est music I own to help her through the pain. She would never admit it, but I think she would appreciate a good chorus of "Screaming Infidelities."

My phone buzzes, and I expect another "save me" text from my college bestie. Home life and Haley are not a match made in heaven. At all. It's comical only because I know she's half serious in her desperation. Like tonight, she's out with her hometown friends. Her socials are full of silly selfies at glow-in-the-dark mini golf. Haley might chafe at being back under her parents' rigid rule, but she's making the most of it. The text, however, is not from Haley or Becca or anyone I want to hear from. It's Andrew. Again. I ignored his initial message when I was out with Becca. While my best friend might be oblivious in love, she would notice if I started texting with Andrew right in front of her.

I read this message despite my better judgement. *Leaving Rob's party now. Swing by and get you?*

My stomach twists at the thought, and not in the usual "this is a bad idea but I'm going to do it anyway, to hell with the consequences" sort of way. This isn't a brush of butterfly wings and a tingle of change. It's wrongness and dread, a parasite rooting its way into my heart.

I type a single word—*Can't*—then delete it. Can't implies that I would if I could. I think of Liz standing up to Julian, demanding what she needed, and channel that strength.

I type the two letters that haven't been in my lexicon with Andrew in over a month.

No.

Chapter 13
Liz

The apartment is a small one-bedroom off a busy road. It's in a nice but not ultra-expensive part of town. It's sleek and modern. The kitchen has nicer granite than my house. Living here would be easy. Standing in the empty living room, I can see how I would decorate the space already—a spot of color there, an artsy photo on the wall, a shoe pail so as not to scratch the hardwood with my heels. Finding a place in Princeton on such short notice with a month-to-month lease option is like winning the lottery. But I'm teetering on making a decision, partly because Mom is shaking her head like I'm crazy and partly because something is missing.

"How soon did they say they can get me in?" I circle back to the kitchen and take a seat on one of the nook stools.

My mom stands there in full Realtor mode. Her black pants are pressed, her white blouse vibrant, and the light scarf hanging from her neck offers a perfect spot of color. She taps her foot a few times, the hard bottom of her heels loud in the empty space, and then tosses me a weary smile. It's the only crack in her professional veneer since I climbed into her car this morning. "Two weeks."

Though her tone is even, I can tell she doesn't want me to rent this apartment or the last one or the one before that. When I told her about the situation with Julian a few nights ago, she was politely surprised. She demurely offered to take me out to a few apartments when she had a break in her schedule. My mom isn't cold. She may not have been sufficiently surprised, but she pulled me into her and let me cry, stroked my hair, made me her calming magic tea. But the woman in front of me is not Mom, and as my real-estate agent, she thinks I'm shopping out of my price range. As my mom, she doesn't understand why I won't take up in her guest room until I have a more solid idea of what I want to do. I don't have the heart to tell her moving back home for me would feel like the ultimate failure, or if I return to the comforts of my childhood home, I might make the wrong choice. I need to know I can do this on my own, that I can be on my own. I need to remember who I am without Julian Madden.

I glance around the space again, still trying to figure out what the issue is. But then it hits me—Zoey. There's no room for overnight guests, and even though I want to be Miss Independent right now, my sister is going to need a refuge and a safe space when the actions of her summer affair come crashing down.

"Is there a two-bedroom available?" I ask as nonchalantly as possible.

Mom eyes me as if she can guess at my reasons behind this inquiry, but only nods. "Yes, but—"

"Then I want that one, and I want to move in next week." I'm breathless by the end of the statement, but I had to get it out before she can tell me all the reasons it's a bad decision.

"Liz, honey, I know what you're doing, but you can't afford a two-bedroom here long-term."

Okay, she definitely knows this is about Zoey. I mentioned to her what I knew, what I feared. But it's not only about Zoey. I glance around the small apartment. There's nowhere to go. Kitchen, bedroom, living room, bathroom. It's spacious enough for one, but the space already feels claustrophobic. "I have savings, and Julian's covering the house expenses. The rest is pretty limited."

We haven't gotten to how we're dividing the bills for the foreseeable future. I honestly hadn't thought about it much in the days since

I declared I wanted space. All of the bills come out of a joint account that we feed money into from our own personal accounts. There's no set split on who pays what. I suppose we'll have to talk about this eventually, but for now, Julian can figure it out, like I had to do when he left me during graduate school with no notice. I survived with only a barista's salary and a broken heart. He's much better off now.

Mom leans on the counter and fixes me with a glare that says she thinks I'm being ridiculous. "Not the point. As your mother, I'm not going to set you up to fail, and as your Realtor, I'm not allowing you to sign on to something, even temporarily, that you can't sustain, no matter how sisterly the cause."

"She needs me, Mom." Zoey's face flashes in my mind, the expression she wears when she thinks no one is looking, the bags under her eyes and the gauntness of her cheeks. My little sister is in pain. A weight is sitting on her, and I know, better than most, how hard it is to remove. Even reconciled all these years with Julian, a piece of that first heart-wrenching, life-altering boulder still remains. And Zoey's situation is much worse. "Her boyfriend slept with her best friend, and Zoey is still sleeping with him in some convoluted attempt to get him back. Dad is never around, and even when he is, he can't help her, not with this. Her mother is god knows where. I can't abandon her."

An emotion flashes across my mom's features, but it's gone before I can place it. Her fingers fly over her phone again, and then it pings with a message. She meets my gaze. "The last place we saw has a two-bedroom available. It's significantly less costly than the unit we're standing in, and they can get you in within ten days."

Another ding. Her eyes narrow. "They do require a six-month lease."

Six months. It seems equally like forever and nothing. But six months from now, it won't even be the same year, and these increasingly hot summer days will be snow-covered. My boss will have flown south for the winter, and all of Julian's flights will be delayed for one reason or another. Will one of those reasons be Sheila? Or some other airport lover?

My stomach sours. Images of Julian wrapped around a myriad of different women flood my mind. Young, old, blonde, brunette, glasses or not. But they all have Sheila's face and her button of a fucking nose. How am I ever supposed to trust him again?

I picture the last apartment we saw—small, modern, not quite as sleek as the one we're in but nice. With a few ritzier pieces, it can be something. There's a pool and a fitness center. A few other people from work live in the complex already. It's convenient, and to my mother's point, I can pay the rent out of my salary if I'm frugal enough. Tack on a guest room, and it seems full of possibilities. "Where do I sign?"

Chapter 14
Cecilia

The clock ticks another minute past eight. Tension settles in my back. *Relax*, I chide myself, forcing my shoulders away from my ears. This is fine. More than fine. It's only a quarter after eight. I don't have to be at the airport for another hour. The car service isn't even here yet. I tell myself these truths as I read the same line in the newspaper over again. It's no use. I hate being late for anything. And even if I'm not technically late for anything at the moment, my schedule is off. My Uber is supposed to be here in ten minutes, and my girlfriend is still blow-drying her hair, which takes her fucking forever. Not that I can't technically leave without saying goodbye, but that's too dickish, even for me.

I top off my coffee from the french press and flip to the next page of the morning paper that I still have delivered. There's something calming about reading actual newsprint. Maybe it's the lack of backlighting and white space that fill the rest of my day. I read one article then another. I flip another page. Finally, the bathroom door screeches open. I will get around to fixing that. Steam billows into the kitchen, carrying Evie with it.

Auburn hair falls in loose curls around her face. A few strands stick to her cheek. She toys with the buttons of her blouse, exposing the lacy bra underneath that should be covered by a camisole. Evie never worries about such things. A fact that makes her damn sexy. I'll be daydreaming of the supple curves of my girlfriend's breasts the entire flight now. My shoulders relax a fraction of an inch. Desire rumbles low in my belly and fissures out through my fingertips. I pull her in for a kiss, letting it linger and play and grow. My fingers trace the swell of her breasts. Evie sighs against my lips, and any frustrations about the late start to my morning vanish.

"I'm so sorry," Evie says, her hands still resting above the waist of my pants. Her fingers trail circles along my skin, sending sparks through my entire body. "But *someone* kept me up late."

I smirk. It's too hard to stay angry at someone who counsels young children. It's even harder when their beauty bowls you over, and their touch sets you on fire. Which is exactly how I feel all the time—lost in a stormy sea with Evie as my beacon in the mist. When this happened and how I let it happen, I have no idea. It's my life's mission to not let anyone get this close, and yet Evie has burrowed deep. No matter how hard I push her away, she is there, and she asks for so little in return. My mind knows it's time to extract myself from this situation or risk losing a piece of myself. But I have no idea how to do that. None of my normal tactics are working, and I'm not masochistic enough to force my hand. "I needed last night to last me my whole trip."

"I could come with you, you know."

I step away from her. She offered before, but I can't. Evie hasn't even met my family. I'm actually pretty sure they think we broke up since I rarely talk about her. So to bring her to comfort my sister in her time of need? Though I suppose meeting my girlfriend of a year would help raise Liz's spirits.

"You have work, and I don't know how long I'll be there."

"I have vacation time."

True.

My phone buzzes with a notification that my Uber is here. And dammit if I don't want her to climb into that car with me. "It's a little late to get a ticket."

I hurriedly pour the rest of the coffee into a to-go cup, add sugar and a splash of milk, and hand it to Evie. She takes it with a sly smile and a warmness to her eyes. "Let me worry about that," she says.

"Evie..." My phone buzzes again. Apparently, I have an impatient driver who will absolutely charge me a waiting fee.

"You go, Cee. I'll clean up and then lock the door behind me."

"Thank you." I kiss her lightly and then shoulder my purse and grab for the handle of my suitcase. I stop at the door and turn back to my girlfriend, ignoring the buzzing of my phone. "I guess I'll see you in New York?"

She grins at me over her shoulder. "Yes, you will."

Chapter 15
Zoey

Tears fall down my temples and past my ears. My hands shake. My breathing is labored and too quick. A weight sits on my chest. I roll over, my cheek hitting the damp sheets. How long have I been crying? Have I been dreaming of him again? Of a different outcome to that first kiss by the pool? To a time before I knew betrayal? I can't remember, but that must be the case. I hiccup around another breath and try to calm my body. I'm not a stranger to panic attacks, but I fucking hate them. I hate that Andrew Singer is the cause of them now. No one deserves that power over me.

I put my earbuds in, finding my favorite Wilderness Weekend song, and let the music wash over me. Slowly, my hands stop shaking, my breathing normalizes, and my chest doesn't feel like it's being crushed by a boulder. Tears still fall, but they are always the last to go. I let them come. I welcome the heartache because anything is better than the crushing weight of devastation. I breathe with the song, letting the music soothe my heart and the lyrics my mind.

I've been to enough therapy to know that panic attacks are a perfectly normal reaction to the shock of loss and betrayal I experienced. I know how to manage and avoid them. At least when I'm awake. Mommy issues and two sets of siblings whom I barely know—Liz being the sole exception—forced me to deal with the weight of grief and loneliness. But none of that has been like this. This instant, soul-crushing loss.

Stop. I sit up, waiting to make sure my head is clear, and then walk to the bathroom. I splash cold water on my face. *I'm fine.* This is fine. I can't ward off my subconscious. In the mirror, a pale stranger greets me. Rejecting Andrew's advances that night felt empowering. I woke up the next day proud and feeling better about my situation. If Liz can break away from Julian, whom she's been with for my whole life, I can get over Andrew. We weren't even together for two years. In the grand scheme of things, it's nothing. But it was everything.

After my rejection text, Andrew went radio silent. Haley went on a cruise with her family, and Becca returned to her love bubble. Liz spent her free time looking at apartments and then buying furniture for her new apartment, reacquainting herself with Princeton, and talking on the phone with her other sister. So now, five days after I fearlessly told Andrew no, I can't breathe from the sheer loneliness of my existence. I'm dreaming about him. Every song makes me think of him. Every day, I have to go to the field where we first kissed and walk the halls where our love story flourished. There's no escape. And no more distractions.

I know who I am. Zoey Reid, the girl not good enough, whose own siblings only tolerate me because we share DNA. The girl who you fuck but don't marry, the state record holder who hasn't even tried out for the Bellewood track team. Zoey Reid *had* potential. So much potential. But she would never be enough. *I* will never be enough.

I force out a long breath as my chest constricts, the vise on my heart tightening another notch. My cheeks are drenched in fresh tears. *No. No.* I cannot have a Zoey spiral. *Recognize the thoughts as false.* My therapist's words come back to me. *Erase them. If you can't erase them, flip them.* I conjure the excited faces of my younger siblings when I step out of the airport each summer. I think of Liz and Becca and Haley. I am not alone.

"You almost done in there?"

I jump at Dad's voice on the other side of the door. Our mornings don't often overlap, but Liz's presence and now absence have affected him too. He's home more and not just in residence but here, making conversation, asking questions, laughing. It's been a nice change of pace. I dab at my cheeks, knowing my eyes are a lost cause. There's no way to hide the puffiness or redness. But my dad isn't one to press when there are tears involved.

"Sorry, Dad," I say, opening the door.

He takes in my complexion and the rhythm of my breathing. "You okay, Zo?"

I nod. "Didn't sleep well. Think I'll go feed Lenny some breakfast."

"You spoil that squirrel," he says as I make my way past him.

"Guess you should've gotten me that kitten I asked for."

His laughter fills the hallway, and then before I reach the living room, his voice rings through the quiet apartment again. "Bread's on the counter."

Nothing is better than a dozen ten-year-olds when you need a distraction. Particularly ones whose sole responsibility this summer is to run. It's a godsend but also utterly exhausting. The day's hot, and we're forced to deviate from our normal routine to run laps around the air-conditioned hallways of the high school. The kids are troopers. I think they like the indoor days better, actually. When else do you get to run through the halls? It's the teenagers who give us the hardest time on days like this. It's too easy to sneak away into stairwells and classrooms and doorways. Which is why I'm wandering the high school, the last place I should be after this morning, looking for two sets of missing teens. Potential for unwanted make-out footage is high.

Max usually takes this job, being the older, more authoritative one of us, but he could tell the tweens had worn me down. So, handing me a bag of mini cookies, he kicked me out of the gym. If only he knew how little this would help me. After a lap of the third floor, where we usually find the offenders, I head outside. It's sweltering, the heat almost oppressive after the coolness of the air conditioner. My skin prickles at the temperature change, and my cheeks tingle. Days like this are wasted on me. Half the town—hell, half the East Coast—will descend on the shore on a day like today. But me? No way. I will blast the air until I need a hoodie and lounge around the house. If you want to see me on a day like today, you better come to me.

I turn left out of the building and head toward the front of the school. I set off at a light jog, but it's like running through soup. Hair sticks to my neck and cheeks where it's fallen out of my ponytail. There's no way campers are outside in this. No one can make out in this heat.

"Zo?"

My feet falter at Andrew's voice. I turn toward the quad, an area so open I hadn't even bothered to look at it when I rounded the building, and spot him. He's balancing on the curb with his hands in his pockets and his eyes locked on me.

"What are you doing here?" I ask, my voice breathless even though I barely exerted myself.

He shrugs. Shrugs as if his presence isn't heartbreaking and exhilarating and coursing equal parts anger, desire, and hope through my veins. I thought maybe he gave up. If it—I'm—not easy, then what's the point? Ardena girls have been waiting a long time for Andrew Singer to be single. It's not like he has to even try.

"Was driving past the school, and I wanted to ask you something." He shrugs again. "Thought I'd see if you had a minute."

I stare at him, the ability to form words momentarily lost. From anyone else, his story is plausible. Becca stopped for lunch the other day. But Andrew—at least this iteration of him—doesn't stop by to ask me questions. He puts in the most minimal of efforts when it suits him.

"So do you have a minute?" he asks, his tone cool and confident.

I nod even though this exchange has already taken longer than a minute and then realize that it's weird that I've uttered only five words in his presence this whole time. I clear my throat. "Maybe forty-five seconds. I'm looking for rogue campers."

He laughs because only a few summers ago, we were the rogue campers. "They're in the front parking lot. I sent them back inside."

"Were they smoking?" I ask, confused why they would be in the front lot, in plain sight and direct sunlight.

"No. Sitting between two cars, sharing a sandwich, holding hands, and looking gooily into each other's eyes." He holds a hand up to his heart. "Tweens in love."

"They had a sandwich from G&L?"

He grimaces. "Looked like it. Does it matter?"

Yes, it matters. If it's G&L, then they absolutely went off campus to pick up lunch, which is strictly forbidden. But I swallow my diatribe for the moment. "Sorry, what did you want to ask me?"

"I'm going down to Wildwood with the boys next week."

This I know. The yearly trip is one of the advantages of having an absentee father who works too much and lets you use his time-share. We took advantage of the small cottage more than once senior year.

I don't say anything. Is he going to ask me to feed his cat or something?

"The guys aren't coming until Tuesday, so I was thinking we could go down for the weekend."

Did he use the word "we" to refer to the two of us? I don't know what my face is doing, but whatever it is, Andrew softens. He tucks a strand of hair behind my ear, his fingers casually brushing my cheek.

"It could be fun. You and me and none of the pressure that comes with being home or at school." He sighs and looks at me through half-lidded eyes. "Things were always so easy with us."

Until they weren't. Until you complicated them beyond belief. My stomach turns because somewhere in him, he believes what he's saying. How can he act like he didn't rip everything we had to shreds?

His eyes drop to the ground before meeting mine again, searching for something. This is one of his tells. He's about to drop the trump card. "Is it so wrong to want that back again?"

Oh my god. I step back. This is Andrew logic. He's not saying he wants to get back together. He's not. He wants me to think it, but it can't be what he means. I start to shake my head because this will break me, and I can feel myself getting ready to say yes. Because I'm an idiot.

He grabs my hand. "I miss you, Zo. Come away with me."

"It's Liz's last weekend. I'm not sure I can get away." The words come out in a rush of panic.

"Last weekend on this earth?"

I knew it was the wrong argument as I was making it, but I had to say something or else I would've jumped into his arms and professed my love for him. My heart hammers in my chest. Why do I want this? *Why?*

"Still..." I hedge, hoping to think up some coherent answer that will at the very least buy me some time.

"Reid!"

Max's voice breaks off whatever rambling thought I'm about to give. Thank god. He stands at the top of the stairs to the school's main entrance, his arms crossed, eyes narrowed. I wonder if he's glaring at Andrew or battling the sun. Probably the latter, but a girl can hope.

"One minute," I call back.

"Forty-five seconds! Lunch isn't going to serve itself."

A smile grows on my face at that. I didn't realize we both used that phrase or that I picked it up from him in our short time as coworkers. This coincidence does not go unnoticed by Andrew. He glowers at his former coach.

"Sorry, I have to go."

"This weekend?" There's a sort of desperation in his voice I've never heard before.

"I'll think about it." Before he can respond, I turn and bound up the steps to Max's side. I don't chance a look back. Seeing jealousy or longing on his face will torture me, and if he's already gone... I focus on Max, who stares down at me with an unreadable expression.

"Everything okay?" he asks as we step into school.

It's a reasonable question, given what he knows about how things ended with Andrew, but it feels heavier than that. We turn into the senior hallway, and for once memories don't come. There's no Claire laughing so hard she cries or Andrew wrapping his arms around my waist and pulling me in for a kiss. There's Max and an empty hallway. My racing heart slows to normal speed, and the disastrous hope that filled me at Andrew's words ebbs.

I elbow Max in the side and give him a smile that's real. "Everything's fine."

He musses my hair and nudges me back as we reach the cafeteria. I can do this. I can say no to Andrew and lose the love of my life and survive. I can. I think of Liz, Haley, and Becca, and now Max, who has become a balm to my scorched edges, softening the sharp pain and dull ache that simultaneously reside in my chest.

Chapter 16
Liz

A partment-white walls, standard gray carpets, and sliding balcony doors—this apartment is a blank canvas of mediocrity. But it's mine, and I can't help constantly squeezing the key tucked into my pocket. Even though they gave me the key a few days early, I'm not ready to move in. One, because none of my furniture is arriving for another week, and two, I told Zoey exactly when I was leaving, and based on her mood recently, I feel like departing sooner might not be well received.

Instead, I'm lying on the floor, staring at the blank walls of my home for the next six months, and imagining what it could be. In the quiet, my creativity has free rein. Painting the walls is a no-go, but I can absolutely splash the walls with color in artwork and statement pieces. There's a funky thrift store over by the Princeton campus. I bet I can find a cool lamp or some retro décor. Maybe I can stop by after work or the next time I go into the office. I've been trying to alternate office days with remote days to maximize the time I have with Zoey, but she's been MIA more than usual. And not with Andrew, as far as I can tell.

My stomach rumbles. Right, because it's dinner time. And I definitely can't eat here. As I pull myself to sitting and adjust my now-crooked ponytail, there's a knock on the door. I stop, my fingers twisted in my hair tie. Who the heck is knocking on my door? God help me if it's Julian.

I scrambled to my feet and then pull the door open to find my sister on the other side. I blink a few times, but no, she's real. "Cecilia?"

"Hey, sis," she says with a smile.

"What in the world are you doing in New Jersey? And how did you know I was here?" I ask rapid-fire as I let her into the apartment.

"What do you mean what I am I doing in New Jersey?" She's not facing me, but I can hear the eye roll regardless. "You left your husband! You signed a six-month lease! Of course I came."

I practically jump into her arms, wrapping her in a tight embrace. "Thank you."

"Tell me everything," she says.

And so I do.

We're sitting on the floor in the living room, our backs against the wall. Cecilia kicked off her shoes at some point during my story, and her hair is up in a messy bun. I haven't seen her like this in a long time. I haven't seen her period. Despite the tension of my story, she seems relaxed.

"I can't believe Mom let you sign a six-month lease," Cecilia says and scans the apartment, her eyes discerning. "And a two bedroom at that."

I debate letting the remark go but find that I can't, even though I'm more than grateful that my sister came home for me. "You know why I wanted the two bedroom."

Cecilia shakes her head. "Yes, but you don't sign a six-month lease so that a wayward college student can have a soft landing when she'll only be around for six more weeks."

"Zoey's not some wayward college student. She's *our* sister." Usually when we have this argument, I'm resigned to my older sister's views, but today anger seethes through me. Maybe because I've been living with Zoey or maybe because I'm angry in general right now, but I can't. Not after so many nights of that sad soundtrack coming through the walls and watching our dad fish for any information on his eldest daughter's life.

"You know I don't see it that way," she says as she gets to her feet.

That should be the end of this conversation. Cecilia won't budge on this, but after Julian's misstep, I know deep in my gut that I would *never* disavow a child, no matter how they came to be.

"Dad broke up our family, Cee. *Dad* cheated on Mom. It's not Zoey's fault she was conceived from an affair."

I feel like a broken record, and I must sound like one. I've said this exact statement more times than I can count in the last seventeen years. Maybe Cecilia and Julian are more alike than I realized, both unable to evolve and settle and be. My older sister certainly has a penchant for running off anything good in her life. Did I marry my sister? Is that subconsciously why I give Julian chance after chance? I wring my hands, hoping to calm myself down, but the anger is already too deeply rooted.

"And"—I point an accusatory finger at Cecilia—"I think seventeen years is enough time to get over the trauma of our parents' mostly civil divorce. Especially because you weren't even there. You were away at college, and I was the one shuttled between parents and welcoming a two-year-old into my life."

"Mostly civil..." Cecilia trails off, shaking her head, but then she holds up her hand placatingly. "I'm sorry, I shouldn't have said that about Zoey." She walks into the dining room. "What are you thinking for this space?"

An hour later, we're at a trendy brewery across the street from the Princeton campus. My coworkers frequent this place. It's a good lunch spot and an even better happy hour option. The Christmas party was even held here once. With a majority of the student body gone for the summer and the workday already over, the restaurant is quiet, mostly filled with lingering corporate types.

On a whim, I texted my mom an invite to join us, and now she sits next to Cecilia and across from me. She isn't even surprised to see her eldest. That fact grates on my nerves, though it shouldn't. I know that even with the miles between them, Cecilia is closer to Mom than I am. It's an inevitable aftereffect of Cecilia following in our mother's footsteps. But knowing they are close and seeing it are two different things. It's like watching my dad and Zoey these past weeks but infinitely worse. Mom and Cecilia don't look alike, per se. Cecilia is dark haired like our dad with dark-brown eyes. Anna is a sandy blonde—natural, not bottled. She has green eyes that both of us wish we'd inherited. At least I won out with hazel, but I've always been the obvious mix of my parents. But beyond looks, there's nothing else they could be aside from mother and daughter. They talk the same way—with their hands. They laugh the same way. Their mouths form matching smiles, and their vocabularies mimic each other's.

"Listen," Cecilia says, her voice tentative and incredulous at the same time. Whatever she's about to say, I am not going to like it. Not one bit. "Don't get mad, but Evie sent me this text from the hotel and asked me to show it to you."

I take Cecilia's phone and glance at the event flyer without really taking anything in—because Evie. I thought things with Evie petered out months ago, as most of my sister's relationships do when they get too serious. Not that Cecilia will ever own up to the fact that she pushes away any good thing in her life and generally seeks out the not-good ones. It's glaringly obvious when you're paying attention, and when it comes to Cecilia, I'm always paying attention. At least, I thought I was. My mom's eyebrows practically reached her hairline at Evie's name, though, so it's not only me.

"Evie?" I ask innocuously.

Cecilia glares at me. "Yes, Evie."

"Is here with you?"

"Read the flyer, Liz."

I swallow my laugh. Poor Cecilia. She's in love, and she can't stand it. I look at the image on the screen, taking in the curly font and awful clip art. *Speed Dating for Divorcees*. Seriously. This is a real thing.

"Wow," I say because there are no words for this.

I hold the phone out to my mom, even though I'm certain she knows exactly what's on it. Her reaction is one of surprise though.

"But she's not divorced," Mom says, clearly intrigued, not aghast. I guess I'm glad they are both being supportive, but really? Speed Dating for Divorcees?

"I'm not even sure I'm going to be divorced yet," I add.

Neither of them scoffs at that, but they also don't show any signs of encouragement. When it comes to Julian, I'm on my own.

"That's what I said to Evie." Cecilia gives me a small smile, as if to let me know she didn't instigate this. "But she thought it would be good for you. You've been with Julian your whole life, and with the exception of that guy you dated right before you and Julian got engaged—who, if memory serves, you didn't even sleep with—Julian's been your entire love life."

I slept with Lucas. A lot. He wasn't some guy I dated before getting engaged to Julian. When Julian showed up at my door after a year of silence with an engagement ring, I'd been falling in love with another guy. I had moved on in a lot of ways. But while I was in Philly ensconced in a lust hole, Cecilia was building her real estate empire in Chicago. To her, my engagement probably looked as simple as kicking Lucas to the curb and falling back into bed with Julian. It was anything but simple. It wasn't even easy. But I'm not about to say any of that in front of my mother or give them any more ammunition.

Cecilia continues, unaware of the highlight reel she's kicked off in my mind. "She thinks you need to remember there are other options out there and that they are, in fact, available to you."

"I like this Evie," my mother says, a mischievous look on her face.

I arch an eyebrow at the two of them. "You're saying I need to find myself a Sheila?"

My mother nods emphatically. "Yes, that exactly."

What in the world? My mother condoning dating while married? Does it count if you're separated? What are the rules here? Will "my mother, who was totally and utterly betrayed by an extramarital affair, said it was okay" stand up in relationship court? Probably not. I try to picture telling Julian I went on a date or slept with someone else. What are the deal-breakers here? Does it even matter if we're not emotionally together?

"Mom?"

"Honey, you and Julian are obviously separated. Why not go on a date or ten?"

"Ten."

She shrugs. "You never know what you'll like, you know, now that you can try all the flavors."

"Mom!"

"What? It took quite a few taste tests before I found one I liked after your father."

I'm going to vomit. Oh my god. I hand Cecilia back her phone, committing the information to memory. Speed dating doesn't actually count as dating. It's more like an interview of several available and probably horny men. Maybe I'll consider it. Later. When I'm not stuck in this god-awful conversation.

I turn to my sister. "I didn't think you told your girlfriends enough about your family for Evie to be so insightful on my situation."

She grimaces and then shrugs. "She's a psychologist."

"Well, since she's here, does that mean we get to meet her?"

We haven't met one of Cecilia's partners in years. She doesn't bring them to holidays or family dinners. In fact, my sister has seemingly gone out of her way to end a relationship whenever that possibility might happen. Including right before my wedding, when she broke up with her girlfriend and brought some random guy to the reception. Which wasn't out of the ordinary to us, but Julian's family, aside from his twin, was definitely confused.

Cecilia's shoulders slouch, and I feel the no coming. Maybe I shouldn't have asked with our mother sitting here. Cecilia is always more reluctant to talk about her love life when Mom's around. It's the one no-go place they seem to have. But then a grin splits Cecilia's face. *Uh-oh.* I'm going to like this even less than the flyer.

"Yes, you can meet her. If you go to speed dating."

Chapter 17
Cecilia

Evie and I need to spend more time in hotels. The pressure I feel building in our relationship releases in this small room. We're us but more. Away from my apartment, I am able to bask in everything that we are and give in to Evie's need to take care of me. Which is why I'm curled up on the couch with a book in my hand, and she's puttering around the kitchenette. I watch her futz with the takeout containers before my eyes glaze over as a replay of last night and what we did on this very couch runs through my mind. Evie pulling the book out of my hand. Evie crawling into my lap. Evie's hands at my waist, hips, lower and lower. Goose bumps rise on my arms.

"You all right over there?"

I blink away the erotica and focus on the real version of my girlfriend. She stares down at me with a grin that says she knows exactly where my mind is, and if I'm good, there will be more tonight. That grin holds dirty promises.

"Fine." I straighten and take the plate of food from the hole-in-the-wall restaurant down the street.

"I would've ordered you something," Evie says, sitting down next to me with a plate of her own. "But I figured you'd still be with Liz."

I shake my head, even though I assumed that until three this afternoon. "She's having dinner with Zoey."

"And you didn't want to join?" Her voice is innocent enough, but she's obviously fishing. Ever since the night I found out about

Liz and Julian and spilled the whole story—my dad, Zoey, Liz, Julian—Evie has been asking needling questions and psychoanalyzing
every response. Once, her interest in my life would've been irritating,
but now, I'm grateful to have someone to share it with. And the more
I tell her, the more I want her to know. Letting her in is terrifying,
but it's also fulfilling. It's been so long since someone really saw me,
since I let someone see the full picture. But Evie does, and she's not
running, which makes me want to stay too.

"Not really. For starters, they're both in the broken hearts club,
and no one wants to be around that."

"Zoey too?"

I nod. "Right before the end of the semester, Zoey caught her
boyfriend and her best friend in bed together."

Evie gasps and then glares at me. But truthfully, I didn't think to
include that in my story about Zoey at the time. I knew it happened,
but in the way I know anything happens in Zoey's life—because Liz
tells me. But hearing Liz talk about it stirred an inkling of sympathy
in my stomach. No one deserves that pain, and yet no one seems to
be able to escape it.

"Yeah," I say, resisting the urge to shrug. Something tells me Evie
would read way too much into it. "I was not dealing with that on top
of the awkwardness of the whole situation."

"The whole situation?"

It's a psychologist follow-up if there ever was one, down to the
deliberate innocence in her voice. She might as well have asked how
I feel about that. I almost give her a snarky answer, but the truth rolls
out of me instead.

"Liz said something to me the other day, that I should be over
our parents' divorce because it's been almost two decades and that
the divorce was mostly civil, considering."

Evie sips her wine, and I can see her mind running through
everything that falls under "considering." I'm not going to get the

girlfriend answer, not tonight. Not when she's staring at me as if I'm the best project that's ever fallen at her feet. "That seems like a valid assumption."

I think of all the weekends my mother came to see me that year after the divorce, after the Zoey bomb. I was a junior in college, living the quintessential college life despite being a professor's daughter. I lived off campus in an apartment with my two best friends. My father was on sabbatical that semester, which seemed weird timing. I wondered—still wonder—if he knew. Had he heard whispers of his former TA being pregnant and then signing up for the Peace Corps? Had he worried endlessly at night that his world could come crashing down? Does it matter? Whether he knew or not, I can't get past the endless tears my mother cried on those weekends she visited. The only place she could grieve without Liz as a witness. Liz, who hadn't complained about spending weekends with our father or babysitting her new sister, was falling in love with Zoey and Julian at the same time. She had fallen seamlessly into her new life.

"My parents' divorce might have been civil, but it wasn't as easy as Liz remembers. Our mom went to such great lengths to make sure Liz didn't see her upset. And my sister, god love her, believed my mom and loved my father and Zoey, as if it didn't hurt my mom every time one of their names came out of Liz's mouth."

Evie narrows her eyes and puts her wineglass down on the table. "Liz was... seventeen? I highly doubt she was that oblivious to your mother's feelings."

I open my mouth to protest, but Evie silences me with a look.

"Did you ever think that, maybe, as hard as that time was for all of you, Liz was making the best of it to survive? Just like your mom was hiding from Liz, maybe Liz was hiding from your mom."

The weight of that possibility hits me like a bar across the chest. Julian makes too much sense in that light. Liz couldn't be sad when our mother was devastated. She couldn't be angry since I had that covered. Liz had to be brave, and Julian held her up through it all. *Ugh.* This is why I don't tell Evie things. It's impossible to be righteously angry when your anger might be misplaced.

"I'd prefer the girlfriend answer. Please."

Evie rolls her eyes. "That bitch."

I laugh so hard tears sneak out. Evie almost never curses, a holdover from working with young kids all day. I kiss her lightly. "Thank you."

With that conversation effectively dead, we turn to other topics. Evie tells me about her day wandering around Princeton and meeting up with some old friends. I add in stories about the latest requests from a young client who wants a fixer-upper. Spoiler alert—they will not fix it up. Twilight falls, and we're still on the couch talking and laughing and touching. It's a perfect night, on top of a series of perfect nights. Two weeks of perfect nights. Not that I'm counting.

"So..." Evie starts after depositing our plates in the dishwasher.

I do not like the sound of that. "Yes?"

"I got you something." She perches on the edge of the couch. "But don't make it a thing, okay?"

I cross my racing heart. We're not gift givers, and I have an uncomfortable feeling about Evie's hesitation. She stares at me for a moment longer, gauging my mood, before finally pressing something small, pointy, and cold into my hand.

"I want you to have this for when we're back home." She says it assuredly, clearly, unrushed. She's been thinking about this for a while.

A key. *Wow.* It sits on my palm almost accusingly. Set. Point. Match. I close my fingers around it. It's not the first time Evie offered me a key, but it *is* the first time I think I might want to keep it. What is it about this woman? I literally can't quit her. I've tried, and somehow here we are. I don't allow myself to get into situations like this. It's rule number one. But I have no intention of returning to my own cold bed when we get home unless Evie wills me away. And I know she won't. Not when she's handed me a key to her apartment.

This is a gross overreaction to Liz's marital woes. I'm aware of that. But the news shook me. That and the fact that Liz ran to her *other* family. To Zoey. How many days was she in Ardena before she called me? Those were probably the hardest moments of my sister's life, and she didn't let me in until I flew across the country and demanded answers.

I tear my gaze away from the key clasped in my hand. Evie's eyes are full of love and hope. My stomach flutters.

"Thank you," I say, taking her hand.

Maybe this is the answer. Maybe letting Evie in is as simple and complicated as it has to be. Because sitting on this couch, Evie's hand in mine, I can almost pretend I don't care about anything else.

Chapter 18

Liz

The seating situation at work is slightly better today. Instead of being shoved into a storage closet, I'm in an actual office with a window, a chair that can be ergonomically adjusted, and a standing desk. The space still reeks of old man cologne, as if the stench has latched onto all the things left behind by the former occupant. As an added bonus I can also smell whatever hellish food someone is microwaving across the hall. The kitchen in this suite is mecca. Coffee gurgles all day, milk aerates, the microwave beeps, and people whisper. Closed doors aren't exactly a thing here. Sure, if you are on a call, but there's an unofficial—and literal—open-door policy. Still, it's better than the closet. And after I bought an infuser and attacked every surface with Lysol wipes, it's doable for now. The admin promises to have the boxes, papers, and other things out in another week. I'm not holding my breath.

People slouch past my office in a steady stream and are always straighter on the return. The magic of coffee. I watch the parade for a few moments, flipping through spam emails. There are so many every day. Half, I don't remember signing up for, and one, I know I've unsubscribed from several times since they email me three times a day. And yet, here is my second email of the day, right above a message from my mother. She probably sent another self-help article. My mom went from never texting during the work day to sending several articles a day by email along with a constant stream of texts. I'm positive if I look now there will be a message on my phone. Something like: *Checking in. Still want to see your new place. Pictures only do so much. Stop buying secondhand furniture! I know a guy.* If it wasn't absurd, it would be funny.

I scroll to the offending marketing email, ignoring my mom's latest intrusion, and click the unsubscribe button a little too forcibly. It feels good. I jam my fingers onto the keys to type in my reasoning.

"I hope I'm not on the other end of that email!"

Great, it's Angie from HR, a frequent kitchen whisperer. She couches her extended coffee breaks as part of the employee wellness initiative because "breaks and human interaction improve workplace morale."

"No, no," I say, sitting back in my chair. "Taking my frustrations out on a marketing email."

"For real, girl. Some companies are more persistent than herpes." She steps into my office and shuts the door. *Crap.* "Anyway, I wanted to check in... I saw your new address come through."

I expected this to happen, but I'm still not ready for it. The fact that we moved from our house in the suburbs to a popular Princeton complex is a red flag that something's wrong. Whether it's Julian losing his job or me moving out. But I felt uncomfortable leaving my old address as my primary address at work. He's still my emergency contact, so I hope that will squelch any rumor mill gossip. Watching Angie watch me now, though, I can't help but wonder what it'll look like if I change my address back in six months? Or what it'll mean if I don't have to.

"Everything's fine." I don't put that false brightness into my answer that requires energy I don't have right now. "Julian and I are..." Tears prick behind my eyes, and my chest constricts. Who would've guessed that this would be the hardest part—telling people, admitting defeat. It's awful. "Taking a moment," I say finally.

My life feels like a soap opera—the prime-time ones, not the day-time ones, at least. I can see the marketing campaign. *Will Julian and Liz find their way back to each other? History says yes, but this time Liz might say no.* Where are the #Lilian shippers when you need them? Back in West Dover, believing the fairy tale. But true love's kiss isn't going to fix this one.

"I'm sorry, Angie," I say to her awkward silence. "I think I'm going to get some air."

B arnes & Noble is quiet this early in the day. The lunch-break browsers are still enjoying their ten o'clock coffees, and the stay-at-home parents already have their kids at music or ballet or pre-K readiness. I let the scents of paper and ink and wood wash over me. It's soothing for my frazzled soul. It always has been.

As graduate students, Julian and I lived around the corner from a bookstore. It was a small indie and perfect. In the weeks after Julian left me, the crowded aisles became my refuge. It was the one place in all of Philadelphia that calmed me. Jane would find me there and drag me home, forcing meal after meal upon me. The owner would thrust bottles of water at me and let me take home more books than I could carry.

The similarities between myself at twenty-four and myself now are heartbreaking. And next time, because I'm coming to accept that there will always be a next time with Julian, will it be an actual physical betrayal? I'm not sure I'm willing to live my life waiting for a next time anymore.

Fuck. I swipe at my cheeks. So much for the calming effect of books. With a sniffle, I turn down another row of shelves. The book I was reading—a slow-burn romance about daemons, vampires, and witches steeped in a mystery about a missing book—still sits on my bedside table in West Dover. It's going to stay there for the next six months, if not indefinitely, which means I need to buy it again because I must know what happens. Will the vampire return from Oxford to confess his forbidden love for a witch?

Except ten minutes later, I still can't find it. It has to be in stock. It was recently given the television treatment and became quite popular. I know it's sitting on a table in plain view—they always are—but I can't do another lap of the store, and I have a meeting in fifteen minutes. I glance at the man leaning against the help desk. Khakis and a polo, what looks like a phone strapped to his belt loop, a jawline for days. He has to work here.

"Excuse me," I say, walking toward the desk, "can you help me find a book?"

The man looks up with an easy smile, amusement coloring his gorgeous golden eyes. Good god, I will buy a book every day for the rest of my life if he works here. Soft eyes, five o'clock shadow at midday, lips that tease me with their suppleness. I try to calm the burning I feel crawling up my neck. *Calm down, body! It's not like we've never seen a hot guy before today.*

"I'm happy to try." His voice is as smooth and lust-inducing as his body.

I hold my phone up to show him the book in question. He nods, and instead of walking around the desk and typing something into the computer, he heads off toward the cash registers.

"I'm pretty sure I saw this on the table up front with the other books that made the *leap from page to screen.*"

Oh my god. He does not work here. It's obvious as he scans the store for the table rather than walking right to it.

"Oh," I say, my voice high and slightly manic. "I thought... You had that phone. I'm sorry."

He smiles again, unconcerned, and pulls the phone off his waist. "Bravo delta, what's your location?"

It's a freaking walkie-talkie. "I'm so sorry."

He laughs, his eyes trained on the table in front of him. He turns and hands me my book. "Not a problem at all."

My cheeks burn, but there's no helping it now. "Thank you."

"I don't know why they don't leave any on the shelf when they put them out on these tables. It's infuriating and confusing." He holds out his hand. "I'm Spencer."

The walkie-talkie streams static before I can answer. The high-pitched voice of an adolescent boy comes through. "Bravo alpha, the target has been located."

I watch their exchange warmly, unable to ignore the fact that Spencer's eyes never leave mine as he handles the walkie-talkie. After a moment, I turn to my book. I could get lost in those eyes forever.

"Good work," he says into the device. "Bring her in to the check-out line, captain."

"Yes, general, sir."

I look up again as he hooks the device back onto his pants. "My son forgot his copy of *James and the Giant Peach* at camp and seemed to think he could get away without doing his weekend reading."

I nod as if I know anything about children. Sure, I'm the cool aunt to Jane's kids when I need to be, but by definition that makes me too cool for summer reading lists.

A child, maybe eight or nine, walks up to us then. He clutches two books to his chest, the Dahl and a manga with a name I vaguely remember—*Naruto*. "Dad, can I get this too?"

"Sure, buddy. Can you say hi to..."

"Liz." I offer the boy a smile. "And you are?"

"Ryan." He points to the book I hold. "My mommy has that book."

"All right, bud," Spencer says, and I swear a look of chagrin passes over his face. "Let's go pay and get through these chapters. I don't want to spend our whole weekend together reading about an orphan who lives in a magical peach."

Ryan sighs dramatically. "No spoilers, Dad. That's like the first rule of life."

Spencer rolls his eyes and gives me one last smile, his eyes locking on mine. "Enjoy your book, Liz."

Chapter 19
Cecilia

"Stop fidgeting." Evie cups my cheek, and her deep-brown eyes meet mine. "I've never known you to be nervous."

That's because I've never introduced you to my family. "I'm not nervous. Liz is late."

Evie rolls her eyes, clearly seeing through my pathetic excuse for a lie. "By five minutes."

The door to the restaurant opens, and then Liz is there, an excited smile on her face. She's come straight from work. "Sorry, sorry," she says. "Route 1 traffic was a bitch. It took me like fifteen minutes to drive two miles."

"It's fine," I say and slip my hand into Evie's. My heart is in my throat. I don't do this, and yet now that it's happening, it feels inevitable and right. Keeping separate lives is a burden that I didn't understand until this moment. "Liz, this is my girlfriend, Evie. Evie, this is my sister."

"It's about time," Evie says, nudging me with her shoulder. At the same time, Liz laughs and exclaims, "Finally."

Right. They're going to get along great.

Two hours later, our dinner has long since been cleared, the wine's run out, and we still chat easily. Evie leans forward, taking in everything my sister says, her hand never leaving mine. Liz sits back in her chair, more relaxed than I've seen her since I've been here. For my part, I have no idea what they're talking about. But I love this moment. It's unexpected and everything I thought I never wanted, and yet it's been more than perfect. I'm not sure why I've been avoiding this.

"Wait, wait, wait!" Evie's voice pulls me back to the conversation. "Cecilia used to do what?"

Uh-oh. There are any number of stories that my sister could be sharing about our childhood. The glee behind Liz's smile is disconcerting and gives it away. I want to throttle my sister. This inside look into my life is something I haven't given anyone since my college boyfriend. But letting Evie all the way in has opened a long-sealed door. Every day its rusty hinges loosen further. Maybe this time, with this woman, things can be different. Maybe *I* can be different.

"Play wedding," Liz says through a giggle. "She did it often enough that our parents got her a fancy white dress. She would decorate the living room, put on classical music, and make our next-door neighbor marry her. I, of course, was maid of honor, which really meant I had to do whatever she said. She is quite the bridezilla."

I glance at Liz, taking her measure. She's not drunk. We only shared a bottle of wine between the three of us, and that was with more food than was healthy. She's happy.

Evie's eyes are bugging out of her head when I turn to her. And true, this doesn't fit with the woman she's known for the last year. "And this went on for how long?"

"Oh, maybe a year?"

"And what happened to your husband?"

I blink. It's been ages since I thought about Dan. Dan, who had been my first kiss, my first love, my first everything. "We eventually dated for real. His family moved to Chicago about halfway through junior year, and that was that."

It most certainly wasn't that simple, but time and distance and maturity have given me a different spin on the situation.

"You never saw him again?"

I shrug. "We kept in touch at first. You know, the whole 'It's only a year and a half, and then we can go to college together.' He visited once for junior formal, but even then, we knew whatever it had been had passed."

That's true but also a lie. We broke up when he moved, and I hated him for it. But we'd been friends for so long, we tried to stay that way, but when he came for the dance, he'd already been dating and I'd already figured out that maybe I liked girls as well as boys. I wasn't willing to compete with girls halfway around the country, and he wasn't willing to compete with girls at all.

"The divorce was quite amicable," I say. We're even friends on Facebook. Not that I'll ever let that slip in front of Evie or Liz.

Evie laughs but then clears her throat. "Sorry to break up the party," she says, "but my car is here."

I glance at my watch. The night went too fast. I'm not ready for Evie to head to Philly and get on a plane to Chicago. Not without me with her.

We gather our things and walk outside. Liz pulls Evie into a big hug, and Evie promises to visit again soon. It's heartwarming but also ridiculous. My sister is such a meddler.

Liz gives me a pointed look and then heads off toward the car to give Evie and me some privacy for our goodbye. Once my sister climbs into her car, I pull Evie into me. Our lips meet, and it feels like coming home. After a week in our hotel room, night after night cuddled together, nothing of our normal lives to interfere, I'm not ready to sleep on my own. I've been feeling like this all day. As if this goodbye might break me, even though we go days without each other back home. I spent the hour Evie went down to the fitness center to examine these feelings. I never examine feelings. I've never even wanted to. But I did. And the truth was plain. I don't want to go back to a relationship defined by distance. I also don't want to lose myself in Evie. Balance and patience are going to be key. I can't change overnight. I'm still the same woman with the same hang-ups, and eventually something will pull me away. But, by acknowledging these realities, maybe I can mitigate the fallout.

"I wish you didn't have to leave," I say.

She kisses me lightly. "I know. I wish I could stay longer, but I can't miss another week. My clients need me, and I have to prep for a placement trial."

"You're so *good*."

She meets my gaze with a quizzical look. I don't blame her. I'm not usually effusive with my praise. "You okay, Cee?"

I nod and pull the key I had freshly minted this afternoon out of my pocket. I press it into her palm. "I hope you'll use this when I get back."

Evie wraps her fingers around the key without looking down at it. Her eyes are watery with tears. "Thank you. This means... a lot to me."

I smile and don't flinch away from the emotions playing across her expression. We both understand the enormity of my actions and the gesture I'm making with this gift. "I'm sorry it took me this long."

Chapter 20
Zoey

"**Y**ou have an overnight bag. Why do you have an overnight bag?" I ask, closing the door behind Becca. I don't remember planning a sleepover, but then it's been a *week*. Which Becca knows, and it's not like we need permission from our parents—or even each other—to crash. We've been sleeping at each other's houses for over a decade.

"Oh." Becca glances around for Dad, who isn't here, and then leans in conspiratorially. She's totally not spending the night. I'm about to be an alibi. "Ben's parents are out of town for their anniversary. My mom doesn't know, but you know how she is. I made like I was spending the night with you now that Liz is gone."

Like I need a reminder that my sister officially moved across the state this morning, just as we were finally getting close. "So you're sleeping at Ben's tonight?"

Becca's smirk extends into a full-on grin. "I don't think there will be much sleeping."

I stop in my tracks. With how Becca and Ben have been dancing around her virginity all summer, I honestly stopped thinking she was going to hand it over. But that smile...

"Are you saying what I think you're saying?"

"Last hours as a virgin!" Becca whispers the words as we plop down on my bed, like her mother can hear her across the houses. "Any advice?"

"Close your eyes and think of England?" I duck in time to avoid being hit in the face with a pillow. "Relax and try not to overthink it. Let it be what it's going to be."

"Can you not overthink losing your virginity?"

"You can try," I say, hugging the pillow to my chest. "I built it up so much. You know, junior prom. Andrew and I were in love, and we had the whole Wildwood cottage to ourselves..."

Becca leans forward even though she knows every detail about that night. "You said it was perfect."

I shrug. "Yeah, I mean, it was nice and meaningful. Our whole relationship shifted after that night. But when I think about Andrew, even when we were still together, I don't usually think about that first time. There were so many more important moments. Maybe not as big as the first time, but I think that's the point."

She nods, but she's already overthinking how not to overthink. She bites her bottom lip, and behind her glasses, her eyes are unfocused, her hands absently playing with the hem of her shirt. There's no one quite like my bestie.

"Did you want to do something before the big night?" I ask in an attempt to bring her back to reality.

She shrugs. "It's Friday night. Everyone's going to Lola's."

Ah, Lola's. I've meticulously avoided the café since getting home. A party here or there I can tolerate, but being forced into a tiny late-night coffee shop with small booths and even smaller minds is not my idea of a good time anymore. Not when all anyone wants to know about are Andrew and Claire and how I "let" that happen. Yeah. Because I totally suspected my best friend was going to fuck my boyfriend and let them hang out, regardless. Nothing like a small town to give you a complex. It's no wonder I'm still sleeping with Andrew.

"We can go," I say, hoping my voice sounds resolute. I'm tired of hiding, and it's not helping anything. Plus, *I* didn't do anything wrong. Andrew and Claire were awful to me, and yet I'm the one hiding while they party and go to Lola's every weekend.

"We don't have to, Zo." She almost looks ashamed, but I'm not fooled. "I know it's not your scene anymore."

It was never Becca's scene. Not until Ben happened over Christmas break. My whole high school career was a balancing act of hanging out with my varsity friends, including Claire, without hurting Becca's feelings or making her feel left out, and now Becca's the one staying behind to appease me. I will not allow it.

"I want to go. I'm not some scorned woman who needs to hide away due to the shame of my husband's infidelity. I'm a college kid whose ex-boyfriend is an ass."

"True, but—"

"I know Claire will probably be there. I'll be fine." I would in no way be fine. The last time I really saw Claire, she was pulling her clothes on as I tried not to vomit. But we live in the same small town, and we go to schools within the same ten-mile radius. Our running routes intersect. Our lives overlap enough to be close but not claustrophobic, as Claire put it when we decided on the neighboring schools.

"You're sure?"

"Yes, Bec. My options are literally hang out at Lola's with my bestie in her final hours of virginity or watch *Outlander* with my dad."

Becca cringes because there are few things more awkward than sitting next to your single dad during the endless sex scenes. "Right. Lola's it is, then."

The air is thick with coffee and carbs and sweat. Too many Ardena students and alum are crowded inside. The noise level is a decibel above loud. A few heads turned at my entrance but not many.

Thank god. Maybe the flaming end of my relationship has run its course. More likely, it's not as exciting without Andrew or Claire also in attendance.

I'm squished into a booth with Becca and Ben. There's so little space that I'm practically on a first-name basis with the wall, and the other side of me is knocking into Becca with every breath. She's doing the same to Ben, who is practically falling out of the booth. How many nights had I sat like this with Andrew and Claire, never wondering, never concerned when we mushed together? My whole life is here. At least, my whole Ardena life. It seems small in a way it didn't over Christmas break. I could tell you something about everyone in this room, and for most of the patrons, something meaningful. Growing up ensconced in the drama that is my family, I loved this tight-knit town. I needed friends and community to compensate, but now I'm not so sure it's a good thing.

I scan the space again, my eyes landing on Andrew's best friend, Rob, and his usual crew. Andrew isn't there. He doesn't go out the night before Wildwood week. He spends the night with his mom and packs and repacks and checks the schedule and tinkers with his car. Andrew is a lot of things, but careless isn't one of them. Which is why, in the darkest hours of the night, I wonder if he wanted me to catch him. Cheating is heartless, but doing the deed in a dorm room I frequented twenty minutes before I was meant to arrive? That's careless in a way that Andrew is not, that any person cheating cannot afford to be. These are the questions that still haunt me and that I can't ask. Why Claire? Why let himself get caught? Why come back if he wanted to be away from me so badly? Why?

Stop.

My heart races, and in my lap, my hands shake. I cannot spiral here. I cannot cry in front of my world. *Breathe.* The whys might never get answered. Andrew isn't going to tell me freely, and I am never going to ask him and break my heart again. Whatever the answers, they will be the end of everything. There's no going back once I know why. Nothing to chase but a devastating truth. But then, was there ever really a possibility of going back? Would getting back together with Andrew make me happy? Or would it be a stopgap until it comes crashing back down? I force the questions from my head. Andrew and I are not getting back together. Not tonight. Probably not ever. I squeeze my hands together until they stop shaking.

"Zo." Becca nudges me with her elbow. I turn to her and hope she can't see the panic waiting under my skin. She's so happy that her eyes barely take me in. She's irrevocably in love. Finally. "We're heading out. Do you want us to drop you off first?"

I want to be nowhere near alone with Ben and Becca pre the first time they do it. "No, I'm good. Be safe."

Becca gives me an incredulous look that says *obviously, you dummy*. "We'll debrief in the morning." She giggles at her own bad joke. "Pun totally intended."

And then she's gone. Becca's—well, more accurately, Ben's—crowd isn't exactly mine. I know these people, went to school with most of them since kindergarten, but spending time alone with them? I wish I could spot one track friend in the room, but I don't. Someone slides in next to me, and while I'm not cramped against the wall, I'm most certainly trapped. I focus on the conversation. Pledging. They're talking about pledging. Perfect. Many schools have rules about freshmen joining Greek life in their first semester or at all, but Bellewood isn't one of them. The only letters I wear tonight hang around my neck, a gift from Andrew, but there's no way I'm giving up my letters. I untuck them from my shirt.

"I'm a Delta Sig." Several sets of eyes turn toward me because, of course, that's the first thing I've said all night to the group. "What do you want to know?"

An hour later, the group is still going around in circles. It took me a minute, but soon after I jumped into the conversation, I realized everyone around me goes to Rutgers. While my feedback on the process was appreciated, it was not particularly relevant. Delta Sig isn't a house on campus. And though Dad teaches there, he knows nothing about Greek life. I'm not even sure he can properly identify my sorority despite all the letters I have in our house. When the guy next to me goes for more coffee, I slip out after him.

I need a breather. Talking about my sorority is one of the few things that make me feel normal, that has no Andrew strings attached, but it also makes me miss my sisters and Bellewood desperately. Even after my life blew up, running the loopy paths of campus and into town, avoiding the ones I knew Claire frequented, was one of my few reprieves. Haley, my sorority big sister and roommate, was the other. She is exactly who I need right now. She would talk sense into me and would never let me off the hook for sleeping with Andrew. Not that Becca would. But Haley's reaction would be fierce, whereas Becca's would be disappointed.

I step into line for the bathroom. It's relatively short—a small miracle. Lola's has two single-stall, gender-neutral restrooms. The owner always laments on Friday nights about how he's going to upgrade, but he never does and probably never will. Some nights the line for the restroom winds far enough back that people who would never order another drink or pick up food find themselves standing in front of a display case. Lola's is not Ardena Café quality overall, but a Lola's apple crumble is a joyous thing in its own right. Thankfully, the case is far behind me tonight.

Despite the ache in my chest for my sorority sisters, tonight's been a good night. It feels normal in a way that home hasn't in a while. Maybe surviving the rest of this summer won't be so hard. Maybe, instead of surviving, I need to reclaim my place and realign my expectations. Determination swells in me. I can do that. Ardena is my home, and that doesn't have to be a bad thing. I'm Zoey Reid—not Andrew's ex-girlfriend or Claire's former best friend or the girl my classmates whisper about when I'm not in the room. My whole life has been about redefining the narrative, thanks to my mother and father's affair. If I can turn that story, I can turn this one.

The bathroom door opens, and my heart stops. A chill enshrouds me. I gasp for breath even though I'm breathing too fast. Claire's eyes meet mine, and I take a step back, but there's nowhere to go in the small space unless I literally flee. And that will not help redefine the narrative. Instead, I count to ten and force my breathing back to a measured rate before facing my former best friend.

Chapter 21
Zoey

Claire's lost weight, and there are bags under her eyes. The stress kind, not the partying kind. Her usual effervescence is dimmed. Pain lances across my chest. I wince against both the unexpected sympathy I feel and the similarities between Claire's appearance and my own. My best friend—*former* best friend—is in pain, and I hate it even now. But she did this. She broke my heart into a million pieces and shattered my whole world. Claire doesn't get to be in pain.

"Hi." Her voice wavers on the single word.

I don't say anything. I can't. My body is frozen in place, and the only thing holding me together is my silence. I don't know what I thought seeing Claire would be like, but this feeling as if I've been sucker punched is not it.

"Haven't seen you here in a while," she says, trying again. "But I guess you knew Andrew wouldn't be here since he's leaving for Wildwood tomorrow. Rob still thinks it's weird that he insists on going down before everyone else."

This is peak Claire awkwardness. Not many people see this side of her—lonely, hesitant, rambling. Claire puts off that she's cool and collected, energetic with too much sass. But I know better. She continues to ramble. Most of it doesn't compute, but I gather that she's here with her on-again boyfriend Rob, who is also Andrew's best friend. *Only Claire.*

I feel eyes on us the longer she blocks the bathroom door. But still I can't move. I'm not even sure I'm breathing. I clasp my hands to keep them from shaking and so I don't smack her in front of all these people.

"Excuse me?" A voice from behind me cuts Claire off midsentence. Claire turns burning eyes on the girl, who when I chance a glance behind me, I realize can't be more than a sophomore. But she meets Claire's gaze head-on before transferring her attention to me. "Are you going to use the bathroom?"

"Yes, sorry." I slip past Claire and into the bathroom. Once inside I let out a breath and then another. My forehead is damp and my hands clammy. I'm weak on my feet, and if I wasn't in a public restroom, I would have already sunk to the floor. It took everything not to confront Claire. How can she stand there and talk to me as if we're long-lost friends? As if I don't hate her with every fiber of my being?

I turn on the water and splash my face. Before I straighten, the door opens and Claire steps in. She shuts and locks the door behind her. Why didn't I do that? *Fuck me.*

"Are you really not going to say a single word to me?" She grips the doorknob, as if I'm going to bum-rush her to get out. And it's not the worst idea I've had tonight.

"I have to pee," I say finally.

She shrugs. "Then pee. It's not like we haven't peed and talked in this very bathroom before." When I don't move, she crosses her arms and leans back against the door. "Fine, tempt fate to give you a bladder infection, but I'm not moving until you talk to me."

"I have nothing to say to you."

"Oh, I highly doubt that."

The rambling girl who was caught off guard by my appearance is gone. This is Claire as everyone else knows her. This is her fierce and unforgiving and in control. If I want to be mad, that's fine with her, but I better at least scream about it. My therapist suggested something similar. But will it really make me feel better? I don't think it will. I've decided how I feel about Claire. We're done, forever. Screaming about it will only open up those feelings again. But a part of me wants to do it, wants that release.

Claire's phone lights up, and a photo of Rob appears.

"I can't believe Rob can stand to look at you, let alone touch you." My voice is incisive. It's not yelling, but it'll do. Hurtful words come easily in a way they never do with Andrew. They both betrayed me—I know this—but Claire was my best friend, and breaking that trust is so much worse.

"I told him his penis is bigger than Andrew's and that he was better in bed." She looks up from her phone, her gaze locked on mine. "Between you and me, though, Andrew is superior in many ways."

My stomach churns, and I will my body to hold it together. Throwing up on Claire is unacceptable. That would mean losing today's battle, and I will not capitulate. Anger burns under my skin. My hands curl into fists, and I force them back open. Punching Claire is also unacceptable. Karma will come back to her. It always does.

"But apparently you're not superior." The words are out of my mouth before I can even consider them. The rational part of my brain knows this is a bad idea. But anger wrapped its arm around rational and pulled it deep down into a cage where I can no longer hear its pleas.

"And why's that?" she asks, her tone suggesting she has no idea what I'm about to drop.

My lips curve into a smile. It's malicious and cruel and not me but also me *after*. "Because I'm the one he's still fucking."

Chapter 22
Cecilia

"Tell me more about this guy." I curl my feet up under me and balance my wineglass on the arm of Liz's couch.

She did a superb job furnishing her apartment quickly and on budget. I'm impressed by my little sister's know-how. It's almost like she's been paying attention all these years. The small space looks put together and cozy. The armchair in the corner makes you want to lounge with a book, and I can imagine cuddling with Evie on the couch. The galley kitchen is the standard, but Liz added pops of color to it with dish towels and utensil holders and a few of those clever signs—"Many people have eaten in this kitchen, few have died." It's not my style, but it screams Liz to me in a way that her house with Julian never did. Regret scratches at me. The apartment is Liz without Julian.

Liz glares at me from the overstuffed armchair. She's been in a fabulous mood since she showed up for dinner, but now the stress is showing. It's etched in her face and in the set of her shoulders. And even though she hasn't said it, or even really shown it, she's hurting. A lot. Julian is the love of her life. Until now, that's always been enough.

I sip my wine, swallowing down my worry with it. "Tell me about this guy."

"It wasn't anything, Cee." She fiddles with her wedding ring. "Besides embarrassing."

Liz's cheeks are pink, her eyes downcast. Embarrassing or not, my sister felt something. That's probably the problem itself. Happily married people don't feel things for random bookstore dads.

"You are allowed to think another guy is good-looking, Liz."

"I know that."

I'm not sure she does. I'm not sure of anything, honestly, because she's been tight-lipped about it all. But if Liz is planning on making this "break" permanent... I can't stop my brain from starting an endless loop of Ross and Rachel. Will that be Liz and Julian in a few months? Fighting over what happened during their time apart and if their marriage vows had still applied? I'm not even sure if I want them to get back together. What I want is for my sister to be happy and cherished and loved. And she is those things with Julian most of the time. But, if I'm honest, I'm getting tired of looking past the rest of the time.

"Are you going to take your ring off?" Probably not the best icebreaker, but if Liz turns her ring any more, she is going to burn through her finger.

"I don't know," she says, finally looking up at me. "I mean, I'm still married."

"Technicality."

"You're right. And I know Julian was off doing god knows what with god knows who all the other times we broke up, but we were kids, Cee. We're not kids anymore. This is my *marriage*."

"He's the one who forgot that." I lean forward and take her hand in mine. "Wear the ring or don't. Sleep with Hot Bookstore Dad or don't."

"I don't even know his last name!"

"My point is," I continue as if she hadn't protested, "you don't owe Julian anything right now. This next six months is about you and what you want."

She flops back in the armchair and worries at her bottom lip. "What if that's not Julian?"

I shrug, though I feel anything but nonchalant about that response. "Then it's not Julian."

Liz pulls the ring off her finger and places it on the table in front of her. I'm nauseous with anxiety at her action and have equally never been prouder. I resist the urge to pick up the ring and instead find myself awestruck by the gleaming white line on her ring finger. The evidence of her marriage will be there for quite some time. As if Liz notices it, too, she tucks her hand under her leg.

When she looks back at me, her eyes are dry and steady. Maybe after leaving and signing a lease and changing her address, taking the ring off is a formality. But no, her lip quivers, and her free hand clutches her wineglass like it's holding her together.

"I can see how Evie managed to stick around so long," she says, effectively changing the topic.

I'm about to protest, but her expression as she stares at her ring stops the words in my throat. "It's only been a year."

"Seemed pretty serious tonight." She grins. "I mean, you gave her a key."

I narrow my eyes. "Were you eavesdropping?"

She laughs. "Of course."

"You know I don't do serious," I say in an attempt to wave away the heart emojis that have replaced my sister's eyes. "But I do care for her."

She rolls her eyes. "I think that's the wrong four-letter word."

Love. The word always makes me think of Liz and Julian. In a way, their imperfect and resilient relationship became my definition. They are one of the few couples I've gotten to watch grow over the years, from teenagers to post-grads to married adults. All the while, I flitted from one partner to the next, never finding a person who made me want to use the L word or let my guard down. Until Evie.

"I have told Evie that I love her."

I remember that night. I think about it often. What made me tell her when I withheld from so many before. It was shortly after I rejected her request to move in together. I thought I was days away from getting dumped. Hours, if I was being honest. Evie was in a foul mood, unusual for her. Midway through our argument, she stopped and asked me point blank if I loved her. Because even though it was eight months into our relationship, I had yet to tell her, despite the fact that she'd told me months ago. Her vulnerability in that moment caught me off guard. "Yes," I told her. "I love you more than I ever thought I could. More than I have loved anyone in a very long time." And that was that. Evie sat down, picked up her wineglass, and returned to our regularly scheduled program. Because she knew how much she'd won in that moment.

"She also understands that I don't need to flaunt that particular emotion constantly," I say to my sister's incredulous expression. "But these last three months, when she pushes I don't necessarily want to pull away."

"Good," Liz says with a giant, cheesy smile. "You deserve happiness."

I scoff at the notion. "Love does not define my happiness."

"Semantics." She rolls her eyes. "You deserve to love and be loved, Cee. I'm not sure why you think otherwise."

"I don't think that."

It's technically the truth. It has nothing to do with deserving love or not. My father wrecked my mother after decades together. I saw the fallout, and I'm not willing to risk that level of heartbreak. I honestly don't know if I can survive it. But this isn't something Liz has ever understood.

"What happened with Mom and Dad," Liz says as if she can read my thoughts, "shouldn't define your future. Hiding from love will not keep you from getting hurt."

Okay, maybe she understands more than I think. But Liz is the hopeless romantic, and I am who I am—not hopeless or romantic.

Liz's cell phone springs to life. She glances at the screen, surprise coloring her expression. When I see Zoey's name on the screen, I understand why. It's Saturday night, and Zoey is a college student with an active social life, but she is also a girl with a debilitating attraction to her ex-boyfriend.

"Zoey?" Liz asks, picking up the phone.

She doesn't walk out of the room, but she also doesn't put it on speaker. I watch her, her expression turning to annoyed concern. After a moment, she steps farther away, though I can still hear her half of the conversation. An inkling of disquiet gnaws at me. There's always been a wall between me and anything having to do with Zoey, but I don't like the worry lines on Liz's face.

Liz's voice cuts through the quiet, shrill and nervous. Her eyes meet mine over the back of the couch. "Zoey, what's happening?"

Chapter 23
Zoey

Twelve hours. Twelve blissful hours. Two in the car on the drive down to Wildwood, Wilderness Weekend blasting, our favorite road snacks between us. It felt like old times. The second we crossed town lines, Andrew's shoulders relaxed, his hand found mine, and he smiled—the first real and easy smile I'd seen from him in months. At the beach house, we fell into bed. We've hardly left it since. Beach? What beach? This is our love shack.

All the worry about my brash decision to go away with Andrew after leaving Claire flummoxed in Lola's bathroom was pointless. This lazy, slow, and emotionally charged lovemaking is exactly what Andrew promised. And everything I've been missing. When he said the words outside the high school that day, I didn't believe him, but it's clear that we've made it back. To each other, to love, to what could be. Everything I know of the past few months, of his infidelity, doesn't matter. Whatever Claire was, Andrew and I are together and in sync and perfect. Again. Finally. Maybe he needed to lose me to realize what we had couldn't be replicated. Isn't that the saying? Isn't that Liz and Julian's whole story, ignoring this current part.

"You were right," I say, rolling onto my side, Andrew's T-shirt hugging my curves. Andrew's still naked, the sheet pulled up only as high as his hips. Our entwined legs stick out of the bottom of the tangled sheets, mine tan from days on the track, his from days on the beach. My body trills at the sight, and my heart patters its normal, happy beat. I feel truly calm for the first time since April.

"About what?" he drawls sleepily. His eyes scan my partially clothed body with a frown.

"We needed this." I kiss him, letting our lips and tongues play. "I forgot what we can be when we're us. Being here, spending this time with you..." I put my hand over his heart. Warmth radiates through me, and I'm so giddy I have to suppress a rising giggle. "I'm glad we found our way back."

"Zoey."

"It's not going to be easy." I continue as if he hasn't spoken. I have to get this out. This is my chance, and if I don't take it, then what the hell have I been doing all summer? "Honestly, it's going to be messy, and no one is going to like it, but I love—"

"Stop." The word is forceful and filled with a mix of panic and aggression. My heart, which has been doing this fluttery prance in my chest, loses the beat. "Don't tell me you love me. That's not what this is. You knew that from the start."

"Whatever we agreed upon..." I start, trying and failing to keep the tremble out of my voice. He doesn't mean it. He can't mean it. "It didn't include weekends away and sex so intense that I felt everything we feel for each other deep in my soul. I felt it, Andrew." I take his hand in mine. "I feel it. I didn't believe you when you said we could find this feeling again, but we did."

"No, we didn't." He sits up and yanks his hand out of mine. "Is it too much to ask for one weekend? One lousy weekend where we could have fun, casual sex without slinking off to a shore motel or fitting it in while my mom's at book club?"

The hope from minutes ago, along with the bravado at asking for what I want, evaporates at his words. I knew. Of course I knew. But for that moment, I let myself believe that this could be real.

"And what if I want more than that?" *What if I deserve more than that?*

"There isn't more than that," he practically growls. He reaches for his boxer briefs. "There hasn't been more than that for a long time."

"Then why? Why would you seek me out? Keep coming back? Invite me here?" Here where we lost our virginities and cemented ourselves in each other's histories for all time.

He stares at the ceiling and pulls at his hair. His body pulses with agitation. "Because it was easier than having to court some townie for a few months. And you were *so easy*. I mean, that kiss by the pool was a moment of weakness. I did miss you. But then you *liked* it. You suggested we go someplace more private. I barely had to try. One look at Claire, and you practically mounted me in public."

That's a harsh-but-true retelling of the events of that night. If I'm honest, I didn't think Andrew was insightful enough to know why I decided to sleep with him for half the summer. But if I didn't kiss him back that night, if I let the moment pass, would we be strangers now? But I did kiss him. Because it felt like I would never know anything but heartache again, and that moment undid me. And I wanted to win. I wanted desperately to know that I was better—*am* better—than Claire in every single way.

Andrew walks to his open suitcase and pulls a new shirt over his head. "You can't fuck me into loving you again. You couldn't do it when I actually still loved you, and you definitely can't now."

The room narrows down to Andrew's dark and cruel eyes. Eyes that were once familiar but now feel like staring into the unknown depths of an abyss. *Who is this boy?*

I blink back tears. "You can stop, Andrew. I get the point."

"Do you?" He thrusts his legs into pants. "Because I thought I made it clear by sleeping with your best friend. I mean, how could we ever go back after that? What self-respecting person forgives her boyfriend for fucking her best friend? And yet, here we are."

His words hit like bricks. He picked Claire. Intentionally. Tears spill over, streaming down my face. I don't even try to stop the flow. My body shakes. My mind rejects this latest truth, one worse than all the others. Claire wasn't some organic and horrible mistake. It was calculated and planned. And by the person I loved most in the world. How did I misread the situation? How did I ever love him? Why does some sick part of me love him still?

"I'm going down to the beach," he says, not looking at me.

"The beach?" My voice is hoarse and raspy from the crying. It sounds like some other girl's voice.

"Yeah. There's a party." He pauses, nearly out of the room. "And Zoey, I would suggest not being here when I get back."

The front door slams a few seconds later, but I can't move. I can't breathe. My mind races through everything I thought I knew about the events of the last few months. All this time, I blamed Claire. Claire must have come on to Andrew. I blamed my best friend for the ultimate betrayal. How that betrayal came to pass, I didn't know. I didn't want to know and would hear no explanations. I knew there was something more to the situation, something that I steadfastly ignored all summer, but I couldn't have imagined this. That Andrew handpicked the one person who could irrevocably tear us apart.

My hands shake, and my legs barely support my weight as I fumble in my bag for my phone. I stare at it, nothing but a blur through my endless tears. Too many emotions pile onto my already broken heart. My mind can't process them all, and my body can't take this shock. My fingers tremble as I scroll through my contacts. Too many secrets leave me few options. No Becca, no track family, no Dad—definitely not Dad. Haley, the person I could call, is halfway across the country. I scroll past the H's, thinking of the one local person who might understand.

Chapter 24

Liz

Wildwood. With Andrew. Is Zoey out of her mind? *Yes.* And heartbroken and still desperately in love with someone who doesn't love her. When I left Thursday night, she seemed fine. More than fine. She declined my invitation to spend the week at my new place, citing work and Becca. Was it all a ruse?

"Where are you exactly?" I ask over the sound of Zoey's sobbing. It's not even crying. My sister's heart is being regurgitated through tears. I can hear the shattering of her soul. My heart clenches, and tears trickle down my own face. "Are you safe?"

"Yes, I'm still at the house." She sniffles. "He went down to the party at the beach."

All I want is the details, every last detail, but Zoey won't be able to bear it. Not right now. All that matters now is that my sister needs a way out. The what, why, and how the hell this happened can wait.

"Zoey, hold on one second, okay?" I hand the phone to Cecilia. "Talk to her for a minute and give me your phone."

"What am I supposed to say?" Cecilia hisses, her hand covering the mouthpiece.

"Just do it."

Not caring that I'm invading her privacy by rifling through her purse, I find Cecilia's phone and punch in the passcode she's used since college. Does she remember that it's the last four digits of her ex-boyfriend's cell phone number at this point? I hope not. Though she's a Reid sister, and long-held, misplaced romantic feelings seem to be a prerequisite.

I type Jane's number into the phone, hoping I'm remembering the calendar correctly and that she is where I think she is. Where I very well might have been this week. One town over from Zoey.

"Cecilia?" Jane's voice is heavy with trepidation because why would Cecilia call her?

"It's me." I push back the longing at hearing my best friend's voice. "You're down the shore, right?"

"Yes, Liz. Why?" My name sounds odd, but I don't have time to process a reason.

"I need a favor," I say. "Well, Zoey needs a favor."

"Zoey?"

"I can't really explain," I say too quickly. "But she's in Wildwood, and she needs a place to stay until I can get to her. Can I send her to you?"

"Of course, but..." Jane cuts off amid rustling sounds. I wonder briefly if she dropped the phone before another voice fills the line.

"Liz?" Julian. I've never been so happy to hear his voice. He will take care of Zoey, no question. He always has. "What's going on?"

"Andrew." The one word conveys everything necessary even though Julian doesn't know about my sister's current entanglement. "I'm going to have her Uber to you, okay?"

"No, I'll go get her. I'm texting her to send me that dickwad's address."

This is why it's so hard to move past him. Julian's solid and dependable and good. He knows exactly what I need without me having to ask. And, I note, he's not off fucking Sheila right now.

"Thank you."

"Thank me if I don't punch that kid in the face."

I laugh, but then turn my tone serious. "No punching."

Before our banter can kick in—because I know Julian's response would've been "A little bit of punching? What about a good slap?"—I hang up and retrieve my phone from Cecilia. She is talking to Zoey, though the conversation is stilted and about something innocuous, as far as I can tell.

Zoey is still sniffling on the other end of the line, but her tone is more upbeat than before, and the sobbing has stopped. Cecilia calmed her down. Hell has officially frozen over.

"I hear you are going to speed dating for divorcees," Zoey says.

Freakin' Cecilia. I try to laugh, but with Julian's voice still in my ears, speed dating is the last thing I can think about. I miss him. And as much as my mind is winning the battle, my heart wants to drive home and run into his arms *Notebook* style. I want to forsake all that is logical in the face of true love. *Fuck.* These thoughts are exactly why Zoey is sleeping with Andrew. Pop culture has trained us to believe in the exception. And it's easy to believe they can be the best version of themselves when their light is on you and only you. But too often we find ourselves left in darkness. We both need to stop forgetting the pain of that abyss.

I clear my throat. "Julian is across town and is going to come get you."

"But you're coming, right?" She sounds small and fragile and so, so broken.

"Yes," I say, my heart growing full even as it breaks for her. "I'm coming, Zoey."

Chapter 25
Cecilia

Liz scurries around the living room, shoving things into her purse and slipping into her sneakers. "Let's go."

She's serious. She wants me to come with her on a two-hour drive to pick up the half sister I never wanted.

"Isn't Julian getting her?"

"Yes," Liz says, her patience waning. "Until I can get there."

"Shouldn't Dad be dealing with this?" I hear the bitchiness in my voice, but I can't tone it down. Liz is in so deep that she can't even realize she's asking me to do the unthinkable. I do not involve myself in Zoey's affairs.

She narrows her eyes and juts her hip out. Totally pissed. *Great.* "She called *me*, Cee."

"It's at least two hours from here. You can go in the morning. She'll be fine with Jules and Jane."

That is apparently the wrong thing to say. Her pissed-off face goes to full-on anger in an instant. It's a face I'm all too familiar with. There's a special button that only sisters can press, and I clearly jumped on it.

"What is wrong with you?" she hisses. "Zoey has literally never done anything to you in her entire existence."

A fire blazes behind her eyes, a sisterly indignation I've only seen on Liz once before, and then it was given on my behalf and aimed at my ex-boyfriend. I never thought it would be turned on me. How could I when I only partly accepted the fact that I have a second sister? A half sister whose facial features reflect my own more than Liz's ever have. A half sister I can barely stand to look at, let alone save. But that look on Liz's face. If I don't recognize Zoey now, I'll lose Liz forever. Not some clean-cut estrangement, but a painful and desperate loss that will wear at me for days and weeks and months until I can't remember what a real relationship with my sister feels like.

"I know that." The words are but a whisper, but the admission is more than I've ever given. It does little to appease my sister.

"That asshole slept with her best friend then sought Zoey back out for a summer fling, and there's absolutely no doubt that he will bring another girl back to that house to prove whatever point he feels necessary."

"You're right."

If she hears me, she doesn't show it. "I'm driving there now, Cee, before this catastrophe gets any worse."

How could it get worse? Zoey dug herself a monstrous hole, and finding her way back out will be messy and painful. It will break her before it ever builds her back up. She is going to have to lose him again, and for keeps. Liz has never been able to do that with Julian. But I have. Our dad's betrayal left me broken and confused and so untrusting that I pushed my college boyfriend away until there was nothing to come back to. Before Evie, he was the last love in my life, and I lost him for keeps because of me. If I hadn't already been broken by my family's trauma, it might have been the worst pain I'd ever felt.

"Either get in my car or get out of my way," Liz says, finishing her tirade.

"Let's go then," I say, conceding, making my choice. Because I will always choose Liz.

She blinks, and her expression softens. Her shoulders sag, and her arms drop to her sides. "Seriously?"

"Someone's going to have to keep you from pummeling that kid."

She nods, unspoken acceptance passing between us. This is enough. *For now.*

Chapter 26
Zoey

The gentle creak of the rocking chair against the old wooden porch soothes me. I hadn't been able to find words when Julian showed up or after he secured me in the car and went in search of Andrew or when he came back, cheeks flushed and anger radiating off him. Even in the safety of his sister's home, words beyond pleasantries escape me. Emotions too strong to verbalize swirl inside me still. They are bursting to be released but also holding me hostage.

Finding Andrew and Claire together was a swift, clean-cut wound. Two of the most important people in my life were there, and then they were not. At least that's how it felt. There weren't talks to save either relationship. Their absence became a haunting reminder of what once was. But the second I kissed Andrew by the pool, the clean edges of the wound dirtied with infection, healing ceased, and now I'm septic.

Coming down here was a mistake from the beginning. I knew it when he asked. I knew it when I showed up at his house this morning. Going wasn't about Andrew or my misguided feelings. It wasn't about getting away from Ardena. It was always about winning. I wanted to beat Claire, and this was the only way I knew how, a fact that makes me completely and utterly pitiful.

A flash of Andrew's face malignant with anger brings back the night's memories. I cringe away from them, literally and mentally, desperately pulling anything but that look of disgust to mind. That only brings the image of Claire riding Andrew. *God, no.* Why does my brain hate me? *Please. No.* My fingernails dig into my palms, the pain bringing me back to myself.

Julian stands in front of me. He offers me a beach-themed coffee mug.

"Hot chocolate."

"It's ninety degrees out," I say, taking the mug.

"I thought it would make the whiskey more tolerable."

I shoot him a look. "Liz isn't going to like that."

"It's her idea," he says with a warm smile. Whatever he's done, he loves Liz in his way. "She's about thirty minutes away."

I close my eyes, a new and overpowering emotion pushing through the devastation—guilt. Liz and Julian have decided to part, and my stupidity is forcing them back together. What pain will this cause my sister? What hope might this give Julian?

"I'm sorry." I sip the drink. The chocolate does cut the alcohol but barely.

Julian sits down in a rocking chair next to me and puts his feet up on the ottoman. "You don't have anything to be sorry for."

I scrunch my nose in disagreement. "That's not true."

He only nods and continues to rock. His eyes scan the street. We're far enough from the main part of town that it's quiet here with only a few stragglers returning to their homes. Even the horse-and-carriage rides that pass by all day on historic downtown tours are done for the day. I've never been here before, but I remember Liz talking about the tranquility of this town and how whenever she arrived, she immediately felt at peace. After only an hour, I understand. There isn't a better place I can think of to lick your wounds and contemplate life.

The air between us is heavy. He wants to ask what happened. I want to know what went down when he disappeared for several minutes to go find Andrew. Neither of us is going to ask. Instead, we rock in a shared silence. It's familiar and comforting. This is how things have always been with us. Julian has been in my life as long as Liz, and he adopted me without question into his care. Even more so as he grew from teenager to young man to man. Unlike the other people in my life, he has no history with the Reids that doesn't include me. There's no awkwardness or might-have-beens. There's me as a natural and forever part of a complicated family. It's something I value. Something I will greatly miss if... no, I can't think about what Liz and Julian separating will mean for me. It's not about me. And really there's no question—Julian will fade away. He'll start a new life, and so will we.

After a long while, Julian stands and scans the street again. There's not a soul out there, but he pats my shoulder in farewell, regardless. "Liz should be here in a minute."

"Julian?" I ask tentatively. He stops at the door but doesn't turn around, as if he can guess my question. And he probably can. "Was he with another girl when you found him?"

"Yes," he answers, still facing the door. "Yes, he was, Zoey."

Chapter 27

Liz

Zoey's voice fades out. I lean my head back against the porch rail, my knees bent, my hands hanging loosely between them. She doesn't deserve this. People are callous with their words sometimes. Don't they realize the power and pain that words hold? Words dig in, burrowing deep into the subconscious, only to reemerge at your weakest moment. I blink back tears. Tears won't help anyone, but they fall regardless. My sister's pain is my pain. You never forget your first love, for better or worse. I married mine, and yet every time I hear the song that was playing when Julian broke up with me at prom all those years ago, it hurts. We were slow dancing, wrapped in each other. I was in love, and he said goodbye. It was another two years before we reconciled. Two years of that song being in popular rotation. Of wanting to vomit every time that damned Lifehouse track played. That loss of innocence, that last moment of being your whole self—it's soul altering.

Zoey had to lose that piece of her heart twice. I want to go down to the beach and shake some sense into that kid. What gives Andrew the right to play with anyone's heart like this, but especially Zoey's? Zoey, who loves him completely. Even now, it's tangible how much she loves him.

"Why didn't you have your car?" Cecilia's voice clashes against the quiet of the night.

With the silence broken, sounds come back to me—unseen crickets and tree frogs, horse hooves clomping on the next street over, the scratch and squeak of the rocking chair against the worn wooden porch. The question's been on the tip of my tongue since Zoey started her story, but after that ending, it doesn't seem particularly important. But then, Cecilia's always been more pointed than me.

"Oh," Zoey says, pulling her feet onto the seat of the chair. "I thought it was weird too. I offered to drive so that he could hitch a ride back with the guys, but he insisted on driving us. It didn't seem important to argue at the time."

"Hindsight's a real bitch." Cecilia smirks.

I palm my face. What is wrong with my older sister? I open my mouth to smooth out the comment, though I have no idea how, but then Zoey laughs. A small hiccup at first, but then a giggle escapes, and soon she is laughing hard, her hands grasping at her sides. She is bent over herself, hair covering her face. When she sits up, her cheeks are wet and red enough to be seen in the porch light. The smallest bit of fight has returned to her eyes.

Maybe bringing Cecilia isn't the worst idea I've ever had.

"Well," I say, pushing to my feet, "I'm going to thank your hosts, and then we'll be on our way."

"Should I come too?" Zoey asks, her voice hoarse.

It's probably the more polite thing to do, but I want to see Jane so badly, my body aches.

"No, I got it."

Walking inside the house is like entering another time and not because it's a Victorian with at least one known ghost. So much of my life is here. The Maddens have rented this house for this week for longer than I've known Julian. When their mother decided she didn't want to come anymore after their father's passing, Jane picked up the mantle. Jane and her husband, Michael, and Julian and I always split the week or came together. Then when Jane had her own family, they came for the week. Every year. It's how I knew to call Jane in the first place.

Jane. My best friend. If I leave Julian indefinitely, our friendship may be collateral damage. Jane and I made it through all the other breakups. What an abnormal thing to be able to say about your husband—all the other breakups. It always felt like perseverance, like Julian and I won something that others couldn't quite grasp. Our love was special and so real that we couldn't stay apart. If we weren't together, a part of ourselves was fundamentally missing. But listening to Zoey's story tonight, feeling her pain, it compounded my emotions surrounding the Sheila situation. I could've been Zoey if Julian were a crueler person, if I were weaker. But distance gave me space to make what I thought was a sound decision each time I took Julian back. Zoey went from small college campus to small hometown, both swirling with memories of a love gone wrong and a best friend lost forever.

I can't lose Jane. The thought alone leaves me feeling hollow. But I can't stay with Julian because of the fallout. I knew going in that I was risking my friendship with Jane, and I chose Julian. Jane and I survived his high school idiocy and went on to be college roommates. She saved me when he left in graduate school. But there were never legally binding documents to untangle and assets to divide. There wasn't Jane's pre-engagement warning to not marry her brother or her declaration that if things went south, Julian had to have her allegiance, no matter the circumstances. And we both knew with Julian, there would be circumstances. There wasn't an email log of conversations with another woman or a six-month lease on an extramarital apartment. Life became significantly more complicated in the last five years.

"Hey," Jane says before I've even kicked my shoes off, per the house rules. The sight of her alone is a balm—messy bun, slippers, beach loungewear, and a book tucked under her arm. My Jane. She pulls me into a one-armed hug, and it's like coming home. "I was coming to find you."

"We're heading out in a minute." I step back even though I want to hold on forever.

"She'll be okay." Jane's expression softens. "We all survived our first loves."

"I know, but it shouldn't be *this* hard."

She meets my gaze. A whole lifetime of unspoken words passes between us because it's always this hard. We just don't remember it that way.

"Maybe for Zoey, it has to be. Maybe this is the only way she'll ever be able to move on." She smiles lightly, her eyes glossed over in a memory of her own. I can guess at it. I was there for the end of Jane's first love, for the tears and the cocktails and the rebounds. How can these moments feel equally close and like they were lived in another life by another person? A Julian-less life.

"I'm going to have to call in reinforcements," I say, letting out a sigh, "and change her number."

"It's that bad?"

I nod, hating that this is my sister's truth. "If he texts her again, she won't be able to resist. Because—"

"That can't be their ending." Jane shakes her head, her lips pressed into a thin line. "We let her spend too much time in the editing room with Julian."

"Yes, we did," I say with a laugh.

Outside, I can hear Zoey and Cecilia's low tones. I'm not sure where Julian went, but I haven't seen him since I arrived, and his shoes aren't by the door. Maybe this is his way of giving me the space I asked for. He helped, but he doesn't need to be here when I am. A part of me wants to wait it out, to hug him and thank him. But if he wanted that, he would be here.

Instead, I give Jane another hug and then turn to go. She stops me with a hand on my shoulder. I can't read her expression, which is a first.

"When you leave him," she says, a shadow passing over her face, "be kind about it, okay?"

"I haven't decided anything." I twirl my wedding ring, which I remembered to slip back on before leaving.

Jane gives me a sad smile. "Yes, you have."

Chapter 28

Liz

I flop back onto my couch, kick off my shoes, and toe at my socks. After four hours in the car tonight, it feels good to be free. I flex my feet and wiggle my toes. Some of my stress falls away as the tension in my feet releases. Zoey's tucked into the guest room. Cecilia's rifling through the fridge, although she's not likely to find much. All I want is to sleep until Zoey wakes up, begging for nourishment and her phone back. She is not getting the latter. Tomorrow will be a long day—the day after is always worse. Sleep offers peace, peace that crashes into reality seven seconds after you open your eyes.

"Here." Cecilia waves a plate over me. "You need to eat something."

"It's not healthy to eat after midnight," I say around my small bite of sandwich—peanut butter and jelly, my favorite. "Especially something with this much sugar."

"Would you eat the sandwich?"

I take an extra big bite. The sugar is a jolt to my system. When I finally swallow, Cecilia hands me a glass of milk. Big sisters can be a splendid thing.

"Thank you for coming with me tonight."

She waves this away. "You're going to call Dad in the morning?"

"Yes, I'll need him to change her number."

She sits down across from me, leaning forward, elbows on knees. "That's not what I mean."

"I'm going to let her stay, Cee, if that's what she wants." And a part of me selfishly hopes she'll stay. The nights are long when you live alone. "I'm not going to hand her off to Dad and throw her right back to Ardena. She needs time away from all of it."

"I believe she has a job."

"Cee."

"I think you're overreacting a bit." She bites into her bottom lip. "Projecting your frustrations with Julian onto her."

"I'm not—"

"She made a stupid decision, Liz. If she drove herself, this wouldn't even have been a thing. Andrew would've been a complete jackass, and she would've gotten in her car and driven home to cry it out over ice cream and sad movies. Like the rest of us."

I roll my eyes. It's similar to what Jane said, in its way. "The rest of us weren't still sleeping with our exes."

"Listen, if you need to ask her to stay, ask. But she is not your responsibility, sister or not," she adds when I start to protest. "She picked wrong, and it sucks any way you look at it, but she's nineteen. She'll rebound."

"I know." I put the now-empty plate down on the coffee table. "But I want to give her a safe space to do that in. Dad is not equipped to handle this level of heartbreak. Do you remember what he was like when Julian broke up with me the first time?"

That is, of course, the wrong example because Cecilia has no idea what our father has been like for the past seventeen years. She doesn't know how my dad took me to the mall for ice cream and retail therapy three days after the prom debacle. Zoey was strapped into her stroller and begging for every princess doll at the Disney Store. I cried over sundaes at Johnny Rockets because of how many dates Julian and I had at the mall. My dad went misty-eyed talking about how men, no matter what age, didn't know a good thing until it was gone. And then he said words I have never forgotten—"I miss her every day, Lizzie. Some mornings I wake up, and I think I hear you and Cee down in the kitchen, or I roll over and expect your mother to be there. I'd give almost anything to have not hurt you." I didn't have to ask why it was *almost* anything. He had instinctively reached for Zoey, ruffling her hair and handing her a slice of grilled cheese. My dad would give anything to have his family back, anything except his daughter. It wasn't even a choice.

"No," Cecilia says stonily. "But you're right. He's much better at causing heartache than coping with it."

"Cee."

She holds up her hands in supplication. "You're going through something big, Liz. I don't want you to get so caught up in Zoey's drama that you neglect your own."

I snicker. "My own drama?"

"Hey, you are the one who has a way with words."

But apparently not tonight. "I appreciate your concern, and I promise I'm not shoving my potential divorce in a corner. But there's no easy answer. Do I miss Jules? Yes. Do I want to go home and talk his infidelity and character flaws to death? Not at the moment. I didn't realize this at first, but this"—I wave around the apartment—"is about me. I get to be the one to choose now. I always thought I did whenever I took him back, but not really. Now, I get to go back or move on, to feel or not whatever Jules felt whenever he left, to understand the pull that always drove us back together."

"And you are going to start this exploration of your feelings by taking up with a heartbroken nineteen-year-old?"

I slip my wedding ring off for the second time today. It's easier this time but barely. My pulse quickens, but I steadily place the ring down on top of the copy of *Humans of New York* my mom gave me as an apartment-warming gift. The card had been blank with a kitten on the front. Inside, in my mom's big looping handwriting, it read:

There's more to life than fairy tales and heartbreak. Find it. And a post-script demanding an invitation to see my new place. Classic Mom.

I run my hands down the tops of my legs and grip my knees to keep my hands from shaking and my toes from tapping. Jane's words run through my mind. What made her think I made any decisions? Jane knows me so well that I wonder if I did decide and don't know it. All I do know is I have to embrace this moment in my life because, either way, it's going to change everything.

I look into my sister's worried and tired eyes. "And by signing up for speed dating."

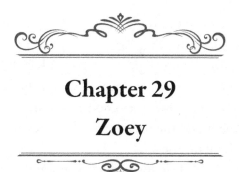

Chapter 29
Zoey

Monday comes too soon. I'm exhausted, even after spending almost all day Sunday in bed. My body hurts, my head aches, and every thump of my heart is laced with memories. Yesterday, in between all the crying, Liz handed me a decrepit laptop and some headphones and told me to write it out. So I did. And for a few minutes afterward, with Wilderness Weekend's saddest album ringing in my ears, I felt relief. It didn't last, but it did force the truth from me. My relationship with Andrew is over. My head and heart finally agree. But my head doesn't know how to forget years' worth of memories overnight, and my heart? I'm not sure it will ever work properly again. All heartbroken teenagers probably think that. Hearts shatter every day. The earth still spins. And I still have to get up and go to work.

So unfortunately, I'm up at the butt crack of dawn to drive the forty minutes back to Ardena from Princeton. If I'm lucky, I will see approximately no one I know, Dad will still be asleep, and Andrew will still be in Wildwood with whoever he picked up Saturday night. Panic stirs under the surface at the mere thought of his name. But Andrew isn't stupid or cruel enough to show up Monday morning and try to talk to me. At least I pray that's still the case. The last thing I need is to bitch-slap him in front of half the athletes at Ardena High. As if we weren't the source of enough gossip this summer.

When I finally pull into the high school parking lot, one hour and two coffees later, it's full. Parents are lined up to drop off the younger kids. Most of the high schoolers walk or bike every day. I watch the line of cars moving slowly through the lot. Whoever is handling drop-off today isn't very good at it. If not for the heat wave breaking last night and the promise of blue skies all day, those parents would be honking for sure.

Even blue skies and clouds so fluffy you want to cuddle up with them can't brighten my mood, however. I grab my water bottle from the back seat and slip my sunglasses back down onto my face. I tighten my ponytail. It's another day, another football field, another high school. *Breathe, Zoey.*

"Zee! Hey." Max's voice brings me back to attention. That and the nickname. I've never gone by Zee, but from Max, it sounds right. He stands by the hood of my car, his eyes crinkling in concern. A sheen of sweat already glazes his body, and his hair, longer than I've ever seen it, is matted to his forehead. "Where have you been?"

I glance at my watch. No, still early. "What do you mean?"

"I've been trying to get in touch with you since yesterday."

"Oh." I hand him the scrap of paper with my new number on it and try to sound as casual as possible when I say, "I have a new number."

He examines the paper, his lips curving into a frown. "Everything okay?"

"Not really." I shrug. "But I'll survive." *I hope.*

"Hey, hey," he sings.

I pull a face. "Real funny."

He grins. "Come on. I don't know what stupid thing Andrew did this time, but I do know that you will survive it."

I hate my life. My cheeks burn, and my voice is stuck in my throat. He knows. And why wouldn't he? It's only my darkest secret.

"I have eyes, Zee," he says to my stunned silence. "Now, let's go."

I nod, my voice still hiding somewhere in my rib cage. Had it been *that* obvious?

The question still hangs heavy by the end of the day, but I must admit I feel better. Max paired me with the rising junior-varsity potentials—fourteen-year-olds. There's a lot of drama with them but so much talent. This camp is the best thing you can do if you want to be called up to varsity sooner rather than later, and these kids want it. Our training is invaluable and targeted, and with a limited number of runners each session, these kids get a personalized approach to their program. I, of all the staff here, understand the importance of this summer session. It's what shaped me, molding me into the record-setting runner I became for Ardena. It started here. Like so many other things.

I stop on the thirty-yard line. It's a football field. Nine years from now when we all pose for our ten-year high school reunion photo, will I even remember this is where Andrew and I shared our first kiss? Probably. Will it still hurt? Not in this way. Maybe not at all. Claire and Andrew and this awful summer will be far behind me. It will be a memory of that pain, of the loss of something you don't realize you have until it's gone—the innocence of first love. You have to survive your first love. I step off the line and walk toward the parking lot. And I will.

Chapter 30

Liz

There's a line for speed dating. A line of divorcees, young and old, extending out the door. Walk-ins are frowned upon, which means that all these people had the same idea I did, that arriving five minutes before the start of the event was a good idea. I figured there was less of a chance that I would back out if I didn't have time to think about it. I'd get in, and the event would start. No time for chickening out. That was the plan. I didn't account for the line. And apparently, neither did the man behind me, who keeps shuffling from foot to foot and muttering under his breath. Maybe I should've taken the organizer's advice and gone to dinner here beforehand.

The line inches forward until I'm finally standing at the check-in table.

"Name, dear?" the woman asks. She's older than I am—maybe my mom's age—with sun-kissed skin, deep-brown eyes, and hair an unnatural shade of blond.

"Liz Madden."

Her acrylic-tipped finger scans the list in front of her. "Ah, yes, here you are. A newbie. I'm Kara. I run this shindig and the support group."

I saw the host organization's name—Divorc-ease—on the event registration page but didn't think much about it or what it might be. It's hard to imagine sitting in a meeting with someone I didn't pick at speed dating, but there must be rules to make sure things don't get awkward.

"You should come to the next meeting." Kara holds up a diamond-bedazzled hand. "Might meet your future husband."

I try not to laugh at the fact that the support group is run by an engaged woman. Wow. "Maybe." I take my name tag from her. I step to the side, and Kara's attention is already on the next victim.

As it turns out, speed dating is slow going. Three guys in, and five minutes is now an eternity. Guy 1 was shy with bad teeth. I prattled on about living in Princeton to fill the silence, but it was still forever. Guy 2 was hot, and he knew it. He worked in finance and had plenty to say about himself. His suit probably cost more than my couch. I wouldn't be the least bit surprised to find out he gets manicures. This latest guy isn't too bad. Shaggy brown hair, hipster glasses, nice jeans, and a polo with the Princeton logo. He's a professor, which is intriguing until he says, "of history." Now I feel like I'm speed dating a younger version of my dad. The timer dings, and Guy 3 slinks off to the next woman. Thank god. Maybe this wasn't the best idea. I flip to a clean sheet of paper and write a big number four on top.

The setup tonight is good. Each table is separated by a curtain to prevent previewing the next date. The men move, which is a nice touch. There's something liberating about having my pick of men, even if they do have to choose me back. There's another ding, and I hear the shuffle of feet that signals my next date has arrived. I look up from the spiderweb I'm drawing in the corner of my paper—maybe I will ensnare this one in my web—and smile at the man standing in front of me.

Holy shit.

I blink, my smile faltering. The man blinks back at me, recognition dawning on his face.

"How are you enjoying your book?" Hot Bookstore Dad sits down and places his forearms on the table, his hands tented. His eyes don't quite meet mine.

He's nervous, I realize. "Almost done. I was about halfway in, but I left my copy..."

He raises an eyebrow. "Someplace you weren't willing to go back?"

"You make it sound scandalous," I say with a laugh.

"A man can hope." He extends his right hand. "Spencer Williamette." He pronounces it like the river in the Pacific Northwest.

I take his hand. "Liz Madden."

"It's a pleasure to meet you again, Liz." His green eyes light with intrigue. At the bookshop, I was wearing my wedding ring, and he had his son. But tonight, a sexy confidence comes off him in waves. I cross my legs underneath the table as his eyes dance with mine. This isn't friendly neighborhood dad Spencer. This is a man seeing something he likes. Something that is now seemingly available to him.

I match his flirty gaze with one of my own. Game on.

The rest of speed dating is a blur. It's possible there were a few promising dates in the back half, but my mind is already checked out and focused on the plans I made with Spencer. As soon as the lady collecting our match sheets grabs mine, I sneak out. The streets are full of life. I love the Princeton downtown, equally quaint and collegiate. I glance down at my phone before turning the corner. Zoey is spending the night in Ardena with Becca. That's her story at least, but I'm choosing to believe her. There's been no covert texting or sketchy alibis since Wildwood. And if Zoey is with Andrew, she's an adult, as Cecilia pointed out. Andrew is Zoey's mistake to make.

Spencer Williamette stands outside the restaurant. He doesn't fidget or shuffle. He isn't even looking at his phone. I take him in, the same and yet different from the man I met at the bookshop. Then he was friendly in the way that you are when someone you find attractive mistakes you for a bookseller. He respected my wedding ring. Tonight, standing in a fitted button-down, slim straight-leg jeans, and black leather shoes, he looks like my own perfect mistake. One I want to make, maybe more than once.

My insides feel like mush as I step into his line of sight and offer a smile. I haven't been on a date in almost a decade, since high school, really. In college, there wasn't dating. You made out at a party, and you either were or weren't a couple after that. And with Lucas, we fell from friendship into a couple without really trying.

I wonder how long it's been since Spencer's been on a date. In our five minutes together, he told me he's been divorced for two years. But I can't imagine doing this with a kid. He has to be doubly careful with whomever he brings into his life because it's not only his life. The thought gives me pause. I'm not the best option for Spencer. There are so many strings attached. Relief washes through me. What if I *had* been pregnant? What if that test said Pregnant and then I found Sheila? It's possible my decisions would've been wholly different.

"Hello again," Spencer says, taking my hand and breaking into my spiraling thoughts.

His face is relaxed and open, and I want to be here so badly. I push Julian and strings and doubts away. Spencer has picked a nicer restaurant in a town full of nice restaurants. They have a killer bar burger that I would die for right now, but the bar is crowded, and there's no outside seating. I rarely miss being shore adjacent, as I was in my youth, but tonight, it would be nice to sit outside and share a drink, the cooling ocean breeze on our faces in the lingering summer daylight, sand between our toes. Princeton, for all it has to offer, doesn't have that.

"Do you want to get out of here?" I ask before he even opens the door.

His eyes shoot up in surprise before he notices my less-than-suggestive expression. "What did you have in mind?"

I shrug because I have no idea. "You want to walk? It would be a shame to waste this night." As if on cue, a light breeze tousles my hair.

He offers me his elbow. "Works for me."

And so we walk, in silence at first, before expanding on the basics we shared during our first five minutes. Tidbits turn into stories and laughter. I'm comfortable with Spencer in a way I'm not usually comfortable with people. He laughs easily and smiles often. Every story he tells is genuine, and he listens to me, asks me questions. He wants to know me. I glance around at the other people walking tonight. How many of them are doing the same thing on these same streets? How many others snuck out of speed dating's social hour to meet Guy 4?

We turn the corner into Palmer Square. In the winter, everything will be lit up, and a tree will brighten the dark nights. Now, everything is lush and green. The fountain glows, giving off the feeling that we aren't in Central New Jersey, steps from a major university, but in the smallest of historic small towns.

"How many times have you been to speed dating?" I keep my tone casual. The answer doesn't really matter unless this is a ruse. Not that I get that vibe from him. What I do get from him is the same sense of wonder I have at this turn of events, at the kismet that brought us together, as if we both realize what a gift a night like tonight is. Chance encounters, serendipity, fate—whatever you want to call it—seem to be working in our favor.

"First time, actually. Though Kara's been trying to rope me into it for a while now."

"You're in the support group?"

Spencer nods. "I know how it seems. Trust me, I never thought I'd be in a divorcee support group, but"—he smiles—"Kara was my neighbor when I first moved out. She brought me cookies as a welcome gift and was always friendly, asked after Ryan. One morning, maybe three months after I moved in, there was a flyer under my door with a note that said she was picking me up at seven and I had better get a haircut before then."

Having known Kara for all of seventy-five seconds, I can totally see this happening. Kara is an adopter, and Spencer, it seems, was one of her projects. Something tells me I'm next.

"And you went?"

"Yup, and it was surprisingly fun. I mean, it's sad to admit, but by that point in my life, all my friends were husbands of my ex-wife's friends. My social life went to her in the divorce." His face turns serious. "My whole life had been wrapped up in my son, and there was this gaping hole where he had been."

I move my hand from his elbow and slide it into his. His fingers slip between mine, and a shock of electricity runs from my fingertips all the way up my arm. "How often do you see him?"

"We split the week and alternate weekends now. Neither of us wanted to be a dick about it, but when I first moved out, the papers hadn't even been drawn, and Natalie had him almost all the time."

His pain, even now, is evident. Those months—I hoped it was only months—haunt him. How much did he miss in his son in that time? I don't know what it's like, seeing the daily changes in your own child. How from day to day, new things emerge, big and small. But I watched Zoey grow up intermittently, and Jane often shares a similar sentiment when she talks about her boys. My heart wrenches at the thought of the boys. Will they still be my nephews if I end my marriage, or am I forfeiting watching them grow into men if I walk away?

"I'm sorry," I say, though it's wholly inadequate.

"Yeah." He squeezes my hand. "The group was really helpful in getting me back out of the house, but I have been able to avoid speed dating until now."

"What changed?"

"I guess I felt ready to date again," he says tentatively. "My ex-wife and I... It wasn't anything bad. We... We wanted to be in love and perfect for each other and in sync. We caved on things when we should've pushed. We settled for less than we wanted for ourselves. And that caught up to us. Especially after Ryan.

"There's less time for each other when you have a kid, and to survive that, your relationship has to be strong. You need to have accepted each other's flaws for real, not have ignored them or lied to yourself that the other person would change if you willed it enough. Nothing quite brings out the worst in someone like not having a full night's sleep for six straight years."

He's rendered me speechless. It sounds too much like what I could say about me and Julian and our rom-com-esque love story. But Spencer's not looking for a response, and the silence between us grows comfortable as we continue to walk.

"Is Kara still your neighbor?" I ask a few blocks later.

He shakes his head. "I moved out of Northgate about a year ago."

I laugh as the name of my apartment complex comes out of his mouth. Of course that's where he lived and where Kara lives.

"I moved *into* Northgate recently."

He smiles, and it's warm and sweet and too sexy. There's a hint of all the things that could've happened if we were still neighbors. What a sexy summer that could've been.

"Small world," he says.

I look away, my cheeks flushed, at the certainty that all my dirty thoughts are on full display. "Where do you live now?"

The question is innocuous enough, but after that sexy smile and all its promises, it feels heavy with expectation and innuendo. And I'm not ready for what that means. Whatever I expected from speed dating, it wasn't Spencer and conversation and hand-holding. It wasn't him pointing to a house two blocks away and claiming it as his own.

"It's a rental, but it has a yard, and Ryan loves being able to walk into town. Sometimes, he's nine and worried about all that comes with being a kid, and other days, he's engaging anyone in Princeton apparel for details on their college experience."

"Princeton is a pretty good dream to have at any age," I say, thinking of the young boy from the bookshop quizzing a freshman on the street.

"Spoken like an alum?"

I shake my head, as if my Rutgers-professor father would've paid for Princeton. It was only scholarships and sheer force of will that got me out of town and state, and even then, it was only to Philadelphia.

"Drexel," I say, remembering how the seventy miles between campus and my house felt like a thousand. I was never so happy as the day I lugged half my belongings into the dorms with Jane by my side, which was saying a lot considering how heartbroken I was then and how much my best friend resembled my ex-boyfriend. Damn twins.

"Not to be forward..." Spencer runs a hand through his hair. "But did you want to come back to my place?"

I freeze, my hand loosening against his. The smallest of hiccups escapes my lips. It is forward. Very forward. And what does it mean if I go back to another man's house? What are your rights as a separated wife?

"Liz." Spencer reaches for my hand again and offers me a wan smile. "For a drink. I can get the fire pit going?" The corners of his lips rise in a half smile. It's the sexiest thing I've seen in my life. "I'm really enjoying talking with you, and I don't want the night to end, but I also already ran a 10K today."

I laugh and glance down at my smartwatch. I'm also several thousand steps higher than most days. I turn so I'm facing his house. "The fire pit sounds nice."

Chapter 31

Liz

"First kiss," Spencer says with a glance in my direction.

I lean back against the plush cushions of Spencer's couch with a smile. We opted to stay inside with wine and charcuterie after the mosquitos invaded. "John Nutledge. Seventh grade. Truth or Dare."

Spencer's eyes gleam with amusement. "And how was it?"

"Ugh." I groan. "All tongue, no kiss."

I'm not sure how we got to playing twenty questions, but we're deep into it now. Somewhere between white and red wine, we silently agreed to skip the niceties, and I love it. The last time it was this easy with a guy was on a cruise ship almost two decades ago.

I nudge him. "And your first kiss?"

"Sydney Stall. We were thirteen, best friends, neighbors and such."

"And how was it?"

He laughs, a not-so-sheepish smile brightening his expression. "Better than John Nutledge, I'm sure."

The air in the room shifts, a tension surrounds us, a spark electrifying the night. Between one breath and the next, I know he's going to kiss me. Spencer hasn't moved, and his expression is still playful, his gaze fixed on me, but it's like he's screaming his intentions. His fingers play with the curls that have fallen over my shoulder. Every nerve in my body piques as a single finger grazes the bare skin of my collarbone.

"I have to tell you something," I say as his eyes go half-lidded and he leans in.

"Let me guess." He pulls back but takes my hand in his. "You're still married."

I hang my head and cover my face. *Fuck.* After a moment, Spencer moves away from me, and my skin goes cold, as if an icy breeze blew through this perfect summer night.

"Trust me," he says. "Your wedding ring did not go unnoticed the first time we met or your lack of one tonight."

"Then why hang out with me?" *Hang out?* Seriously, am I thirteen?

"Because you don't seem the type to use speed dating for divorcees as a way to lure men into your bed. And..."

"And?" I ask, lifting my head. At least he doesn't think I'm a deplorable person.

He shakes his head. "Tell me about your husband."

The word sounds dirty from his mouth despite the fact that he says it evenly and calmly, as if the woman he was about to kiss having a husband is a nonissue. Well, clearly not a nonissue, but if Spencer were the one with a wife, the rug would've caught fire with how quickly I would be at the door. But he only stares at me, waiting for an explanation.

"We're separated," I say since that seems like the most pertinent part. "It's been about six weeks." The number startles me. How is it only and already six weeks? "I found out he was talking to another woman, someone he met while traveling for work. And there's only been one kiss between them, but he wanted something more to happen, and emotionally... When I confronted him, he had that look in his eyes, the one he gets when he's about to run. I hadn't seen that look for years... When I saw it, I knew, and I couldn't wait around to be left or cheated on, so I walked away."

Spencer leans forward, his hands clasped between his knees. He looks over at me. "Then this isn't a hall pass kind of thing?"

I hate that phrase. A hall pass. Is that what Julian thinks he's giving me? A pass to take some time since he's taken so much in the past? Anger swells in my chest, and my cheeks brighten. I steel myself for a battle. Except Julian's not here, and Spencer is waiting for an answer.

"No," I say, attempting to keep my tone neutral and not let on that there's a fire kindling inside me. "It's not a hall pass. We're separated. I moved out. I'm free to do whatever I please. There's no set timeline or plans to discuss reconciliation. It's not like when my lease is up in six months, I go home and this never happened."

Those words hit me hard. This isn't temporary. Whatever happens next, this moment is not a stopgap. "My marriage is ending. And I don't know if it will—if I want it to—begin again."

I watch Spencer, this man I hardly know and yet feel like I've known for much longer than the few hours we've been together. His face is shadowed in thought. The gold of his eyes has darkened to amber, and his lips are pressed in a line. What is it about this man? He's my type—brown hair, golden eyes, tall, refined dad bod—but it's more than that. His life shows on his face—a crinkle there, a worry line here, a faded scar that runs down his jawline where the first signs of stubble have sprouted. I cup his face, the scratchy little hairs exciting each and every nerve in my hand and beyond. One simple touch, and my body lights up.

His gaze slides to mine. His expression is open and questioning and nervous. My love story never had those looks. From that first kiss on the deck of a cruise ship, Julian had my whole heart. But here, tonight, what happens next involves a real risk. And Spencer has to consider the risk for himself and his son.

"Maybe I should go." I stand quickly and shoulder my bag. I don't look back until I reach the door. I can't. If he's still staring at me like that, I won't be able to leave. With one hand on the doorknob, I turn with what I hope at least appears to be a real smile. "Thank—"

"Liz."

He's been saying my name all night but not in that way. Not with a hint of exasperation that is far too familiar for our short-lived acquaintance, and that makes my insides quake. And he hasn't been close enough that goose bumps rise on my arms.

I look up at him, almost a full head taller than me. How nice would it be to rest my head on his chest? That's always been one of my silent complaints about Julian. He isn't tall enough for me to rest my head naturally over his heart, and forget it if I wear heels.

Almost of its own volition, my hand goes to Spencer's chest, fingers splayed across his heart, which beats a steady rhythm. When I look up again, his eyes are on mine. He cups my face, his fingers again tangling in the loose strands. Desire shoots through me, real and honest and overwhelming. Spencer leans down, no hesitation this time, no coy statements, his fingers soft on my skin, his breath against my lips.

I close my eyes and lean up on my tiptoes. Our lips meet, and that desire explodes. It courses through me, pushing the kiss from soft to playful to deep. I wrap my arms around his neck. His one hand cradles my head while the other rests at the sliver of bare skin at my waist.

A perfect kiss. It's been too long since I had a perfect kiss. For so long, I thought I'd had my last first kiss, but thank god I was wrong. If this kiss never ends, I will be okay with that. His tongue dances with mine, and I can't think. I lean farther into the kiss. My body is alive, and it wants more, please. I sigh against his lips as he explores my mouth with his own, dancing with me as if we've been dancing forever.

He pulls back, stopping for one last peck. "Shall I walk you to your car?"

It's an invite and an out. Spencer is clearly in, but he's letting me decide. My body begs me to say yes. One night of pure pleasure with this sexy stranger is everything I need in this moment. But my mind can't see through to the end. Would I really be able to do it? I'm not the casual-sex type, not when I was single or rebounding. And whatever I am now, I'm not sure that includes sex on the first date or potentially a one-night stand. Though, maybe it doesn't have to be black and white. There's an entire spectrum of colors between being walked to my car and falling into bed.

I let my bag drop to the floor and pull him back toward the couch. "Ten more minutes?"

Chapter 32
Cecilia

There's always an ache in my chest after a trip back home. A longing for a life I might have had if things hadn't turned so awful all those years ago. It's why I don't often return unless Liz beckons. Whether that makes me cold or a coward, I'm uncertain, but either way, in the week I've been home, I've talked to my mom more than I have in a long time. Evie's used her key every night, and despite every principle I've followed since leaving the state of New Jersey, I'm already planning another trip.

I offered to cook for Evie tonight. Living alone, I've picked up quite a few skills in the kitchen. But I'm keeping it simple. Marinara from the Italian deli downtown simmers next to a pot of boiling water while the meatballs bake. Garlic bread waits on the counter for its turn in the oven. I stir the penne absently, glancing out the window to check for Evie's car. Again. Whatever case she's working has kept her at the office late all week. She can't talk about it, a side effect of being a counselor for wayward children, but I don't doubt she's telling the truth. I can see the effects of it in the set of her shoulders and the tiredness dulling her eyes.

My phone buzzes, and I jump to answer like a little kid offered a fudge pop, but it's not Evie. I need to get a grip.

"Hi, Mom." I tuck the phone between my ear and shoulder.

"You got your sister's invite, right? You're coming? I told her you would come back for it."

I laugh at my mom's flustered excitement. She wants to see Liz's place something awful. Almost as much as she wants to meet Evie, especially now that my girlfriend is sister-approved. "Yes, Mom. I'm figuring out the details now."

"And Evie is coming."

I smile. It's been too long since I've seen my mother excited about anything like this. "I'm going to ask her tonight."

The timer dings, signaling that the meatballs are ready for the gravy.

"What are you making?" Mom asks as I put her on speakerphone and slip a pot holder on. A wonderful blend of Italian spices greets me when I open the oven, and I breathe it in.

"Macaroni and meatballs," I say, dropping each of the mini circles into the gravy pot.

"Oh, one of your best dishes," she says approvingly. "Good thinking. I'll let you get back to it. Let me know what she says."

"Will do, Mom." I'm almost enjoying her meddling.

Ten minutes later, the kitchen is full of a chorus of timers. I click on the first one—drain the macaroni—before turning to the rest of the tasks at hand. Plate the meatballs, toss the salad, put in the garlic bread. Have I even set the table yet? Take off the apron and fix my hair. A key sounds in the door. Too late. The sound is unfamiliar but exhilarating. I purposely locked the door behind me so that I could hear this smallest of sounds. It's fast becoming one of my favorites.

Images pop into my mind uninvited. Simon, my college boyfriend, coming into my apartment with his boisterous laugh. *Honey, I'm home.* He said it every time he let himself in. Even the day he came in and found me sitting on the floor in the middle of the living room, tears streaming down my face as I stared at a photo of a certain two-year-old. He sank down next to me, the *home* dying on his lips. It was the beginning of the end for us, for me.

I shake the thought away, but another one opens, this one not a memory but a reenactment. Zoey, not the wan, heartbroken girl I know now but an excitable, vibrant teenager with a warm smile that I only recognize from photographs. In my mind, one of those awful teen soaps Liz loves to watch plays out. Zoey keys into her best friend's room like she does every day, except on this day her life as she knows it is changed forever. Zoey's features, a mirror to my own, crumple, and she morphs back into the ghost of a sister I've just met.

"Cee?"

Evie's voice shakes me from the weird movie playing in my head, but the message has already seeped in—a key can be dangerous and comfort a hazard. But any relationship involves risk. Relationships don't work if you don't entrust your heart to another person. I've lived that truth for almost two decades now. Never trusting, never letting anyone in. It's exhausting. Perhaps even more exhausting than letting Evie in, but I never got hurt. Sure, I've been left by partners who wanted more, but I'd never truly been hurt. Not like Liz, who seems to finally see in Julian what we all suspected long before, or Zoey, who can't breathe without reopening a wound, or my mother, who lost a lifetime. For the first time in forever, my heart is opening. Behind the love and the lust and the growing sentimentality at normal, everyday sounds, fear is nesting, a memory of loss rising to the surface. Evie can hurt me.

"Cee, something's burning." Evie nudges me out of the way with her hip and throws open the oven door. She sounds exasperated, annoyed even.

"Sorry." I stare at the burnt garlic bread, the sound of the final timer reaching me. I stare into Evie's wide brown eyes as she jams a finger into the off button on the timer. Her eyes look different today. Less enamored and more steadfast. Evie's burrowed in, and I have finally let her stay, but I can't fight back the question that keeps bubbling to the surface. Now that Evie has me, will she still want me?

While the garlic bread wasn't salvageable, the rest of dinner turned out well and seemed to lift Evie's mood. Or at least halfway through her first glass of wine, the scowl dissolved into a general look of discontent. There might have even been a smile when I brought out dessert. I'm pretty sure the mood has nothing to do with me, but I've also rarely seen Evie like this before. Everyone has moods, but we've kept our lives separate for so long that it's easy to mask the bad ones. How many times had "not in the mood" texts passed between us? How often had I ignored the signs and Evie buried her feelings?

"Liz sent proof of existence," I say, trying to get my girlfriend engaged in something that isn't the awful reality television that she acquiesced to watch.

She shifts on the couch, tucking her legs under her. A spark of interest lights her features. "Oh?"

I hand over my phone with the photo my sister sent pulled up of her and the guy she'd met—or re-met, as the case may be—at speed dating with the message, *He does exist!*

"A second date." Evie nods approvingly. "Speed dating for the win."

I glance down at the photo again. Seeing my sister with someone who isn't Julian is weird. Something stirs in my stomach at the painful nostalgia, as if I'm in an alternate universe where everything is slightly off. But her smile, cheesy and toothy and quintessentially Liz, is the first real smile I've seen on her this summer.

"She invited us to an apartment-warming dinner in a few weeks. I was thinking maybe we could fly back out? My mom will be there, and thought... I know it's soon, but I feel like I need to be there to support my sister in this decision."

Evie's gaze drifts to her lap. "I don't think me going with you is a good idea."

I consider playing it off but take her hand instead. "I thought you'd want to meet my mom."

"I do," she says. "But it's a housewarming, right? Zoey will be there?"

"Probably." I shrug, though there's no doubt she'll be there. It's a fact I've come to terms with these past few weeks.

"Probably? Doesn't she live with your sister?"

"She does *not* live there. It's a temporary arrangement for the summer."

"As is Liz's apartment."

Wow. I take a breath and swallow my annoyance. It's a good thing that my girlfriend finally feels comfortable enough to be bitchy, I think. "Okay, fine, Zoey will be there. Why does that mean you can't come?"

"I think it might be good for you, Cee, to spend time with your family, together. It might help you move forward if you make an effort to wade through the awkwardness."

"You could've just said you didn't want to go."

"It's not that. I want to meet your mom in a situation that's going to be less stressful for you." Evie pulls at her cuticles, something I've never seen her do. "Zoey. Your mom. Liz's new life. And me. It seems like a lot."

"Okay." Her reasoning sort of makes sense, but it still feels like she's stalling. "Well, my mom's been pestering me to come for a visit. What if I can get her to fly out for the weekend?"

I'm not sure why I say it or where this sudden urge to push comes from. But Liz's invite was addressed to the both of us, and in that moment, I decided. On Evie. On letting her all the way in. On introducing her to my mom. All of it.

"I'm going home this weekend," Evie says, still not looking at me.

I swallow my pride and nudge Evie's chin until her eyes meet mine. "Do you want me to come with you?"

Evie's eyes widen, and her shoulders stiffen. I've surprised her. Good. We're in uncharted territory, and now she knows it for certain. There's a joy in this moment but also turbulence. She didn't expect me to offer to go with her. She didn't even mention it, and I realize, maybe too late, that Evie might never have told me about her trip home if not for this conversation. We don't spend every weekend together. In fact, with my open-house schedule, we don't spend most weekends together. How often has she gone home without me knowing? Her family knows about me, in the same way that my mother and Liz knew of my girlfriend, but Evie's never invited me home. Not once. A fact that I appreciated since we never had to have *that* conversation, but now, it seems intentional.

"I..." Evie swallows and then starts again. "I don't think that's the best idea."

The words sit in the space between us, heavy and suspicious and laden with doubts. I take a breath to steel my nerves. I've been here before, and this tentative distance only ever leads to one outcome. Foolishly, I never expected it from Evie.

"What's going on here?"

She looks at me then, her eyes bright and wide, searching. I barely blink as the seconds drag on. What is she deciding?

"My grandmother is going to be there," Evie says finally. "And she doesn't know..."

I straighten. We've had this conversation. We have to have had this conversation. There's no way we got past the first date without being clear that we were both far from closeted.

"Your grandmother doesn't know or your whole family?"

"My grandmother. She's like ridiculously religious and old, and my mom didn't want me to tell her when I first came out." She reaches for my hand, and I let her take it. Her touch is gentle, tentative, and the vulnerability in it sends a shiver up my arm. "It sucked after getting up the courage to tell my parents, but it never mattered because I never had someone I wanted to bring home. And then I did, but you would never have come. I wasn't expecting... It can't be this weekend but soon, I promise. Okay?"

I cup her face with both hands and bring my lips down to hers. Understanding and compassion and love mingle in my veins. This is real. This is *love*.

"Yes," I whisper. "That's more than okay."

Chapter 33
Zoey

Max clicks the stop button on the timer. Surprise colors his face as he holds the stopwatch out to me. It's an impressive mile time and a huge improvement for Millie since the start of summer. Between me and Max, we might be able to mold Millie into Ardena's next star.

I lean back against the fence. We've been watching the freshmen and sophomores run all day, event after event. This is the part of the summer where we identify those who can use extra training, who can move onto the varsity squad before their time. It's time to find the next Zoey Reid—at least that's how Max put it, a goofy grin wrinkling his brow.

I motion to the stopwatch. "Your diamond in the rough."

Max laughs, and he's so close that I feel his arm shake against mine. He looks down at me. And I swear there's a spark of excitement in his gaze that isn't related to the timer. There's a softness as he takes me in—loose ponytail and red cheeks from the number of races I've run today to challenge the varsity hopefuls.

He tucks the strand of hair that blows across my face behind my ear, but his touch doesn't linger. "Think you can get her to break your time?"

My time has already been broken. That's the way it is with state records. There's always someone, somewhere faster. It's hard to hold on to records for long. But I still have one of the fastest times in state history and hold all the section, county, and school titles. Seeing someone break them will be bittersweet, but if I get to pick who it would be, Millie is my choice.

I glance at the timer again. It's still far off. "Not by the end of summer, but I bet you can get her there before States." I look up at him, narrowing my eyes. "Don't rush her. Even getting close in the next few years will get her the scholarship she needs to get out of Ardena."

"Always thinking ahead, Zee."

My lips quirk in a half smile. That nickname. "I *am* an Ardena Heat success story."

"Yes, you are, Superstar."

"Former superstar," I correct. I haven't matched my record-setting time in quite a while.

His brow furrows. "Why aren't you running at Bellewood?"

The question is one I've been asked before—by my old coach, by the Bellewood coach, by my honors program advisor, by Andrew, and Claire, and Becca. Some people would do anything for a spot on a college squad, and I walked away from all my offers. Bellewood is a Division III school so it's not as if I passed up a scholarship, but the spot was mine—no questions, no tryouts—and I didn't want it. Half my teammates broke their backs for a D3 shot and never achieved it. Even Claire, the second-best runner at Ardena, didn't make the team at her school.

But endless practices and travel, I didn't want that life. It's why I turned down spots on Division I and II teams. College sports aren't like high school sports, where you take a bus at three and are home by eight. Even if they were, what would I have given up? Being a member of the honors program? Pledging? Mock trial? I can't imagine my life without Haley and the rest of my sorority sisters, and the thought of sitting in English 101 and rereading *Heart of Darkness* puts me to sleep.

"I love running," I say with a shrug, "but it was never meant to be more..." My eyes catch someone in the distance. It can't be, but yes, the girl is waving and wearing Greek letters and is most certainly not Becca.

"Yes, Little, it's meeeee!" Haley's voice carries across the field, and my chest swells at the sound. She falls into a mock curtsy when only the track itself stands between us.

I cross the short distance and throw myself into my roommate's arms. Everyone is watching us, but I don't care. I've been home for months, and this is the first time I've felt at home. I hold on to her, not ready to let her go. "What in the world are you doing here?"

"You needed me," Haley says into my hair. "And once I was able to reasonably arrange it with my job, because I'm a responsible employee *and* a dedicated Big, I hopped in Dexter and drove straight here."

Dexter is her ten-year-old Corolla. It's an old-lady car if there ever was one, and yet it has more life than any other car I've been in. Everything about it reflects my Big Sister's personality, from the disco ball hanging off the rearview mirror to the fuzzy covers on the front seats to the stuffed animal collection—mainly unicorns, so many unicorns—sitting in the back window.

The vise that's been around my chest since Andrew and Claire loosens a notch. My breathing feels almost normal.

"Thank you."

"Of course, Little." Haley pulls back but keeps her hands on my shoulders. Her eyes rake over me and then past me before narrowing in what I know to be mischief. "Please tell me that's Max."

I laugh and glance over my shoulder to where Max is studiously staring at his phone. He never uses his phone on the track. But he understands, like he did when Andrew showed up here, that this moment, though public, deserves privacy.

"Max," I say, turning to face him. He looks up with an amused expression. "This is Haley."

"Ah, the illustrious roommate."

"Roommate, Big, bestie, all-around amazing person." Haley mimes the tipping of her hat.

He grins, and it's honestly breathtaking. "Zee talks about you all the time."

Haley's eyes shift to mine at the nickname, but her smile remains steady as we cross to the sideline. "Of course she does." She plops down on the ground, her back against the fence, and waves as if she's the queen. "As you were."

Max leans into me, his shoulder bumping mine. His breath stirs the loose hairs by my ear as he whispers, "Bossy, much?"

Goose bumps sprout on my arms. His eyes are penetrating and playful, and I fight the urge to lean into him and do more than touch shoulders. Does he feel it, too, or am I suffering from heat stroke?

I lean away from him and force a smile. "You have no idea."

An hour later, we sit on the hood of my car, watching the last of the high schoolers still on the track. Hanging out at your school over summer break seems weird, but I understand the pull. At this time of day on a Friday, everywhere else has been taken over by summer camps or tourists. The school, even as the heart of the town, is an escape from Ardena.

"What's there to do in this town?" Haley asks, lying back and shielding her eyes from the sun.

"Not much," I say. "We can try to hit up the beach around dinnertime, or I'm sure everyone will be at Lola's tonight."

"There are some good running trails at the state park," Max adds from his perch by the driver's side door.

Haley scoffs. "Don't you two spend all day running?"

"Mostly watching people run," I say.

"Even worse."

"You guys can come to my place," Max says hesitantly. "I'm having a game night with some friends. Bring a snack to share and whatever you like to drink."

I stare at Max, who is looking at a spot on the roof of my car with keen interest. He's never asked me to do anything outside of running and work. Yes, we've had breakfasts and lunches, but all of those were within the constraints of our jobs. This is purely a social invitation. To his house. With his friends.

Haley nudges me after a moment, and I turn away, blinking against the glare of the sun. She has her "I want all the details" face on. Which means that whatever is happening between me and Max—not that anything is happening—I'm not imagining it. Those subtle touches are apparently not so subtle. Except most mornings, I still wake in a panic or in tears. My tears vary from awful remembrances to dreamland happiness that doesn't exist in my waking life. I know I don't want those things when I'm conscious. There's no going back. If I accepted that sooner, maybe Wildwood wouldn't have happened. But healing takes time, and in sleep, my mind and heart are still battling heartache. So no matter what effect Max is having on me or what Haley thinks she's seeing, it can't really be happening. Right?

"That sounds fun," I say, far too late after the initial request. "Any holes in the snack department?"

Growing up with only a dad, I've become pretty resourceful in the kitchen. I can usually scavenge enough from the apartment to make something edible without having to go to the store unless it involves cheese. We're always lacking cheese.

"Brownies," he says immediately. "No one ever makes them. I've been surviving on those prepackaged cosmic things, but they aren't really brownies. There are no edges or center pieces that are all gooey."

I giggle at his simple request. "Do you have a preferred brand?"

Chapter 34
Zoey

Haley and I stand in front of the door to Max's apartment with a plate of brownies, courtesy of the Dough Boy. He lives in a complex off the main road. We're too far from the beach to see the water, but the ocean still salts the air, and the scent lingers. I pause, my hand poised to knock. Anxiety ripples through me as it has all afternoon at the idea that we're crossing some line that our easy bantering at work never does. Max is a teacher at Ardena, and though I was never taught by him and am no longer a student and no one at camp seems to think anything of the two of us always attached at the hip, this moment gives me pause.

But then Haley knocks, and Max answers, his smile as big and bright as ever. His eyes linger on me for a long moment, and I'm glad I decided to throw on a V-neck tee instead of my usual tank top.

"We brought brownies as requested," I say, holding them up.

He takes the plate, his fingers brushing against mine. Our eyes meet, and something unspoken that I can't identify passes between us. Maybe it's an acknowledgement of this step we're taking. I don't know. It's not intense but hesitant, almost questioning. Does he regret the invite? Does he feel like we're teetering on a line too?

"Nice." He steps back to let us in. "You totally weren't getting in without them."

The apartment is small. From where I stand, I can see most of it. It's exactly how I imagined—running shoes by the door, a bike hanging on the wall, secondhand furniture mixed with newer pieces. Hints of his life are everywhere, from concerts tickets to Greek letters. There's no obvious pictures of his ex but a few of his family. After only seconds in his space, I feel like I know him better.

"Everyone, this is Zoey and Haley." He turns toward us. "This is everyone."

I survey the group, spread out amongst every spare seat of the living room. There's no one I know. My anxiety dissipates a little more. Haley, per usual, jumps right in, shaking hands, getting names. She sinks onto a pillow Max has sitting on the floor and falls right into a conversation with a blond guy in board shorts and a polo and a woman with a pixie cut and a maxi dress.

"Can I get you anything to drink?"

Max stands close enough to me that I can smell his cologne. He doesn't wear cologne on the track, and I've grown used to his scent of sweat and soap and what I know to be Head and Shoulders from living with my dad. Tonight, though, he smells clean and musky, more his age. His hair is carefully coiffed, and the sleeves of his button-down are evenly rolled to his elbows. This isn't Coach Evans or his teacher persona. This is him with his friends, which I am now, apparently, counted among.

"Umm." We brought beer, but it was handed off with the brownies and is nowhere in sight. Max holds an IPA, and there are wineglasses in the living room, but alcohol right now seems highly unappealing. "Water for now."

"Hey, man, do you have any salsa?"

I freeze at the familiar voice and slowly turn to face one of Ardena's freshman English teachers and the advisor of the yearbook that I helped put together since sophomore year. My stomach drops. This is what all my anxiety's been about, though I'm just realizing it.

"Joe," Max says in an easy tone. "You remember Zoey."

"Mr. Turner." I swallow, cringing at how awkward his teacher moniker sounds from my mouth as I stand in the middle of Max's apartment. "Nice to see you again."

Recognition registers on Mr. Turner's—Joe's—face immediately. He leans back on his heels, his eyes traveling from Max to me and back again, most likely taking in the lack of distance between us. His lips press into a thin line before he nods at me. "I think you'd better call me Joe."

Max's hands clamp down on my shoulders, and he squeezes lightly before releasing me. "Okay, water, salsa. Got it."

And then he's gone, and I've never wished so hard for a beer. Joe stands with me, one hand in his pocket and the other clutching his beer. His gaze travels around the room before returning to me.

"So," he says finally, discomfort evident in his voice, "Max said you work at the camp together."

I start, but nothing comes out. I'm too lost in the fact that Max has mentioned me to his friends. His invite seemed off the cuff this afternoon, but maybe not? While uncomfortable, Joe doesn't seem surprised by my presence.

My phone buzzes in my back pocket before I can formulate an answer. I glance down at the screen, expecting it to be Haley from across the room. My roommate has saved me from situations like this numerous times. Well, maybe not exactly like this. But it's Cecilia's name on the screen. I didn't even know she had my new number. "Sorry, I have to take this."

Joe nods and retreats back to the kitchen. I shuffle forward and glance around for a quiet spot. There's not a lot of options, but I move to the far side of the room, which holds a small dining set with a laptop set up.

"Cecilia?"

"Are you with Liz?"

"No," I say, spotting two doors off the room. One is the bathroom. The other has to be his bedroom, but my options are slim, and I don't want to have a conversation with my sister in the middle of the party. I shut the door behind me and sit down on the edge of Max's neatly tucked bed. "I'm in Ardena for the night. Is everything okay?"

There's a rustling as if Cecilia's settling in. My heartbeat ramps up. What's happening right now? "Everything is fine. Sorry." She actually sounds contrite. "What do you know about this guy Liz is seeing?"

Of course. Cecilia would never call to talk to me. Not about anything other than Liz. She didn't even check in on me after the disastrous weekend in Wildwood, though I know Liz updated her for at least the first few days. Did Cecilia ask? Did she even care? I remember my oldest sister's soft voice on the porch at Jane's house. There was worry there. She talked about getting over first loves—real ones—and how it was awful any way you looked at it. She told me about Simon. Liz does an excellent job of keeping each of us apprised of the other, but Liz never mentioned that Cecilia's first love exploded because of me. We really are three sides of a triangle. Broken as the lines between us are, we're ever connected, whether we like it or not.

"I know the basics and that when she comes back from seeing him, she's happy." I pause. "I thought you wanted her to date."

I noted over the last week that Liz was tight-lipped about Spencer on her calls with Cecilia, so I stop myself from giving the details I've gleaned from sharing a living space. Like what he does for a living or that Liz stays up talking to him almost every night. And most importantly, that they've seen each other much more than the two times she's mentioned to Cecilia.

"I did want her to date." Cecilia's voice is high and tight. "But I didn't think..."

That she would meet someone. The words fall unspoken between us. Is it better or worse if Liz meets someone special? Sleeping with a random guy seems tawdrier than dating someone, but the whole point of this experiment is for Liz to realize that there are other people out there. That after all these years, someone else can love her, want her. It's exactly what I'm going through. I can't go sleep with some rando to shake Andrew away. If it were that easy, I would have done it already. But I can't. And we weren't married or together for a lifetime.

"She needs to do this in her own way," I say quietly. *Or she'll always wonder. Either way.*

"I know, but it's my sisterly duty to worry." The irony of her statement is painful. I feel it in my gut. Has she forgotten who she's speaking to?

"I understand." I try and fail to keep my tone neutral.

Cecilia clears her throat. "How are you dealing with everything?"

Wow. I'm not naive enough to think the question means her sisterly worry extends to me. One inquiry doesn't negate all her silence. And even if I answer, she doesn't know Haley or Becca or Max. She doesn't even know Andrew or Claire. But still she asked.

"I'm fine," I say stiffly. "Andrew—"

The door opens, and Max stands there, eyes wide. His gaze travels from the bed to me and then down my body. Each second feels like a mini eternity.

"Are you okay?" he mouths silently.

I try to smile to reassure him, but getting caught in his bedroom seemingly talking about—or worse, *to*—Andrew is too awkward. Our eyes lock, and I wave him over.

"I have to go, but try not to worry," I say to Cecilia. "Liz is a big girl." I hang up, hoping that that last line dispels any possibility that I was talking to my ex.

"Sorry to interrupt." He sits down next to me, close enough that our knees touch.

I bump his shoulder with my own. "I'm the one in your room uninvited."

"You, Zee, are welcome in my bedroom anytime."

The air shifts between us, static and tension sparking. Goose bumps rise at the nickname or the comment—I can't tell which. He's never said my name like that before. I hold his gaze for several seconds, during which I'm brilliantly aware of all the places our bodies touch. Max isn't drunk, and though I saw him with a beer, no alcohol is on his breath. But I can't imagine him saying such a thing otherwise. Max, despite the nickname and the touching and the honesty, hasn't alluded to anything more than friendship aloud. If Haley hadn't spent the entire afternoon asking a zillion questions about me and Max, dissecting every moment of our time together this summer, I might've thought I was completely delusional or suffering from transference and latching on to the first guy who cared at all. But she saw it. And now this.

"What's going on?" he asks when I don't respond to his comment. He doesn't, I note, move away.

"My sister called." I've mentioned Liz and Cecilia and the craziness that is my family before, but I don't expect him to fully grasp my meaning. "My other sister."

His eyes narrow in understanding. "That's *interesting*."

He remembers. Of course he does. The corners of my mouth quirk. "That's one word for it."

He smiles and tugs on the loose ends of hair that hang over my shoulder. His fingers brush the bare skin of my collarbone. Electricity shoots through my veins. The touch is nothing like anything we've shared. Coherent thought abandons me. Every nerve in my body is focused on his skin on my skin. I breathe slowly, and his fingers rise and fall but never leave me.

He feels this too. It's written all over his face. His hand circles the back of my neck, and he tangles his fingers in my hair. I sigh and lean into him, closer than we've ever been—not close enough.

"You okay, Zee?"

Zee. There it is again. The single syllable like an oath. Blood rushes through my body, waking up parts of me that had long since gone dormant.

"No one else calls me that," I say instead of answering his question because I am not okay in the best of ways.

His fingers move across my skin in a caress until he's cupping my face. His touch is soft against my cheek but scratchy from too much time outside handling sports equipment, and the tiniest of movements bring me to the brink. He runs a single finger across my lips before bringing my face up to his.

"I know." I can feel each letter of his response. A sliver separates us, keeping us on the safe side of the line. But I don't want to be safe.

"Max," I breathe as his lips finally touch mine.

The door swings open, screeching on its hinges. The sounds of the party come back to me. Max jumps back, his hands dropping into his lap. We stare at each other for a second before he turns to focus on the person in the doorway. Joe, I realize.

"The pizza's here, man," he says warily. And I can't blame him. A little over a year ago, I sat in his classroom, organizing homecoming photos for the yearbook. Now, we're at a party together.

The Max whose gaze meets mine is not the same man who moments before kindled my desire. He's the Max I know from the track and from breakfast, but there's a shadow over him now. He stands without a word and walks out of the room.

Chapter 35

Liz

My hands shake as I arrange the charcuterie. I take a small sip of wine and turn my attention back to Spencer. He's in one of those man sprawls on the couch, arms behind his head, sunk deep into the cushions, legs long and wide. Inviting him over felt natural and completely right when I did it this afternoon after finding out that Zoey was staying in Ardena for the night. But now that he's here in my apartment and there's no chance of interruptions, my body is equally burdened with anxiety and desire.

We've spent a lot of time together in the past few weeks. If he's not with Ryan, he's with me. And we've gotten close to having sex enough times that I feel the way his eyes track me as I move through the kitchen, and I know exactly where to touch to make him moan, and yet something always stops us. Mainly me. But tonight, there's nothing to stop us. He's here in my house, and I'm wearing a little red dress that cuts in all the right places. I want him to stop telling me a story about his son and instead drag me into the bedroom, leaving our clothes strewn across the floor.

I look back up at him, ready to engage with his story, but he's watching me with this uncanny smile.

"Having an acid flashback?" I ask, looking around my small apartment. He mentioned upon entering that my space is pretty much his in reverse.

He laughs. "No, I was thinking how nice this is. Thanks for having me."

His voice dips on that last part, and his eyes meet mine, saying all the dirty things he doesn't. Apparently, my innocuous text about having dinner instead of going out was not as innocuous as I suspected. He clearly read right through the subtext to my actual request—*do you want to skip dinner and bang*—because he's dressed in a button-down with the sleeves rolled up and brought fancy wine.

"Of course," I say, returning to my appetizers. "It's nice to have a guest that's not family here."

"Does it feel real now?"

I nod. "Almost too real but in this amazing way. I feel less like a squatter and less like this is some weird immersive camp experience."

"Well, I'm honored that you invited me into your home."

Into my bed is more like it. I count to ten and then look up at him. It's never uncomfortable between us, and I'm not going to let tonight go that way. It will or won't happen.

"You might rethink that when you see this charcuterie tray." I slide some crackers onto the platter I got at the thrift shop on my way home.

He shrugs. "I lived on pizza rolls and Caesar salad kits for the first four months after my separation."

An image of a scruffy, sweatpants-clad version of the well-put-together man in front of me pops into my mind. A baseball hat sits low on his head, covering too long and unkempt hair. Though I've only known him a few weeks, I suspect this depiction is right on.

"Well, I'm glad your expectations are low because I'm not sure I even have a second serving platter for the main course."

He walks toward me then peeks at the tray I've placed on the counter between us. "You can't replace a lifetime of kitchenware in a few weeks." He comes up behind me and wraps his arms around my waist. My pulse quickens at his touch, at his lips at my ear and the quick beat of his heart against my back. "I like the dress."

My head falls back onto him as he kisses my neck. His hands snake their way up my stomach, skimming my breasts. I turn in his arms. "I thought you might."

His eyes seek mine, looking for approval, for consent. I hold his gaze and give an imperceptible nod—*yes, please, yes*—before bringing my lips to his. He pushes me back against the counter and fits himself between my legs. I feel him, all of him, everywhere. My body is on fire. I unbutton his shirt and push it to the floor. My hands go to his chest and then down farther, farther, until I hear him moan under my attention.

Our lips never part, each dip and breath deepening the kiss, urging us closer. He kisses down to my chest, pushing the straps of my dress off my shoulders. His fingers slip under the soft material, and a spike of desire shoots through me.

"Shall we take this out of the kitchen?" he asks as my dress slips farther down.

"I don't know." I undo the button of his pants. "The cold cuts are creating quite the ambiance."

"True." He slips the straps of my dress off my arms and watches as it falls to the floor. "But I like to take my time."

His eyes rake across my body, and he picks me up, his lips coming back to my chest. He steps out of his pants and kisses me again. It's dizzying and desperate. I want him inside me now.

"Bedroom's last door on the right."

I breathe him in and wrap myself tighter around him, if that's possible. He smiles against my lips and carries me from the kitchen through the living room and into my bedroom. His mouth never leaves my body, moving from lips to ear to neck to breasts, until finally he lays me back on the bed.

I look up at him, this man who has shaken my whole world, and pull him down on top of me.

Orange streaks the sky as the sun starts its ascent into morning. I sit on the small balcony of my apartment with a steaming cup of coffee and a blanket covering my legs, even though the morning is already warm and sticky. I wasn't able to sleep after Spencer left around midnight. My favorite pillow smelled like him. I loved it, but I also hated it. I changed the sheets, but then the bed felt cold and empty. Finally, I picked up my book—the same one Spencer found for me that first day—and decided to read until I fell asleep. Except I didn't fall asleep, and then I finished my book. So coffee and the sunrise. Why not?

All these hours later, I can still smell Spencer on me, feel his touch, remember how I trembled as he pushed me over the edge. It was a perfect night. A more-than-once night, and if he didn't have to leave because of some event with Ryan the next morning, we might never have stopped. I rub at my eyes with my free hand before leaning forward over my knees. I know what's keeping me up, and it's not doubt or worry about Spencer. We were good together, more than good. I haven't had sex like that, well, ever. But I didn't see Julian behind my eyes when Spencer trailed kisses down my spine, and when Spencer's lips met the softest parts of me, I didn't have to swallow Julian's name. With each thrust, Spencer shattered the already-splintered glass holding me in place. I didn't miss my husband for one moment of the entire night. I'm not undecided on my marriage. I'm in mourning.

Chapter 36
Zoey

"Tell me again."

"Absolutely not." I roll my eyes behind my sunglasses and switch positions on my towel. The last thing I need is a sunburn on top of everything else.

Despite all my whining about the tourists, I agreed to take Haley to the beach—on a weekend, no less. It's crowded, but we snagged a spot nearish the water and away from anyone too obnoxious. Liz and Spencer decided to come as we were packing up the car. It's been a fun day. Over twenty minutes ago, Liz dragged Spencer to the board-walk for funnel cake, and they've yet to come back, providing Haley the perfect opportunity to bombard me with more questions about my almost kiss with Max. As if I didn't spend all day yesterday over-thinking it.

"Come on," Haley whines from her supine position, "your for-mer teacher slash new hot coworker told you that you were welcome in his bed anytime, and then tried to kiss you. If there is ever a time to dish."

"It sounds like you have a full understanding of the situation."

"But what if he had kissed you?"

"What if he had kissed me?" I repeat incredulously. "What do you mean? It's not like we were going to strip our clothes off and have sex with six people in the next room."

Haley grins. "Not without locking the door first."

"You're ridiculous."

Haley rolls onto her stomach and rests her head on her arms. If she stays like that too long, she's going to have wicked tan lines. It would serve her right for being nosy. "Your sister, by the way, totally slept with that guy."

Gross. It's obvious, but still... gross. In the last two days, Liz is different. It's like some wall came down and not one built this summer. She's looser and louder and somehow brighter even with the sadness that still sometimes shadows her eyes. My sister is happy in a way I'm not sure I've ever seen before.

"Yes, thank you for telling me. *Again*."

"I'm saying if your sister can get it on with that dude while still married—"

"They're separated."

"You can totally make out with your former teacher."

"He wasn't my teacher. Ever."

"Semantics."

"Not in the least."

Haley's head pops up, and I'm certain she's glaring at me behind the designer sunglasses she paid far too much for on the boardwalk. "When you explained him to me, you literally said he was one of Andrew's football coaches and taught geometry."

Why am I cursed with a Big who remembers everything? Why? It's easy to forget that Max isn't my coworker at Ardena Heat but a coach and teacher at the high school. We almost never interacted at school. It took several texts with Becca and a look through my yearbook before I remembered he taught math. And Max only knew me by my association with Andrew and a mile time. Even now that we're friends, our lives don't overlap outside the track. We exist in this safe little bubble where nothing matters but what's happening that day on the field. At least we did until the party.

What's tomorrow going to be like? Back at work for the first time, that kiss hanging over us. Joe's scowl burned into my memory. Max walking away. And Haley there to witness it all.

"Do you think people will care?" I clear my throat. "That he works at the high school?"

"Some people," she says with a shrug, though her eyebrows pop up over her sunglasses. I guess my question is a declaration of sorts. A pretty big one considering Haley drove halfway across the country to help me grieve my cheating ex-boyfriend some more. "But it seems to me that you met pretty organically outside of school and over a year after graduation. And no one is going to believe anything less than kosher was going on while you were with Andrew. I mean, you two were..." Her face scrunches as she searches for the word. "*Repulsively* in love. Literally sometimes looking at the two of you made me want to vomit."

I giggle and ignore the fact that something less than kosher *had* been going on while I was with Andrew. We *were* repulsively in love, particularly in high school. Claire shared the same feelings as Haley on the matter more than once. An ache flares deep inside me. I don't want my relationship back, but that doesn't mean it doesn't hurt or that I don't miss it. Because I do miss a lot about my life, myself, before I walked into that dorm room. But grief is a process, and my therapist advised me to allow myself to feel whatever I feel, accept it, and carry on. There's no guilt in missing someone you loved. There's also no guilt in moving on.

"But seriously, if you like him..." She trails off as Liz and Spencer return, carrying not one but two funnel cakes and a basket of fried Oreos.

My sister hands me the fried Oreos with a knowing look. Liz does not share funnel cake; Spencer's lucky he got a bite in. I pick up an Oreo and reach for the other funnel cake, but it has magically moved from the towel to Haley's lap. She doesn't like to share, either.

"See!" Liz points at her plate and the pile of powdered sugar coating their towel. "I told you we would have to share if we only came back with one."

Spencer laughs and pulls Liz into his lap. His hands linger at the bare skin of Liz's waist. She smiles and wraps her arms around him, wiping powdered sugar off his face. I look away, a different ache building in my chest. This isn't the sister I've always known—reserved because a little kid was around, and then comfortable in a long-term relationship, and then married. Yes, Julian would come into a room and have only eyes for his wife. Or Liz would plant a kiss on him when she passed between rooms, but this is unlike anything I've ever seen from Liz. It's like she's coming alive right in front of me. It's exhilarating to watch but also such a deviation from what I know. It gives me hope for the future but crushes the idea that first love can conquer all.

Haley bumps me with her shoulder, and the smell of sugar overpowers the saltiness of the ocean air for a moment. She grins and leans in close. "Totally did it."

I stifle a laugh by shoveling fried dough into my mouth.

"So," Liz says, eyeing me suspiciously, "what do you two have planned for the next few days?"

"Work," I say, grateful that she's back on the blanket. "Hanging out with Becca, maybe Grounds for Sculpture one night."

"Make sure you make a reservation at Rat's if you go to Grounds for Sculpture," Spencer says. "Best food around and beautiful at night."

Haley nods along to all of this, absently playing with her food. She glances at me, a small smile forming on her lips. "And then on my last night," she says, and I cringe because my Big has no filter, "we're burning everything Zoey still has from Andrew in effigy." The statement is met by silence. "It's cleansing. Dr. Goodwin agrees."

Liz's face registers surprise at the name of my therapist out of my roommate's mouth. But Haley knows pretty much everything about me. We're not friends but sisters. Big and Little. We're bonded in a way that it would be weird if she didn't know the name of my therapist.

"Okay." Liz shrugs. "Don't leave any burn marks that would negate my safety deposit."

"We're doing it at Dad's. Outside."

"And don't worry," Haley says around a bite of funnel cake, "we've done this before."

Chapter 37
Zoey

The days pass quickly. Between working and entertaining, there's time for little else. Knowing my friend, this was Haley's intention all along. She dutifully sits through my workday, sometimes exploring Ardena or spending a few alone hours at the townhouse but mostly pestering Max with questions. Max, for his part, acts completely normal. He grins at us, sunburned and exhausted, on Monday morning, and it's like the party never happened. Except it did, and I feel the subtle distance between us that wasn't there before. Maybe I'm imagining it. Maybe I put it there. I don't know.

Now as the week comes to a close and Haley's due to leave for home in an hour, the three of us sit on the bleachers, watching the campers enjoy the midsummer BBQ. It's a camp tradition celebrating the end of the first session. Many of the older campers will be back on Monday for the second session, but for the younger ones, this is the last day of camp. And even though we're an intensive sports camp, the last day still means fun. There's an inflatable obstacle course on the football field, a DJ, a few food trucks with specialty desserts, and way too much barbecue.

"Now," Max says, spearing a piece of watermelon off my plate, "will you please explain to me why you two smell like a smokehouse?"

My cheeks burn. The last thing I want to do is tell Max I spent last night standing over a small fire, burning photographs, letters, and emails that I had meticulously printed and scrapbooked the first year of my relationship. After that, Andrew and I were so inseparable that the need for romantic missives decreased, but from the sheer number of photos I have—*had*—from our time together, you would never know we had extracurricular activities or friends. We really were repulsive.

Watching my memories burn last night, I was stoic. That girl with the wide smile and the gleam in her eye didn't feel like me anymore. At the very end of the burning, standing shoulder to shoulder with one of my best friends, the tears came but not for Andrew or Claire or any of it. They came for that girl who loved so completely, so innocently. Will I ever love like that again?

"We had a ceremonial burning," Haley says, her eyes staying on the field, her tone completely nonchalant, as if this is a normal occurrence. Though for us, I suppose it is.

Max chokes on his soda, not expecting that answer. "A what?"

I feel both of them watching me. Because clearly the question is directed at me. It's my story to tell, and Haley's not going to let me lie about it. "We were *disposing* of some things I still had... of Andrew's."

His name sticks in my throat. I avoid saying it as a general rule, but saying it to Max feels wrong. I'm not sure I've ever initiated a conversation about Andrew with him, which is silly. Andrew was a huge part of my life, and as much as I hate it, he'll always be part of my story—that memory I dredge up when people post those silly surveys on social media or whenever first loves come up, or losing your virginity, or any number of firsts I shared with Andrew. And I don't need to feel bad about that or about whatever I need to do to move on. Because last night wasn't about Andrew. It was about me.

"It's a Delta Sig tradition." I meet Max's gaze head-on. I can't expect him to want to talk about an almost kiss if I can't even talk about my ex-boyfriend. "It's a way to cleanse yourself of bad mojo that assholes bring. Haley added that last part."

He holds a hand to his heart, as if I've shot him. "I'm wounded on behalf of my gender."

"Asshole is not a gendered term," Haley says, sparing him a glance. "I call 'em like I see 'em."

"And we've seen 'em," I add with a knowing nod.

Max rolls his eyes. "You two are weird."

"We know," Haley says at the same time that I say, "It's part of our charm."

This only makes Max's grin wider. We have this effect on people a lot. It's why we bonded quickly as roommates and why when I pledged in the spring, there wasn't even another consideration for my Big. It's also why there's no way in hell I'm transferring out of Bellewood. If I have to see Andrew every day for the next three years, watch him date and fall in love and grow and change, I'm going to do it with grace. Bellewood is home. And hopefully, I'll date and fall in love and grow and change too.

I sneak a look at Max. He's leaning back against the bleachers, relaxed and happy. When he laughs, I feel it on the riser below. He glances down at me, his eyes meeting mine. It's a quick look, but it's like he's seeing me for the first time all week. He's all dimples and laugh lines, and I feel that look down to my toes.

"All right, Little." Next to me Haley stands and stretches before reaching for her bag. The week's gone too fast, and it feels like today didn't even happen. "Time for me to hit the road."

I'm not ready for her to leave. For the silence that will descend as soon as she walks off these bleachers. I'm not ready to be alone again.

"Max," Haley says turning to him, "it's been a pleasure."

He holds out his arms, and without hesitation, she steps into his hug. "Pleasure was all mine."

I stand then and pull her into a hug of my own. In a few weeks, we'll be back together. I can do this. "Thank you, Hales. Seriously, this was above and beyond."

"Nonsense." She squeezes me tighter. "This is what you do for family."

"Love you, Big."

Haley steps away and clasps my hand. "Love you back."

W hen the final minivan pulls away from the pickup line at the end of the day, I literally run to my car. The rest of the day lingered, and whatever passed between Max and me in those moments before Haley left dissipated into awkward silence. But my speedy exit doesn't matter. Before I can even find my keys, Max is at my side.

"Zee, wait."

My body jerks to life, and oh my god, I hate what that nickname does to me and the way his voice softens and wraps itself around the single syllable. I will my heart to beat normally before facing him. He's a few paces behind, his expression open but stressed.

"I know we need to talk," he says, closing the space between us. He doesn't touch me, but his hands clench and unclench at his sides. "But Haley was always here, and I didn't know what to say. That night... I shouldn't have. I'm sorry."

Sorry? Of all the things I wanted him to say. Sorry?

"I don't want you to be sorry," I practically yell.

"Then what do you want?"

That's the question. What do I want? To go back in time and erase that stupid moment so we can go back to our friendship? To have him lock the door to keep Joe from interrupting? To have him stop calling me Zee and making my insides melt?

What do I want? My stomach flips, and my heart pounds. I want to know. Unequivocally.

"I want you to kiss me." My feet stay rooted to the ground. It's my request, but it has to be his choice.

His expression changes from uncertainty to surprise to joy and, finally, determination. How can one person feel so much between one moment and the next? And about me? He cups my face, his fingers soft against my skin. Butterflies sweep across my stomach, and my mind goes blank as he closes the space between us. The world narrows. His lips meet mine, part mine, devour mine. And my world explodes.

This summer, Andrew, Claire, the tears, and the mistakes—they all fade away. Max's hand is still gentle on my cheek, but his other grasps at my waist and pulls me in close. He smiles against my lips as my arms wrap around his neck and my fingers tug at his hair. I deepen the kiss. Every part of me is on fire. I'm lost in the scent and taste of him, sweaty and salty and purely Max. I didn't believe, not really, that someone would ever want me again and that I could want them back. But I was wrong. So very wrong. My love life didn't end when I walked into that dorm room all those months ago. It was set free.

Chapter 38
Liz

God, I need to clean the bathroom. I haven't seen this many dust bunnies—*or is that hair?*—in my life. My stomach roils again, and I turn my head from the sight, but it's too late. I retch into the toilet for the third time. How is there even anything left in my stomach? All I ate today is that wrap from the cafeteria, the same one I've been getting every day since I started back at the office. And this isn't the first time I've been sick this week. It can't be the cafeteria, but then what?

"Again?"

I glance up at Zoey standing in the doorway. Her face is pinched in concern, but her cheeks are flushed, and there's an almost fevered glint in her eyes. *Please don't be sick. We can't both be sick.* When I look back at her, the frenzy is gone, and only her usual calm expression remains.

"Hi, sister." I wave because I'm not sure I can lift my head. This is bad.

Zoey squats down next to me. "Can you stand?"

I attempt to lift my head, and my stomach turns over again. "No, definitely not."

Okay." She sits down next to me and rubs my back. "What can I do?"

I glance at my sister. What is she doing here? It's early on Friday night, and she has a life.

"Can you get my phone?"

She pulls it off the vanity and holds it out. Right, because I was getting ready for my date before this happened. I fumble for a minute before finally getting Spencer's number on the screen and putting him on speakerphone.

"Hey, babe," he says after one ring. "I'm just changing my shirt, and then I'm heading to you."

"I'm sick," I croak, glad he can't see me right now with my arm braced against the cold toilet seat. "Stay far away."

"Again?"

Why do people keep asking me that? Yes, again. Still. Whatever. My consternation must show on my face because Zoey laughs.

"Oh. good, Zoey's there," he says. "Is she staying, or do you need me to come?"

I silently plead with my sister. She's holding a fountain drink from our favorite take-out spot, which usually means she's intending to sleep here, but I can't take any chances. No fledging relationship should have to survive vomit.

"I'll be here," she says evenly.

"Call me if you need anything, please. Feel better, babe."

Somehow, Zoey gets me off the floor and into the living room. She forces a giant cup of tea on me and some crackers before curling up in the armchair. I sip the tea, a minty green mixed with chamomile. Magic tea, my mom always called it. I'm surprised our dad remembered such a small thing and passed it on to Zoey.

"Can I ask you something?" Her eyes don't quite meet mine, but I nod, and she takes the deepest breath, as if she's about to ask after the mysteries of the universe and isn't sure she wants to know the answer. "Are you pregnant?"

"What?"

She rings her hands together. "It's... We've lived together for several weeks now, and you haven't gotten your period."

"That's not uncommon for me."

"But now you're throwing up, and last night at dinner, you ate your pickle." Her voice rises, becoming shrill the longer she talks. "You never eat pickles, and when I offered you some of my chicken, you looked at it as if it was rancid milk." She pauses. "Is it possible that you're pregnant?"

Holy. Shit. It's not possible. No way in hell am I pregnant *now*. "I only slept with Spencer a week ago."

And we were safe.

Zoey cringes at my words but presses on. "And Julian?"

I put a hand to my stomach. There doesn't seem to be any extra pounds hiding there, but even if—I can't even think it. It's like my brain skips right over the possibility. Except, well, we weren't safe the night I left or any night before. It can't be. This is some awful, cruel joke.

"I'll go get you a test." She stands, but I hold up a hand to stop her.

"There's one in the bathroom."

Isn't this conversation supposed to go the other way? The nineteen-year-old has the pregnancy scare, not the thirty-four-year-old. I palm my face. My mind swims. A baby. It's everything I want. But not like this. Not now when everything is completely up in the air. But if I'm puking and having cravings, that means I've been pregnant for a while. And if I've been pregnant for a while, then Julian is the father. And if Julian is the father, what does that mean?

"Come on." Zoey holds out her hands, but I don't move to take them.

The thought of standing, of taking that test, is paralyzing. There's no going back after that. I bite hard on my bottom lip, tasting the saltiness of fresh tears. There's already no going back.

"I can't," I say through my tears.

"You can."

Her touch sends relief through me. I'm not alone. Zoey is here. My mom is here. Even my dad. Whatever happens next, I am not alone.

Zoey pulls me to my feet. "Don't worry, Liz. I got you."

We sit with our backs to the bathtub, the test resting out of sight on the vanity. My hands shake, and my stomach threatens to betray me again. Zoey is silent next to me, her hand in mine, her eyes on the timer on her phone. In less than three minutes, that awful digital pee stick will change my life. Pregnant or Not Pregnant.

"Tell me something," I say quietly.

She glances up, her face scrunched as she considers her options. "E is the most common letter and appears in eleven percent of all English words."

"Why do you know that?"

She shrugs, her eyes back on the phone. "Dad and I used to do trivia."

I stare at the ceiling, the only place I can't see the timer or the test. Of course my dad and sister did trivia. I can one hundred percent see them duking it out and winning. "Tell me something that will make time move again."

Zoey shifts next to me, and she squeezes my hand. "I kissed someone who wasn't Andrew today."

Thank god. Zoey needed that kiss more than anyone else in the entire world. Maybe now she can move on for real. I remember every first *after* kiss—John the summer after high school graduation, Lucas, and now Spencer. No matter what, Zoey will remember this boy and this kiss.

"It's about time."

"*Thanks.*"

"It was Max, right?"

She flushes a deep red, and that's all the answer I need. It really is about time. She spends more time with Max than anyone. I'm not even sure she realizes it.

The timer dings, and we both straighten, our eyes going to the sink. I will myself to move, but I can't. The shaking returns to my hands and works its way up my arms. I close my eyes. Never have I wanted to know and not know anything as much as in this moment. It's like finding Sheila's emails but a million times worse.

Zoey pulls me into a hug, but I feel her reaching for the test. She must know what it says, but she doesn't react, only pulls my hands free and places the test in them.

I count to ten and then twenty. Zoey's hands stay on mine. She breathes calm and steady, and slowly I match her breaths. Whatever the result, I will be fine. Whatever the result, I can do this. I open my eyes to a single word.

Chapter 39

Liz

Pregnant.

I'm pregnant. Finally. I stare at my reflection in the mirror. The woman looking back at me looks terrified and ecstatic all at once. Her stomach is as flat as it ever is, which isn't very flat. She's going to be a mom. I'm going to be a mom. If my math is right, from the last time Julian and I slept together, I'm between six and eight weeks. It's hard to gauge since before that, I didn't have my period for two months, but there was the negative test. I was sufficiently Not Pregnant before I decided to have farewell sex with my husband.

My doctor will confirm at my appointment, but I know. Know deep in my bones with every hour that has passed since the positive result. My whole body and all my senses are now tuned to the new life growing inside me. The baby that I wanted more than anything is here.

I put a hand over my stomach. "It'll all be okay, peanut."

Peanut. It came without a thought, but now that it's out there, I can't take it back. It's the name I used last time before it all ended before it ever really began. But it made goodbye that much harder. I breathe deeply. I can do this. It will be fine. I'll make it out of the first trimester. I'll hear that wondrous, fast heartbeat, and all will be right in my world. But who is standing next to me? Julian? And if it is Julian, what does that mean for our marriage? For Spencer? Oh god, Spencer. He's not the father, and I can't help but believe that's a good thing because that would be too much. We're so new. He's handled all of my baggage, counterweighting it with his own, but there's baggage, and then there's an unplanned pregnancy with your not-quite-ex-husband. How am I going to tell him? Either of them?

"Liz?" Zoey pops her head into the room. "Cee is here."

"I'll be right there."

"Does she know that Dad"—she mouths the word—"is coming?"

I shake my head. Please let this night not be a disaster. When I planned it in my head, it made sense. There would be an Evie buffer between my sister and our dad. Cecilia would've been pissed, but with Evie there... I'm not sure I have enough wine, and I can't even drink it. "You know how she is."

"True." Zoey steps into the room and shuts the door behind her. "How are you feeling?"

It's a simple question, but it turns me to mush. Tears fall, and I pull her into a hug. Zoey's become my lifeline this summer. How unexpected. How amazing. "I love you."

An odd expression colors my sister's face—a bit of happiness, a bit of loneliness. Because we don't say those words often enough.

"I love you too," she says, giving me another squeeze.

"Cee!" I squeal as I pull her into a hug. "I can't believe you're here. Again!"

She smiles warmly before hanging her purse on the rack. "You know I would fly one thousand miles for you and then fly one thousand more."

Zoey snorts from the kitchen, where she's transferring a store-bought vegetable tray onto a platter that matches the plate set I used for the dinner. "Your age is showing."

Cecilia's eyes narrow, but her usual irritation is not there. "And yet you got the reference."

Zoey grins. "Touché."

My mom arrives next, and we all filter into the dining room. Laughter fills the space. It's been a common sound with Haley and Zoey in residence the last week, but tonight it's different. This is my family—my mom and both my sisters—at the same table, breaking bread, and laughing. Never in the last seventeen years has this happened. Not even at my wedding. This summer has changed us. Even my mom is at ease. She's always been good with Zoey—better than anyone could expect—but tonight the air feels clear and our baggage handled. When I told her I wanted to have a dinner with everyone, she simply asked if Zoey was still allergic to strawberries, a fact I didn't even know. And probably should have, considering all the times I babysat her.

"Zoey dear, how are you doing? I hear it's been quite the summer."

Zoey blushes at Mom's question but shrugs. "I'm okay. Going back to school will be hard in the same way that coming home was. There are memories everywhere."

"Yes, there are. But you'll get through it." She looks at each of us, stopping for a long moment on me. "We all do."

"I know," Zoey says. "And I have a great support system now. It would've been a really different summer without Liz."

"I don't doubt that." My mom's tone is off, but her smile is real. I've seen her act for clients for years, and this is no act. She's interested in what Zoey has to say, cares about her well-being. "And how is your father?"

What a strange question. My mom almost never asks after my dad, except in that perfunctory way when she knows I've been with him. I watch the two of them, and it's like they're having a silent conversation, but about what?

Zoey's gaze shifts to me and then to Cecilia before coming back to Mom. "He's well. Eating on campus a bit too much now that I'm in school most of the year, but sometimes I think he likes it that way. Keeps him from getting lonely."

"He's hardly lonely."

"What?" Zoey and I say at the same time.

"Your father is a highly esteemed law professor at a top-rated university, ladies. He's quite the catch in certain circles."

I think about speed dating Guy 3, the professor who reminded me too much of my dad. Now Mom is saying that's exactly who my dad is for "certain circles." I can't picture it. My dad has literally never dated in all these years. Sometimes I'm convinced he's still in love with my mom even though she's had several serious boyfriends over the years.

"Are you saying"—Zoey swallows, and her faces distorts in dread—"that someone caught him?"

Mom rolls her eyes. "Many times. Currently, it's a short brunette from the history department. I believe she teaches American History circa the late eighteenth century."

There's no need to clarify that one. Constitutional law is the one thing that gets Patrick Reid excited. And now he's apparently found a peer who can talk the intricacies. I glance at my sister, who looks like she's about to puke up dinner. It's clear she didn't know, which makes sense. Dating seems like something he would keep close to the vest. He's all Zoey has, and he knows it. He feels that responsibility and honors it every day.

"How do you know this?" Cecilia asks, her voice brisk. She was so quiet during all this that I almost forgot she was there.

Zoey's eyes widen and swivel back to my mom, who shrugs. Something passes between them again, and my stomach twists. I'm missing something important here.

"We had dinner recently, as we do from time to time."

"What?" Cecilia and I exclaim together. While our mother has most certainly moved on, I would never suspect that she still has any communication with our dad other than their public interactions.

Cecilia is a ball of fury across the table. This is not good. She fixes my mom with an incredulous look. "But you hate Dad."

"I do not hate your father. I never hated him." Mom takes a sip of wine. "Did I have to divorce him? Yes. Did it break my heart? Absolutely. But seriously, Cecilia, I forgave him years ago."

In the silence that follows, I can hear the echo of my mother's unsaid words—*as you should have.*

"Why?" Cecilia's hands are clenched so tightly her knuckles are white. I want to do something to quell her anger, but my head is still reeling from what my mom revealed.

Mom waves her hand noncommittally, as if she hasn't rocked our understanding of the last decades of our lives. "Anger isn't good for your health."

"Mom," I say before my sister jumps across the table and strangles her.

"For you kids, of course." Her eyes move past all three of us. Three of us. Not two. "Who do you think your father called about Zoey? Certainly not her mother. No offense, dear."

Zoey's laugh is bitter at the mention of her mother, but the look she gives my mom is easy and familiar and holds a history I know nothing about. She glances at me as if in apology before turning back to Mom. "I remember when I wanted a training bra. I thought his eyes were going to fall out of his head."

"Yes, and when you got your period," Mom adds. "Your first boy-girl party. When you met Andrew. It takes a village, and I was all your father had."

None of what's being said computes. My mom and Zoey shopping for training bras? Where was I? In college and getting back together with Julian, but still. How bad were things that my dad would ask his ex-wife to help his love child instead of me? And why didn't they tell us? All these years of tiptoeing around each other, and they were having dinners.

No, I can't get mad about this now. My dad is literally on his way, which Mom knows. Why she's doing this now, I don't know. Cecilia is rage incarnate, and if Patrick Reid walks through the door, she is going to lose it. How do I defuse this situation? I can't. I can't even keep my own frustrations down. Because everything about my life could've been easier.

"Why didn't we know this?" I mean to ask my mom, but my gaze slides to my younger sister, who won't look at me. Because she kept it secret too.

"You never asked," Mom says at the same time Zoey says, "I asked her not to."

"Really?" Cecilia pushes back from the table, her fork clattering against her plate. "We never asked?"

Mom fixes Cecilia with a glare only a mother can give. I haven't seen that face in ages. "What exactly would it have changed? Your anger is your anger. It has nothing to do with me."

"It has everything to do with you!"

Mom shakes her head. "Maybe it did at first, but no, Cecilia. It hasn't for a long time. I'm happy. I've been happy. You've seen me with your father and Zoey at things. Did I ever seem heartbroken?"

"Only all those weekends you spent in my apartment crying so Liz couldn't see."

Too much is happening and coming out at once. I don't know where to look and who to shut up. What weekends are Cecilia talking about? I have no memory of my mother being anything but stoic and stolid after the divorce. Of course I knew she was grieving and heartbroken, but she always put on a brave face. It was like one day all my dad's stuff moved to Ardena, and my weekends went from trying to escape the house to see my friends to alternating weekends with a toddler I barely knew. But through it all, my mom encouraged me to get to know Zoey, to visit my dad, to carve my own path when Cecilia walked away.

Cecilia and Mom continue to go back and forth until the doorbell rings. *Fuck.* I meet Zoey's eyes across the table. She's pale and worried, but she stands and goes to answer the door.

"Who's that?" Cecilia asks, her voice still tinged with anger. Her eyes follow Zoey to the door. There's no stopping this train.

Zoey lets him in, and they stand side by side, Zoey a ball of tension and our dad completely oblivious to what he's walked into. And it's now, in this moment, that I realize my mistake. We've never all been alone in a room together without other people. Maybe this would've worked in a public setting, but even an Evie buffer would not have been enough to wrangle this in. I've spent years making accommodations for Cecilia and, I thought, for our mom. But our parents are friends, and Zoey has been using Anna as a temporary mom when needed. It was all for nothing. All that trouble and stress and drama for nothing.

My dad smiles at me before his gaze settles on the daughter he hasn't seen in five years. "Hello, Cecilia."

Chapter 40
Zoey

There's no time to warn Dad about the shit show going on in Liz's apartment. He literally walks into arguments and then stunned silence, which sucks because I can tell he's nervous. I slip my hand into his and squeeze twice, our patented silent support communication. Cecilia's gaze turns toward us, and it's like spikes digging into me. Liz misjudged tonight's plan.

"What is he doing here?" Cecilia exclaims, glaring at Liz.

"Cecilia," Liz chastises. "Hi, Dad."

"Hi, Lizzie, Anna."

I hate this so much. How was I foolish enough to believe that this summer changed anything? It doesn't matter how much progress Liz and I made. This is our reality. It will always be us versus them. And I am the founding *them*. Dad doesn't deserve this. He destroyed his life to save mine. Why can't anyone see that? If he hadn't owned up to me, taken care of me, where would I have gone? My mom wasn't staying no matter what Dad said. I squeeze his hand again. Whatever happens next, we're in this together.

Liz walks over to us, her mouth set in a thin line. She takes the bag of pastries out of Dad's hand and gives him a kiss on the cheek. "Thanks for these, Dad. Go sit."

No sooner has he taken a seat than Cecilia stands and chases after Liz. My hands twitch in my lap, and my head throbs. What gives Cecilia the right to be such a total bitch all the time?

"Dad," I say in a sad attempt to break the tension and clue him in to what's been going down, "I hear you have a new girlfriend. One in a line of many I've never met."

Dad blushes brighter than the day I first asked to buy tampons. "I see Anna's been telling stories."

There's a teasing in his voice and in the look Anna gives back to him that I wish Liz could see. Cecilia's too angry to appreciate it, but it might give Liz some much-needed perspective. Patrick and Anna Reid may have been divorced for nearly two decades, but they are still connected in some cosmic way.

I knew this in the smallest of ways. The yearly card Anna sent for my birthday. The gift from her under the Christmas tree. The infrequent-yet-significant outings that I desperately needed a woman for but was too shy and ashamed to ask Becca's mom for help. Liz was in college and then graduate school, flitting in and out of Ardena, always with an air of drama around her. She tried—Liz always tried—but it never seemed to work out.

"Can I meet her?" I ask with a grin. "Before I go back to school?"

"Of course, dear." His face relaxes, and his smile, though tentative, is real. "Robin would like that, I think. She knows all about you—about all of you—but especially you."

The sound of pots clanging in the kitchen catches our attention. We can't see Cecilia, only Liz, her shoulders hunched as she organizes the pastries.

"How could you do this?" Cecilia shrieks as if the apartment isn't completely open concept and we can't hear everything she says.

"I mean," she continues, her voice getting quieter, "first you go to Dad—fucking Dad—when you leave Julian. And then you force Zoey on me this summer."

I straighten at my name. What is she talking about? We barely interacted all summer.

"I didn't—"

"Yes, you did. You literally gave me no choice."

Tears come without warning. They won't stop no matter how often I dab at my eyes or how hard I jam my fists into them. There's the story of my life in black and white. I knew it. I knew Cecilia wasn't warming up to me, but there was that moment in Wildwood and then on the phone... But I was wrong. So wrong.

"Zo, come on." Dad stands and extends his hand. "Let's go home."

My heart cracks at the words. Home. Dad has been home since I was two years old, but this summer I started to form another one. I don't want to leave it. Tears blind me as I take his hand. My breath hitches in my throat. I force myself to calm down and dab at my face again. The room comes back into focus, and Liz stands in front of us, tears glistening on her own cheeks. Cecilia stands at the door, her purse slung over her shoulder. She stares at Liz, her hand on the doorknob, waiting. Whose side will Liz take?

"Please don't go," Liz says, her eyes fastened on mine.

The front door slams, and Cecilia is gone. Liz stares at the door but doesn't move. I'm rooted in place, Dad's hand the only thing keeping me upright. Liz picked me.

Anna stands, her chair creaking as she pushes it back. She brushes her hand across mine as she passes and places a hand on Liz's shoulder. She looks between the two of us and finally gives a nod to Dad. "I'll talk to her. I'm sorry. We knew she wouldn't take it well, but this... I'm so sorry, girls."

And then she's gone too. My heart aches from Cecilia's words, but it's also full. I want to throw my arms around Liz and cry until I have no tears left.

"What now?" I ask, my voice scratchy.

"Now," Liz says with a weak smile, "we eat pastries."

Chapter 41
Cecilia

It takes ten minutes for the Uber to arrive. Liz never comes after me. My mom leaves a few minutes after me, and I think maybe I will get answers or an apology or something.

But she says, "You should know better," then walks to her car.

There is one flight from Philadelphia to Chicago tonight. I book it, not caring about my actual return flight that I will have to cancel. I'm in no mood to deal with customer service of any kind.

After I pick up my carry-on from the hotel—thankfully, I barely had time to unpack—the Uber driver drops me off at the airport with a smile I can't return. I tip extra for my mood. Security, boarding, even the flight, are a blur of rushing. I can't calm my mind or my body after takeoff. What the hell was my sister thinking? And my mother... I close my eyes and try to focus on the playlist running on my mindfulness app. But no, my heart still races in rage and confusion and too much hurt.

The sky is dark by the time I land and climb into yet another Uber. It's still warm despite the late hour, and I shuck off my plane cardigan as we pull into Evie's lot. This day needs to end. Now. But the time stays resolutely on this side of tomorrow as I stare at my phone screen and its lack of messages from anyone. Fuck this day. I avoid slamming the door, but barely, and stalk toward Evie's. Another excessive tip will be needed.

I yank open the door to Evie's building, shutting out summer. Where is the key? Evie uses her key often, but I've rarely had the opportunity. The action feels foreign, and my fingers shake as I move past the store cards. Finally, I push the door open. Two heads swivel around to meet me. Evie's dark curls and brown locks are pulled back in a braid. She's with Layla. Neither wears an expression of welcome, but Evie's annoyance quickly transitions into concern, while her best friend rolls their eyes, which is typical but completely infuriating after today. I focus on Evie. If I can get to my girlfriend, it'll be better.

"Cee?" she asks, her eyes wary. "What are you doing here?"

Irritation bubbles under my rib cage. Why give me a key if I can't stop by unannounced? I swallow back the retort because it'll help nothing. I rotate my shoulders and take a breath instead.

"Dinner was a disaster."

"Enough of a disaster that you flew back home?"

"Yes," I reply through gritted teeth. "You have no idea."

"I guess that's my cue." Layla stands then mouths something to Evie before fixing me with a glare that I wholeheartedly return.

We've never been on the best terms, but this open hostility is new. What exactly has my girlfriend been whispering in her best friend's ear? And more importantly, why? Haven't things been good lately?

Layla walks past, and the room turns icy. I consider an apology, but for what? Evie gave me a key. Evie didn't mention she had plans. She only held fast that it was not the best idea for her to come to New Jersey with me. I haven't done anything wrong here. If anything, I'm finally doing something right. I freeze as Layla slips into their shoes. Was my girlfriend in the know? Is that why she refused to come? No, that's not it. Evie is clearly confused and concerned and weirdly agitated by my sudden appearance.

As soon as Layla is gone, Evie motions for me to join her on the couch. Her eyes are narrowed and focused on me. Whatever she sees, she is not pleased. Her expression darkens, and she clasps her hands in front of her.

"What did you do?" she asks quietly after I sit down.

Wow. Maybe this is a bad idea.

"Why do you assume *I* did something?"

Evie's gaze bores into me. She's not going to let this pass. "If you didn't want to talk about it, why are you here?"

"Because you're my girlfriend? I'm sorry I ruined your girls' night. Jesus."

"This isn't about girls' night." She scoots farther down the couch and away from me. "Tonight was important to Liz, and the fact that you're not even in the same state as her doesn't bode well for the outcome."

"You're concerned about Liz?" I exclaim.

"No, I'm concerned about you, Cee." She leans forward, and her expression is sympathetic for the first time since I arrived. But it's fleeting. There's no chance I'm getting the girlfriend answer tonight. "What happened?"

"My mother was feeling chatty."

Evie rubs her forehead, a sign that she's beyond frustrated. "I'm trying here. I really am. But it's been a bad few days, so if you can tell me what's going on without putting it through the Cecilia filter, that would be great."

What. The. Fuck? I should leave. This isn't going to end well. Evie's not in the mood. I'm not in the mood. But if I leave now, I don't think I'll be coming back. And I can't risk that. Not now. I take her hands in mine and give her a once-over. She's frazzled and tired and weary. I've never seen Evie weary. Did something happen on her trip home? I hadn't even asked in the frenzy of my own trip, but maybe I should have.

"My mom and my dad are apparently friends. She's been helping him with Zoey all this time."

Evie sits back with a huff, her eyes fixed on the ceiling.

"And then my father showed up for dessert." Desperation and incredulity war in my voice. I still can't fathom how any of them thought ambushing me was a good idea.

"And you left?" Evie's face crumples, a knowing and sad expression coming over her. Because if I had only left, I would've gone back to the hotel. I wouldn't be here prowling around her living room like a caged animal.

"I mean, I talked to Liz first, but she made her preference clear."

"Did you stop to consider why Liz invited him?" Evie asks, her voice shaking. "Or why your mother did what she did? Or what a night like tonight might have meant to Zoey?"

Definitely not the girlfriend treatment tonight, but it's too late to stop now. "No, because none of them stopped to think about what having my father there would do to me."

"I don't believe that."

"Of course you don't," I spit out. "But I've happily kept my distance from the B-side of the Reid family for almost two decades, and Liz forced Zoey on me when I was there. But I will not let her—"

"Fix you?"

Ouch. Evie's not holding back tonight. "I'm not broken. People are estranged from their parents all the time. It's my right to be angry."

"Are you really still angry, Cee? Or are you annoyed that there's no longer a valid reason for you to be angry?"

I stand and pace in front of the couch. I don't need this tonight. Not on top of the family-sized betrayal I sat through earlier. "I'm angry about all of it."

"And Zoey?"

"What about Zoey?" I ask, choosing to ignore the fact that Evie switched to her psychologist voice.

"I thought perhaps you started to think of her as family."

My stomach turns over. Am I getting used to Zoey's presence in my life? Yes. But she is *not* my family. How can my own girlfriend even suggest such a thing? "She will never be my family."

"And you made that clear to her tonight?" Evie's tone is flat. Disappointment radiates off her. The force of it nearly knocks me off my feet, but I'm not the villain here.

"I'm going to go." I walk toward the door. "I came here for support from my girlfriend, not the third degree about why I don't want my father's illegitimate child as my sister."

"Leave your key."

I stop moving, stop breathing. This is what will break us? "What?"

"I thought we could do this, Cee, but I can't." Her voice cracks. "I need someone who gives back what I put in, and you are too stuck in your anger to really care about anyone else. I told my family about you last weekend. Even my grandma. Because the look on your face when I told you not to come—I never wanted to see it again." Tears stream down her cheeks, and she flicks them away angrily. "And you didn't even ask me about my weekend. Not once this entire week. And the saddest part is that I'm not even surprised."

"Evie." *Please don't do this.* "I can be better."

"What awful thing did you say to your family tonight?" It's barely a question. She knows me all too well. "You were perfectly happy with our separate lives until Liz left her husband and went to stay with your dad and Zoey." Her therapist voice is coming back, but the warble and emotions evident in each word betray her true feelings. "You felt betrayed, and you clung to the only thing you could. And I let you because I wanted you to love me like I love you. But I can't do this anymore." She holds out her hand. "Your key."

I yank the keys from my purse and detach the freshly minted piece of metal from the ring. Tears build behind my eyes, but I will not cry now.

Evie reaches past me and pulls a single key, already off the ring, from the bowl by the front door. She places it gently into my hand and then turns and walks away.

Chapter 42

Zoey

"Hey." Max sits down next to me in the end zone. He moves closer until we're touching and wraps my hand in his. "You want to talk about it?"

I lean my head on his shoulder. "Not really."

It's only been a week since the kiss that rocked my world, but so much changed over the weekend. Walking onto the track this morning, I felt like a different person from the one who asked Max to kiss her. The flop my stomach does upon seeing him is no different, nor is my desire to plant a kiss on him at all hours of the day. But I can't do that at work. Dating's not forbidden—with a staff of mostly teens, that's impossible—but the Ardena Heat gossip mill is the same one that swirls around the high school. The last thing I need is people giving their opinion on a relationship that has barely started.

This moment is the closest we've been all day despite spending hours standing side by side. And it feels good in a way that I haven't felt in a long while. Being able to go from coworkers to friends to this over the course of the summer, being able to put my head on his shoulder and know it means nothing and everything, it all feels right. Andrew and I were never friends. We went from classmates to true loves in the length of a yard line. But Max and I are friends and now more.

He kisses the top of my head and wraps his arm around me, taking on some of the weight. "Anything I can do?"

"This," I say, closing my eyes. My stomach grumbles loud enough for us both to hear. "And maybe some french fries."

"That, I can do."

A while later, I stare up at the sign above the restaurant door—Mack's. It's a bar and grill on the outskirts of town. It's popular, but not overly so and not on a Monday night. Younger teachers from Ardena are known to frequent it for happy hour, and the big Thanksgiving Eve gathering of Ardena alum is always unofficially here. It's the go-to spot for wings at two in the morning. And when it comes to Mack's, you always want wings at two in the morning.

The last time I was here was with Andrew for that Thanksgiving Eve party. We didn't stay long, but he was adamant we make an appearance. Things like that matter to Andrew. Once they mattered to me too.

"Mack's?" I ask incredulously.

"What?" Max grins and pulls open the door. "They have the best fries in three towns."

Untrue. But we can debate the qualities of the perfect french fry another time. Right now, I want to sit on the same side of the booth, hold hands, and steal imperfect fries off his plate with no commentary from anyone else.

"Can we have a booth?" I ask the hostess before she can lead us to a table.

She nods and changes course. Mack's is small. There's the bar room and then one dining room with about ten tables in the middle while booths line the walls. It's always a notch above dark inside, and you can't visit without hearing Bon Jovi or the Boss at least once.

I slide in next to Max once the waitress is gone. If he's surprised by my closeness, he doesn't let on, only stretches his arm out behind me. I lean into him and soak in this moment, glad to have someone to share it with.

"Do you want anything besides fries?" he asks, holding up the menu.

"Wings, obviously." I feel him smile and chuckle. "Boneless, please. And an iced—"

"Tea, unsweetened, no lemon," he finishes. "I know."

Of course he knows. I sneak a glance at him while he peruses the menu. My body hums whenever he's near. It's unexpected. But he's undeniable. Honest. Real. He isn't playing a game.

I kiss him, quick and soft. My lips tingle, and even my toes feel the impact of that smallest of kisses. "Thank you."

"For what?"

"For knowing my drink order."

It's the smallest of things. But he remembered it, and that means something. Andrew still doesn't know how I take my coffee, and my dad is hopeless when it comes to these things.

The waitress comes to take our order, and once she's dropped off our drinks, Max shifts to face me. "When are you meeting your dad's girlfriend?"

I explained the whole ordeal that is my family, starting with pregnant Liz and ending with tears and pastries, over the course of our day. Yesterday, I hosted a group chat with Becca and Haley, unwilling to have to share the story more than once, but other than that, I haven't worked through it. My dad made sure I was okay, but it's not the type of thing we talk about. In the retelling today, though, I discovered bright spots. Liz is having a baby. My dad is in love. I don't have to lie about my relationship with Anna any longer. Liz picked me.

"Next week. I'm spending this whole week at Liz's, if I can. Then I'll be home for dinner with Dad's girlfriend and getting repacked, hanging out with Becca, saying goodbye... and then once this second session is over, I'll hit the road."

"What about me?" he asks, nudging me playfully.

I glance up at him innocently. "What about you?"

"Will we be hanging out before you go back to PA?" he asks, his fingers running circles on my shoulder.

"No." I laugh as his eyebrows rise in mock offense. "We'll be *making* out."

He shifts next to me, his offense shifting into intrigue. "That sounds—"

"Illegal?"

I know who it is the second his voice sounds in the small space. My body goes frigid, and next to me Max is tense.

"Singer," Max says sharply.

"Well, at least highly frowned upon," Andrew continues, his eyes searing holes into me.

I don't flinch or move from my position under Max's arm or look away. Andrew doesn't get to rattle me ever again. "Do you want something?"

"Just saying hi." He motions to someone we can't see, and a moment later Claire appears at his side. Her expression is one of confusion, but it quickly turns stony and even a little snide when she spots me. But I know that face. It's the one she puts on when she's trying to intimidate someone, when she's pretending to be a badass.

Andrew slides an arm around her waist. "We were catching a bite before we head down to the beach house for the week."

"Just the two of us," Claire adds, as if that isn't obvious.

I swallow a retort about Claire loving leftovers. It's not worth it. Honestly, I don't even understand why Claire is trying so hard. In her telling of the story, she won. Andrew realized he wanted her and not me. Losing our friendship paid off. She isn't the villain of her own story. But Claire can't seem to grasp that.

"Well, have fun," Max says as the waitress steps around them to deliver our food.

Max keeps a casual expression the whole time, but as soon as the waitress turns away, his face darkens. I follow his gaze to the front of the restaurant, where Joe and two other teachers from the high school are chatting with the hostess.

Andrew, as observant as ever, smirks at the change in his former coach's expression and glances behind him. "Uh-oh. I wonder what they'll have to say, *Coach Evans.*"

Claire looks from me to the teachers and back again. She brings her arm up and links it through Andrew's. "Come on, babe. If we don't leave now, we'll get stuck in rush hour traffic."

Did Claire give us an out? Or does she hate that Andrew still cares enough to screw with me? Both?

Andrew kisses her temple. My stomach flips. How many times had he done that to me? It's his go-to sign of affection. One that I loved because of its simplicity. And he's doing it to Claire.

"You're right, love." He raps his knuckles on the table. "Good luck, you two."

Max turns to me once they're gone, his expression unreadable. "You okay, Zee?"

"Yeah." And I think it's true. I tuck my hair back behind my ears. "I'm fine. I mean, they're ridiculous, but it's fine. Let them fuck until the cows come home."

"You're upset if you're talking in bad clichés."

He shouldn't know that about me yet, but he does. "I'm..." My voice cracks. *Fuck Andrew Singer.*

"What is it?"

"I was going to say I'm surprised." I pick up a fry and point it at him. "But I'm not, which is worse somehow, you know?"

"Hey, guys," Joe says. We can't catch a break today. I inch away from Max and give my boyfriend's best friend a wan smile—at least I think Max is my boyfriend. Joe's expression at least is pleasant, nothing like the evil eye I got at the party.

"Hey, man," Max says, taking his hand across the table. "You guys strategizing for orientation?"

"You know it." Joe fixes me with a smile. "Nice to see you again, Zoey."

"You, too, Joe," I say, his first name still awkward from my mouth.

Behind him, the two other teachers, who I now recognize, are getting settled. Max and Joe talk, but I'm focused on the teachers. They are dating. No, wait, engaged. It was a rumor my senior year, but no one ever confirmed it. But it's clear now. They both look up then. Ms. James smiles and waves. Mr. Matthews, who was my class advisor for two years, eyes me and Max. It's clear he's noting that we're sitting on the same side of the table and eating off the same plate, but he only nods a greeting before turning his attention to his menu. Maybe Max and I won't be an issue. Liz doesn't care. Neither do Haley or Becca. And Max wouldn't risk his job to make out with me. That would be silly. With his looks, he can have whomever he wants.

"Well, enjoy your dinner," Joe says before heading back to his table.

Max pulls me close again. "Where'd you go?"

"Oh, it's... Joe didn't seem very happy to see me at the party. Particularly when he found me in your bedroom. And the other teachers..."

"Ah." Max links our fingers. "Well, first, there's no rule that says I can't date you as you are a graduate for more than a year and were never under my purview. I checked. Twice. We're not doing anything wrong—legally, morally, or otherwise. I'm only five years older than you, Zee. If you shift our meeting a few years, no one would bat an eye." He sighs and runs a hand through his hair. "Second, Joe's reaction the other night had nothing to do with you and everything to do with my ex-girlfriend."

"What do you mean?"

"Joe's boyfriend is Tess's best friend."

I didn't know Max's ex's name before this moment, and now it's forever seared into my memory.

"But *she* dumped you."

To his credit, he doesn't react to my crass comment. "Yes, but then she tried to take it back, and I turned her down."

"Because of... me?" It feels indulgent asking such a question, but it would certainly explain Joe's reaction. While it couldn't have been fun to run into a former student at a party, it also didn't warrant the chastisement I felt that night, especially since he knows Max and I work together.

"Because she and I don't make sense anymore. Because her deciding to move a thousand miles away when she knew I couldn't go with her was uncool. And yes"—he leans close enough that his breath stirs my hair, and I ache to kiss him—"because of you."

Wow. Way to lay it out there. My cheeks heat up as does the rest of my body. I want to look away, but no matter where my gaze goes, it lands back on Max—his hand in mine, his arm around my shoulder, his lips close to mine.

I take a sip of my iced tea. It does nothing to curb the fire working its way through me. I wish we ordered in. I wish we were sitting on Max's couch, hidden from the public eye. All I want is to climb onto his lap and kiss him for days. There's no Andrew or Claire or Cecilia. No nosy coworkers or end-of-summer deadlines. On that couch, in that moment, we can be Max and Zee.

"Where's your head?" Max asks after I've guzzled half my drink.

The Zoey I've always been would've shrugged and moved on. But with Max I get to be Zee, and maybe, for Zee, the rules are different. Zee asks to be kissed. Maybe I can ask for this too.

"Back at your apartment," I say, fluttering my eyelashes at him.

"Oh?" His eyes widen, and I watch as he works through my statement. "And what are we doing?"

"Making out on the couch."

His eyes darken, excitement and something like nerves playing across his features. It's cute, really. For some reason my candidness has thrown him off. Is it a good thing or a bad thing that suggesting a make-out session sends him into a tizzy?

He waves down the waitress when she's done dropping drinks off at Joe's table. "Can we get this to go, actually? And the check, please?"

Chapter 43

Liz

"Sorry, sorry! I'm here." Zoey skids into the kitchen, still in her work uniform of mesh shorts and an Ardena Heat T-shirt, a Bellewood cinch bag across her back and her hair in a messy ponytail. Quintessential Zoey.

"Hi," I say, not looking up from the sandwich I'm making. If I stay focused on it, maybe my sister won't notice my hands are shaking. I hand her the sandwich and start on a second one. "You really didn't need to take the afternoon off to come with me."

"It's fine," Zoey says, her eyes taking in the sandwich as if she's never seen food before. "We lost track of time."

"Ew."

"Because of a runner, weirdo."

It's probably the truth, but her mischievous smile speaks volumes. And I love it. This is the Zoey I've always known—vibrant and exuberant, silly and happy. There's been little trace of her this summer, the exception being when Haley was here. But her grief seems to be diminishing lately. My sister is evolving into a strong young woman right in front of my eyes. She's always been resilient; she had no choice. But now she is rising from the ashes of first love. For the first time this summer, I can see the other side and who Zoey might become. It's beautiful to watch.

"What?" Zoey asks around a bite of sandwich.

"Nothing."

217

"Not nothing. You were looking at me all doe-eyed." She pauses and adds a few more pieces of ham to her sandwich. "Oh, *hormones*. You were all mothering out on me, weren't you?"

"Maybe." I pour some water into a cup. "I like seeing you happy."

"Famished and sweaty is more accurate, but I guess I'll take it." She slides, literally on her socks, out of the kitchen. "Let me change, and then we can go."

I glance at my watch. "We have to leave in ten minutes."

Almost ninety minutes later, we sit in an exam room. I decided to stick with my regular gynecologist, which meant the ride was long, but the comfort of a familiar face is worth it. Zoey sits in one of the chairs lining the walls. When I asked her to come, I didn't think through the whole process or the part where I have to sit here with no pants on. But she's rallying, chattering on about one thing or the next. I'm honestly not even sure what she's talking about. It might be mock trial or something to do with her sorority. Either way, there are a lot of acronyms to follow.

A soft knock sounds on the door, and then my gynecologist steps in wearing a smile. One thing I've always liked about her is that she seems to remember me even though we only see each other once a year. Usually that means she asks after Julian, but today, she simply nods at my sister and takes a seat.

"Hi, Liz," Dr. Manning says with a warm smile. "Your test came back positive, so let's get in there and take a look."

I nod, but I know that doesn't necessarily mean anything. "Okay."

"Do you want your..."

"Sister," I finish. "And yes, she can stay."

"All right. You can stand here then." She positions Zoey behind me near my head. Right where Julian stood last time I was in this situation.

Zoey puts a hand on my shoulder and squeezes. "You got this, Mama."

"How have you been feeling?" Dr. Manning asks as she readies the wand.

I stare at the ceiling. I hate this part, and I can't bear to wait for the screen to come to life and possibly dash my dreams. "I haven't been feeling great, but I'm taking that as a good sign."

"Yes, an unpleasant one but definitely good."

Memories of the last time I was here waiting to see my baby flash by—the quiet of the monitor, the baby that wasn't. It's too much. I squeeze my eyes shut and try to ignore the cold discomfort. Zoey's hand tightens on my shoulder.

"You can look now."

And I do. On the screen is the tiniest of miracles. Emotions overcome me, and the tears are instantaneous. Warmth surges through me. My baby. Love fills me. I blink back tears and stare at the screen, a smile forming. My perfect little blob with two little feet.

The doctor turns a few knobs, and the sound of a rapid heartbeat fills the room. My new favorite sound. Nothing can ever top that perfect pitter-patter.

"And there we are." Dr. Manning smiles, her eyes focused on the screen.

I reach for Zoey's hand. A weight lifts from my heart, and a completely different one takes its place. One I know will never leave me from now until forever. The weight of motherhood.

"I'm going to do some measurements to get your due date, but the baby looks to be about nine weeks," Dr. Manning says. "And if you want, Liz, you can do your blood work today for prenatal testing. It'll tell you the gender, if you don't want to wait."

I nod, all words escaping me. I'm having a baby. I'm going to be a mother. Finally. Will the baby look like me? Will he or she have Julian's eyes? His smile? Fresh tears fall. *Julian.* I've wanted this for so long, wanted it with him. And we're further apart than we've ever been.

"According to The Bump, the baby is the size of a cherry," Zoey says.

A cherry. That's better than a blob. I take the strip of blurry photos from the doctor. I memorize the information on it. Nine weeks and two days. I run my finger across the cherry. "Hi, peanut."

My first thought after leaving the doctor's office is to drive across town to see Julian. It's Thursday, and he generally works from home on Thursdays. Separated or not, this is his baby. And I want to tell him in person. I need to see his reaction. His real first reaction. But now that I'm here, it seems like a bad idea. Our house looks the same from the outside. The lawn is carefully maintained by people we pay. So even with one of the house's key occupants gone, it looks no worse for wear.

This isn't the neutral ground I thought it would be. And a lifetime of Julian bubbles closer to the surface the longer I sit in the driveway. Some of the memories are real, and some are from his movies. How did our lives get so entangled with fiction?

"Do you want me to come in?" Zoey asks, her voice tight. She's been fidgeting in her seat ever since I said I wanted to stop here. Her trepidation is palpable, even though she's not the one with news to share. But I guess I wouldn't want to witness this encounter either. Whatever happens, she'll know something about us for the rest of time.

"You can stay in the car," I say, fishing my keys out of my purse. "It doesn't look like he's home anyway."

There's always the possibility that Julian pulled his car into the garage, but the chances are slim. He hates backing out and complains about it all the time. Plus, this is prep season for him at work. Without me enticing him to stay home, there's a good chance he went into the office.

The keys are heavy in my hand. I know the exact feel of my house key, where it sits on the ring relative to the cards and fobs and everything else. I find it without having to look. My feet move automatically around the crack in our walkway without having to see it. This is home, and I've never felt more like an intruder.

Inside, the house is quiet. And not the quiet of someone at work but the quiet of someone missing. The air is stale and warm. Too warm. Julian keeps the house frigid during the summer. Half the time, I walk around in a sweater. I eye the thermostat. It's set to away. Worry needles its way into me, followed by disappointment. *Where is he?* Is he with *her?* Did he get tired of waiting for his wayward wife and seek comfort elsewhere? It is, I suppose, his right. I slept with Spencer, maybe even started to fall for him a little bit. But no. Ab-so-fucking-lutely not. Anger blinds me. There's no living room, no house, only white-hot fury. He doesn't get to sleep with Sheila.

I count to ten and open my eyes. The world's a little less red. He could be in Cape May. Or at Jane's. Or traveling for work. The anger resurfaces at the last possibility. Work means Sheila, and Sheila means everything is a lie. *Shit.*

I swipe at my eyes. Sheila or not, betrayal or not, he still needs to know. This is his child, and he deserves to know that. I sit down on the couch. My head throbs. This was an awful idea.

I pull out my phone and dial his number. The picture of him I have saved is familiar and foreign. It's been a weirdly long time since I've seen a photo of my husband. I've avoided him on Facebook, though now I'm wondering if he has a second account. We're still married on social media, irrevocably tied to each other. None of my life this summer has gone online except for Zoey. Spencer is saved only on my phone and in my memory.

The first tear hits my cheek. And it's for Spencer, of all things. Julian's voicemail picks up.

"Hi, Jules. It's me... Liz." *God, this is awkward.* I take a breath that will be audible on the recording. My mind filters through the million options of what to say. They all suck. "I need to talk to you about something. Can you please call me back when you have a chance?"

My hands tremble against the phone, and I finally let the tears fall. If he calls back or texts right away, that means something. But what if he doesn't? What if he delays or doesn't call back at all? I finger the spot where my wedding ring used to be. He'll call. He always calls. I cradle my head in my hands. *But what if this time he doesn't?*

Chapter 44

Liz

I do another lap of the store. My feet tread the same spots, and I pass the same shelves, not stopping to peruse. I've been here for a half hour already. First, I ordered a coffee—half-decaf—and then a cookie. My stack of books is four high, including *What to Expect When You're Expecting*. But that was all in the first fifteen minutes. The cashier eyes me as I stop near the doors again. I survey the parking lot but don't expect to see anything. He would come through the mall anyway. Not that Spencer is coming. Apparently.

There are a few options left to me—save face and let my ghosting of him stand without explanation, show up at his place of employment across the street and demand he speak with me, or text him one last time before reverting back to option one. I pull out my phone. *If you don't come to me, I'm coming to you,* I type before I can overthink it. Not exactly mature, but desperate times.

Fine. His text comes through almost immediately. *Give me five.*

The victory is hollow, but at least it's a victory. I plop my stack of books down in front of the cashier, my membership card already sitting on top. Five minutes barely gives me time to find a seat in the café, and I can't exactly be toting a pregnancy book around when he arrives.

Ten minutes later, Spencer sits down across from me, looking none too pleased. He crosses his arms, and he gazes at the promotional rack behind me with his jaw set. He doesn't want to be here. I get it. Ten days of silence will do that. Especially if you've just had sex for the first time.

"Thanks for coming." *Dammit.* I swore not to say something so inane, and yet it's the first thing to tumble out of my mouth.

"You didn't give me much of a choice."

"You didn't answer any of my texts or calls."

His eyes narrow, and a severe line I've never seen on him before forms across his forehead. "Doesn't feel great, does it?"

I totally deserve that. After finding out I was pregnant and the debacle at my apartment, I disappeared for ten days.

His gaze shifts to mine. "I have Ryan this week, Liz. And having to listen to you tell me how having sex with me convinced you to go back to your husband is not something I want to deal with when I'm supposed to be spending time with my son. He deserves better than that."

I blink, pushing away the flutters at what a good father he is. Is that what he thinks? How could he think that after how well we fit and how— I will not think about that night right now. "That's not what happened."

"What?"

"Sleeping with you." I clear my throat and lower my voice. We don't need an audience. "If anything, it had the opposite effect."

"Then what, Liz? You canceled dinner and then disappeared. If it's something with Zoey, I can help. I can be intimidating too."

"It's nothing with Zoey." I clasp my hands and put them on the table in front of me. "I'm ten weeks pregnant."

"That's not possi—" He cuts off as the realization hits him. "It's *his* baby."

"Yes."

He sits back in his chair, and his arms fall from their perch across his chest. The hardness in his expression softens into something else entirely. "Shit."

"Yeah." I hiccup through a laugh. "That was my first reaction."

"What was your second?" A hint of his usual demeanor is in the words, and the vise gripping my chest relaxes.

I wait until he meets my gaze to speak. "Abject fear. And then joy."

He smiles for a moment before his brow furrows again. "Are you going back to him? Co-parenting? What?"

"I don't know. I haven't told him yet." I hold up a hand when his expression turns judgmental. "He's out of town and not returning my calls." What I don't add is that it's been five days since my trip to the house and my voicemail. Julian's lack of response is jarring. "This isn't something to leave on a voicemail or send in a text."

"Fair enough."

"But I couldn't not tell *you* another minute." Tears want to come, but I will them back. "I hated not picking up your calls or answering your texts. But I couldn't lie to you." He doesn't say anything. Maybe I am too late. "Maybe it would've been easier to let you believe I ghosted you."

"That is never easier."

"I know this is too much," I blather on. "Still technically married is one thing, but pregnant with said husband's baby is completely different. I don't expect—"

"I think," he says, cutting me off, his tone edged, "I get to decide what is too much for me."

I nod. "You're right. I'm sorry."

I'm not sure what his words mean, but they don't fall like I expect them to. Spencer being in was not part of the equation. Yes, sure, if it was his baby, but it's not. And this is drama and baggage and whispers and side-eyes. It's not scandalous like my father's affair and Zoey's existence, but it's still fodder. I'm tired of being fodder. I don't even know if Julian is in or out. If my marriage is paused or over. There are too many questions and no answers. Except one. This baby is mine.

"I think," I say, my words careful, "that right now, I need to take a step back. I can't date you like there aren't a million decisions I have to make. I can't go back to Julian as if this summer didn't happen either, because it did. *You* did. You changed everything, Spencer. But this baby has to be my priority. Every decision I make now is for the both of us."

"You know I understand." He covers my hand with his own, the first time he's touched me since this conversation began. And it's still there. All of it—the spark, the wonder, the desire. But it can't be.

"I'm still sorry," I say, squeezing his hand.

"Me too." He stands and kisses the top of my head. His hand lingers on my shoulder. "Take care of yourself, Liz."

Chapter 45
Zoey

"Can you hand me that?" I point toward my desk without turning around. I'm shoulder deep in my closet, stacking old shoes and clothes. I know I did this last summer. How have I amassed this much stuff when I only live here for a few months of the year? Behind me there's a fumbling and then a grunt.

"What, exactly?"

I poke my head out of the closet and grin at Max. He's being a good sport. I point at the purple Greek letters sitting atop a pile of magazines. They're old editions of *Talented* and a *Deafening Silence* that feature articles, many of which were written by another Ardena alum, about the now-defunct Wilderness Weekend. Who knew I was such a pack rat? "The paperweight, please."

"You need this in your dorm room?" he asks, holding it up.

"Haley gave it to me when I crossed."

He drops it into the box at my feet with a shrug and sits back on my bed, picking up one of the old magazines. "I used to love this band."

"Used to?"

He smiles. "Yeah, back in my emo days."

There is no way in hell that Max was ever emo.

"Right." I brush the dust off my pants. "Well, I guess I got rid of those shoes."

We stopped by my house so I could change into my bathing suit before we hit the beach but quickly got distracted by each other. Once we put a pause on *that*—because sex in my half-packed room with no idea when my dad is coming home is not an option—I tried to find a pair of sandals in my closet. But no luck. And now, I'm not even sure we have time for the beach.

"Do you want to do something tonight?" I look up from my phone, where a text from Becca waits. Starting a new relationship a few weeks before leaving for college sucks. I'm constantly leaving someone in the lurch. Becca's heading back to Florida soon, and though we have plenty of time scheduled before then and she's always booked with her own boyfriend, I feel bad. It's not like I can bring Max to Lola's, which means until I leave, I have two separate social lives.

Max lifts his eyes from the magazine and focuses on a photo of us that I printed and stuck on my closet door with all the other photos of my friends and family this summer. "I have to go to this happy hour thing for the freshman faculty. You can come if you want?"

He tries. He really does, but the invite is forced and awkward. "Come to a bar where I can't drink and hang out with my old teachers?"

"Basically."

I walk over and kiss him. The urge to return to our earlier activities trills through me. "I think I'll pass. Even Lola's sounds better than that." I pause and meet his gaze. "Unless you really want me to come."

"It's okay. I barely want to go." He laughs. "Do you want to come over after?"

I freeze halfway to standing. The statement isn't anything out of the ordinary. But it's the way he said it, and it hangs between us as more than a simple invitation. We haven't had the sex talk, but we also haven't gone very far either. Today being the exception, and even then, we were still mostly clothed. But still this sounds like *the* invite.

"Like to stay the night?" I ask, hating the squeak in my voice and the bout of terror that straightens my spine.

The mattress screeches as he stands, and then his arms are around me from behind. His heartbeat is steady while mine pounds.

"To finish watching season three and spend some extra time together before you go back to school." He turns me in his arms and kisses me lightly at first and then deeply. His lips part mine, and I lean into him, bringing my arms around his neck. I don't want the moment to end, but it does. His breathing is husky, but his eyes steady. "You are, of course, welcome to stay the night. If you're ready."

That's the question. If it were a matter of my body, then hell, yes. Every time he touches me, my body lights up. Sometimes I look down and expect my skin to be glowing. But it's not only about the physical. I've only ever slept with one person. And somehow making the choice a second time seems harder and much more complicated.

"If," he adds quietly, "that's something you want with me."

What does that mean? My pulse quickens for an entirely different reason. "Why wouldn't I want that *with you?*"

"You're leaving in less than two weeks, and Bellewood isn't exactly close. I—"

"And our relationship will be ending?" Anger seeps into every word. Of all the things I considered about my final weeks in Ardena, ending things with Max wasn't one of them. Never. We are just starting. "If that's the case, then yeah, why not? Let's end our summer fling with a bang. Literally."

He holds his hands up in supplication. "You're not a summer fling. Or rather, I don't want you to be one, Zee. But I also remember you saying you could never do long distance, and having sex will only complicate things."

I did say that, sort of. It feels like a lifetime ago. "I said I couldn't do long distance with *Andrew*, which was naive and needy and co-dependent. I'm not that person anymore."

There's a steadiness to the statement, and confidence thrums through me. This summer changed me in so many ways.

He reaches for me, ringing his hands around my waist. "No, you're not."

"I don't want you to be a summer fling either," I say and melt into his embrace.

"Good." He lifts my chin, and the tension in the air is thick and electric. If we kiss now, there might be no going back. There definitely won't be a happy hour.

"I do think," I say, resting my head against his chest and listening to the steady beat of his heart, "that I'd like to be in love before I—before we—do that."

His arms tighten around me. "Then come over tonight, finish this ridiculous show you got me hooked on, tease me to death with that kiss of yours, and then go home. Or bring your pajamas, and we'll sleep. We have plenty of time to get to everything else."

"You're sure?"

"I'm more than sure, Zee. There's no rush."

I meet his gaze, hoping that everything I feel in this moment is written across my face. The face he's become so good at reading. I hope he sees the gratitude and trust, the almost love. Because it's there but not quite, and I'm thankful that he doesn't try to rush it. "Then I guess I'll see you tonight."

The party is a mistake. I knew it from the moment Becca suggested we go but could hardly say no to my best friend's pout, considering it's at her boyfriend's house. But after the disaster that was Wildwood and the run-in at Mack's, I've successfully avoided my two nemeses. And I feel it in my bones that tonight won't end well. Something about being back home makes the triangle worse. It's not the scene of the crime, but it's the backstory, the history I can't escape. At Bellewood, at least there's a chance to make new memories and erase that one moment. But here, I feel defined by it. When you love as hard as Andrew and I did, people notice. And when it burns down, they shake their heads and bite their lips. *They should've known better. High-school-to-college relationships never last. What a mistake to trust Claire with her boyfriend.* I heard it all this summer in whispers and shouts. But somehow I rose above. I moved past Andrew and Claire and who I used to be.

Still, I don't want to be at this party. But I'll do it for my best friend. Becca didn't come home a blubbering mess. She returned to Ardena on the arm of one of its most popular athletes. She's reveling in her change, and there's no fault in that. If I came home hardened instead of broken, maybe I could've done the same thing. But I didn't, and it's time to face the firing squad one last time.

"Thank you for doing this," Becca says, wrapping her hand around mine. "It's the easiest way to say goodbye to everyone, and this way, Ben and I can spend our last days together instead of hanging out with the guys."

I refrain from asking if there's actual best friend time mixed into these last Ben-filled days. There will be. It might be an up-all-night slumber party before we get into our respective cars to drive back to school, but it'll happen.

"No problem." I glance around at the people crammed into the backyard.

Beer pong and flip cup tables are set up on one side, a makeshift dance floor on the other. In between, everyone else loiters, drinks in hand. It's a smaller party than most I attended this summer, but Ben has a smaller house. Maybe the selective invite list will make this party bearable. I doubt Andrew would dare come to Ben's, knowing he's

Becca's boyfriend. I spot my former teammates huddled together by the back door. Claire's among them. I never went out of my way to alienate my teammates. There simply wasn't time between Max and Liz and Becca and Haley. But somewhere in the last few weeks, I noticed them texting less and the invitations dropping off. Apparently, my silence meant they could take Claire back into their fold, which is totally fine.

"I'm going to find Ben and get drinks," Becca says. "Do you want to come?"

I'm about to say yes when Claire locks eyes with me. My former best friend nods to the side of the house, where it's quieter. This is such a bad idea. Everything that needed to be said between us has been said. There's no going back. There's hardly forgiveness, not that Claire ever asked for forgiveness.

"No." I give Claire a nod of her own. If Becca notices, she doesn't comment. "I'll hang here. Meet you at the flip cup table?"

"Ugh, you know I suck at that game."

"Exactly."

"What if tonight we dance?"

I shrug. "Sure, but no twerking."

Becca crosses her heart and dissolves into giggles. "Do we even know how to twerk?"

"Probably not."

"All right. See you in ten on the dance floor!"

I watch her disappear into the crowd before I turn and walk in the direction Claire went. A few steps off the main yard, she leans against the side of the house. A floodlight illuminates a small firewood nook.

"What do you want?" I cross my arms impatiently.

"Is this how it's always going to be?" Claire asks, her voice surprisingly contrite.

"What do you want?" I repeat, more harshly than intended.

"I want my friend back."

This can't be reality. Claire can't really think we can go back. This isn't some teen soap where the main female characters have to stay friends for ratings so they somehow forgive each other for constant betrayals.

"We're never going to be friends again, Claire. You slept with my boyfriend. More than once. You didn't even apologize for it, and now you're dating him."

Something flickers behind her eyes, but she only shakes her head. "I *am* sorry I hurt you."

"But not that you slept with him? Or destroyed our friendship?"

"Andrew came on to me."

"Yeah," I say forcing the memories from Wildwood away. "But you let him instead of pushing him away and telling me my boyfriend tried to sleep with you. You slept with him. Repeatedly. You're sleeping with him still."

"You forgave him."

"You're an idiot if you think me sleeping with Andrew means I forgive him." How can she believe that? I don't even know where to begin to forgive either of them. I barely accepted, and I'll never forget. "But if I was with him, he wasn't with you. Those were the rules, plain and simple."

I fix Claire with such a look that she's pinned to the wall. I dare her to refute the statement. To say that Andrew was screwing her all summer. It wouldn't be a shock. Why would he keep his word? But she doesn't.

Instead, she stares back at me with all the sadness of the last few months in her expression. She's not hiding anymore. "You hate me that much that you would keep him from me? I loved him."

"No," I hiss. "*I* loved him. You were his way to get out of a relationship, and now you're his way to try to piss me off. But guess what? I'm not pissed off. I'm happy."

"Then I'm glad."

I shake my head, done with this conversation and this summer and this triangle. "If you want him, take him, Claire. I don't care at this point."

I turn on my heels and start to walk away, but Claire's broken voice stops me in my tracks. "Will you ever forgive me?"

My heart races, and I turn back to her, arms crossed. "Yes, I'm sure one day I'll forgive you. But"—I pause and meet her gaze—"we are never going to be friends again. Never."

With that, I walk back to the party, praying I don't look as frazzled as I feel. I don't want to talk about this or remember it or anything. But one thing keeps playing over in my mind. Claire said she *loved* Andrew, past tense. Are they not together? Was she trying to say she fell in love with Andrew during the affair? Questions for another night. Or maybe never. The answers don't matter. Whether she loved Andrew or not, Claire betrayed me. Our friendship is unfixable.

My phone buzzes, and I pull it out of my back pocket to see a text from Max. My heart skitters and then calms. Max. One of the bright spots from this summer. *Miss you, Zee. Meet you in an hour on my living room couch? (Think all the dirty thoughts you want.)*

I laugh. It's the cleanest dirty text ever. I breathe in the summer air, scented with beer and sweat and cigarettes. None of this high school drama matters. I've moved on. I'm past it. I survived.

Becca skips, literally, up to me and hooks her arm through mine. "Where'd you go?"

"Doesn't matter," I say. "You ready to dance?"

Becca grins and shoves a cup into my hand. "Hell yeah, I am!"

My bubbly and happy and forever friend. God, I love her. I take in the night, the crowd, and my life as I knew it. There's no use looking back. Not when everything ahead of me looks so promising.

I tug Becca onto the dance floor. "Then let's dance."

Chapter 46

Liz

I stare at the folded sheet of paper in my hand. If I unfold it, I'll get the tiniest of glimpses into my future. Girl or boy. Son or daughter. My stomach flutters at even the idea of this knowledge. Maybe Peanut wants me to know. Maybe I shouldn't have had that extra slice of pizza at lunch. Or maybe I'm terrified. Knowing the sex of the baby will make our connection stronger. I can plan and imagine and name in real time. But if things go wrong... Things won't go wrong.

I adjust the vents in the car and let the cold air calm me. After picking up the innocuous piece of paper, I wasn't able to leave the parking lot. They offered to tell me over the phone, but I wanted the control to look or not. Now I'm rethinking that choice. My fingers tremble as I unfold the sheet with closed eyes. I smooth it against the steering wheel and take a few deep breaths, willing myself to look, to take this leap. Tears spring to my eyes at the sight before me.

Balloons.

Bear.

Pink.

Girl.

Daughter.

I'm going to have a daughter. Happiness floods my body. It radiates from my center, through my fingers and toes to my ears and my eyes and back inside again. My mind is fuzzy from the joy. I'm going to be a girl mom. With bows and tutus and ruffle butts. Julian will be excited. Any time we talked about kids, he always imagined a girl with my waves and his blue eyes. Creative and rambunctious, girly and athletic, a princess and a pirate. She could be anything and everything she wants to be.

I reach for my phone and dial his number. It's been over a week since that first voicemail with no call back. I've waited long enough. The first ring sounds loud through the speakers before his voice fills the car.

"Hey, one second."

Typical Julian. As if I still call him all the time. As if we're still connected enough for him to put me on hold.

"Julian."

"Yes, sorry." He sounds closer and clearer. "I'm here."

"Where have you been?" I ask, letting all the petulance show. "I called you over a week ago."

"Oh, I only got your voicemail yesterday. I went to back-to-back shows, and my phone did that thing where it doesn't tell me I have a voicemail until I reboot. And you know I never reboot."

"You're back in town now?" I'm already up here. It's easy enough to swing across town and tell him in person.

"Not yet. I extended the trip into a mini vacation." The words are normal, but the way he says them isn't. There are too many spaces between the thoughts. He's being evasive.

I will not consider who he's on this mini vacation with right now. This is my moment. And I will not let him ruin it.

I switch the call to my handset and prepare myself. Telling him over the phone isn't ideal, but I'm running out of options. He needs to know because I want to tell other people and start living with this new truth. And because, despite everything, I want to share this moment with him.

"I'm pregnant."

"What?" He sounds breathless.

"I'm pregnant," I say again. "Due in February with our daughter."

"Our... *daughter*?" His voice cracks, and I hear him attempt to measure his breathing. "How far along?"

"Ten weeks," I say, my voice barely a whisper. We both know the frailty of the situation and how quickly it can turn. "The heartbeat was strong on the ultrasound, Jules."

I wonder for a brief moment if he'll be angry that I went to the doctor without him, but the hiccup that sounds from the other end of the line is anything but angry.

"You got to see her?" His voice is high and phlegmy, a sound that can't be faked. Julian is crying.

"Yes, I did."

"I can be home tomorrow. Can I see you tomorrow?"

I don't know if I want to see Julian. There are decisions to make and things to consider. There are hard questions that need to be asked. I'm not sure I'm ready for any of it. What I do know is I want it on my own terms and on my own turf. Home court advantage is no joke.

"How about Monday?" I ask. "Can you get away? I'll send you my new address."

"Yes, of course," he says quickly. "Whatever you need, babe."

What I need is a hard dose of the truth. I need to figure out what the hell I want from my life. Despite banishing all thoughts of who Julian might be on vacation with, I know it's time to ask the question.

"I need to ask you a question." I shift my phone to the other ear.

"Shoot."

"Are you on your mini vacation alone?"

The silence on the other end of the line is deafening. I wonder if he'll try to lie, but I don't think he will. He has nothing to gain by lying.

Finally, he clears his throat. "No, I'm not. But that doesn't matter now. We're having a baby. You and me. After everything that happened this summer."

"Yes, but—"

"I love you, babe. That's all that matters. I'll see you Monday." He hangs up before I can even think to respond—to reject or accept his love.

My heart trills at the words, but the rest of me has its doubts. The words were familiar and comfortable and safe but also outdated. It's startling how quickly he fell back in with me while another woman waited. I've never seen his switch flip before. Never understood what drove him back to me whenever he left. But it was instantaneous. From *I'm with another woman* to *You're all that matters* in a blink. His fealty is less than reassuring, and despite what he probably intended, it undermines any faith I have in his words. What kind of person so easily leaves the woman in his bed? The woman who I have no doubt is Sheila. At a different time in my life, I might have found his antics romantic. A sign of how deeply he loves me. Proof that this other woman means nothing. But I'm not that person anymore, and it's a harsh truth that Julian doesn't understand that.

Chapter 47
Zoey

"Don't you have something better to do with your Saturday than hang out at home?" Liz asks teasingly. "It's summer. Go to the beach."

I look up at my sister, my eyes unfocused after spending most of the day buried in a book. Liz showed up an hour ago to spring the pregnancy news on Dad, but he is, per usual, running late. Fortunately, after cohabitating for the summer, I don't feel the need to entertain her, though she's been pestering me since she arrived.

"It's raining," I say, motioning to the balcony doors.

"Exactly." She grins. "Less tourists."

"No. Whiny tourists with nowhere to go."

She rolls her eyes. "Okay, but you have a boyfriend, don't you? A best friend?"

I glance over at her. "Are you trying to get rid of me?"

"No." She laughs. "I'm surprised you've sat here for the last hour reading a book on one of your last weekends at home."

"Well"—I put the bookmark back in place—"Becca is with *her* boyfriend. And my boyfriend is prepping for freshman orientation with a bunch of my old teachers. So I'm here, reading my book in peace and quiet... Oh, wait."

Liz laughs again. She does it easily now. "So Max is your *boyfriend*?"

How did I fall for that? Oh my god. "You baited me!"

"Yup."

I palm my face, hoping to hide the blush that's spreading. I have a boyfriend. After the summer I had, I have an easy relationship with my sister and a boyfriend. Who would've guessed?

I hold up my phone open to a photo of me and Max canoodling on his couch last night with several hashtags—#adventuresofmaxandzee, #instaofficial, #mustbeserious, #boyfriend. "It's Instagram official and everything."

"And Dad approves?"

"Yes. He gave me a hug and said it made sense for me. Dating an older guy, that is."

"Well, I'm happy for you, sis." Liz's hand hovers over her belly. There's barely a change there, but she still does it all the time. I wonder if she notices. "As is your niece."

I whip my head up. "What? Oh my god! A girl? When did you find out? How did you sit here for an hour and not tell me this?"

Liz crosses the room and sits next to me on the couch. "Breathe, Auntie Zoey."

"I'm going to be an aunt." I've known I was going to be an aunt for two weeks now, saw that little blur on the screen and heard its heartbeat. But the reality didn't set in until I heard the word "niece." It gave that cherry complete definition. Aunt. Niece. Besties.

Liz puts a hand on my arm and looks at me with wet eyes. "And, if you accept, a godmother."

Tears spring to my own eyes, and I'm not even embarrassed. Liz has seen me ugly cry all summer. Happy tears are more than welcome. "Yes, of course. Oh my god."

"You said that already."

I stand, dabbing at my eyes, and walk into the kitchen. I rummage through the drawer by the fridge, where we keep scores of takeout menus.

"What are you doing?" My sister's voice comes from the living room and still holds all the amusement it did moments ago.

No, not Chinese. Not shore takeout. Finally, I pull out the menu I was looking for and hold it up for Liz to see. "We're celebrating. We always order Martino's when we're celebrating. What do you want on your pizza?"

The front door opens, and Dad walks in spouting apologies before he even drops his briefcase. He puts his umbrella in the rack and shucks off his jacket before looking up.

"Dad," I say, the landline to my ear, "mushrooms and pepperoni?"

He squints at the menu. "Yes, perfect. What are we celebrating?"

I offer to pick up the pizza to give Liz a chance to tell Dad he's going to be a grandpa on her own. *Grandpa. Wow.* Dad is older than most of my friends' parents, but he doesn't seem old enough to be a grandpa. That's going to take some getting used to.

Martino's is crowded, as I knew it would be. A rainy Saturday night is the perfect excuse to order pizza, and college students, even in Ardena, are notoriously poor. You can't beat the Martino's three-dollar slice and fountain drink with a student ID. Three dollars. It's impossible to get a slice for that little anywhere else in town. I catch the owner's eye so he knows I'm here, and he holds up two hands—ten minutes. Not too bad, I guess. I grab a Snapple out of the fridge and sit down at one of the tables closest to the door and completely out of the way. Not too many people are sitting and eating, but it's still early. I pull my book out of my purse.

"Zo?"

No freakin' way. Of all the people at Martino's on this Saturday night, it has to be Andrew. And he feels it necessary to say hi to me after what he pulled at Mack's. I almost don't look up. I almost immerse myself in the fictional world I've been in all day. But a morbid curiosity gets the better of me.

"Hi, Andrew," I say, holding my spot with a finger.

"Can I talk to you?"

I glance past him, but the line hasn't moved in the two minutes since I arrived. "If you must."

"I guess I deserve that." He sits down opposite me and fiddles with his baseball hat. He's nervous. Well, that's something at least.

"What do you want?"

"Are you going back to Bellewood?"

I stare at him. That can't seriously be his question. But his expression is grave and leaves no doubt that he wants an answer. "Yes, obviously."

"That's what I thought." He takes his hat off and rounds the rim between his hands. "I'm transferring."

"What?"

This has to be a hunger hallucination. Andrew can't be sitting in front of me telling me he's leaving Bellewood days before we're supposed to go back. It isn't the same haven for him that it is for me, but he was happy there. Happy enough.

"I applied to Drexel earlier this summer, after everything that happened in Wildwood, actually. And I got in. They called me today to tell me they found a dorm room for me."

"Wow." Literally no other words will come out of my mouth. The *guy* is leaving. The guy never leaves. "Congratulations."

He looks up at me for only a second before his eyes refocus on his hat. "Maybe I'll be better there."

"Better?"

"A better person. Or at least better than whoever I became these last few months."

This is where, in a normal conversation, I would assure him. But I can't. Andrew might not be a bad person at heart, but to me recently, he can definitely be better. Maybe away from me and Claire and all of it, he can change. Or maybe this is who he really is. I hope that the latter is not the case.

"Maybe" is all I say.

"I'm sorry, Zo, about all of it."

"It's fine." Which is true and not true. "I mean, it's not fine, but I'm choosing to be over it."

He meets my eyes now. "I'm not over it."

For the first time since he sat down, I really look at him. He's tired and drawn, a shell of himself.

"Does Claire know that?" I ask because I can't let myself empathize with him right now.

"Yeah, pretty sure my behavior at Mack's gave me away." He shrugs. "We didn't even make it to Wildwood."

I try not to feel smug. I want to be above such a feeling, but it's hard. A part of me relishes this information. After he purposely dismantled our relationship, he's not with Claire because he can't get over me. The rest of me is saddened by all of it. Any way you look at it, the situation sucks for every person involved. There are no winners here.

"Reid!" the cashier at the front of the shop calls above the din. The crowd cleared as we talked, and my pies sit waiting for me.

I stand and drop my hand lightly onto Andrew's shoulder for the smallest of moments. A touch like this would've sent a jolt of love through me any other time, but now there's only melancholy and a sense of what might've been. "Good luck at Drexel."

Chapter 48
Cecilia

I've never been a wallower. Not really. But it's a Reid trait. I wonder if it's from my father, because my mother turned to work and remodeling, with the exception of those weekends in my dorm. But Liz? It's like all the melodramatic genes were saved for her. She cried for days after each breakup with Julian. She came home from prom, mascara running down her cheeks, her hair askew, barely breathing between sobs. Jane brought her home. And then built her back up, which I can't even comprehend. To be connected so wholly to twins. And Zoey went crazy this summer trying to out-sex her former best friend for a guy I'm not entirely sure she ever actually wanted back.

There have been very few who made me want to wallow, however. It's not my nature. But Evie makes me want to curl up and cry and eat ice cream and do all those ridiculous things. I gave in. Once. Then I cleaned and bought a new wardrobe and organized incessantly. Like mother, like daughter. I rid every room in my apartment of any vestige of Evie, down to the hot sauce brand she likes. Now, whatever is left sits in a box in my hall closet. None of it seems overly important. It's the stuff I would sacrifice to never see my ex again—a sweater, pajama pants, a book or three. But I can't bring myself to throw it away. Maybe I'll drop it off one morning. Leave it on the doorstep like she left my key in that bowl.

I sit at the kitchen table with a glass of wine and open the Zoom meeting on my laptop. While I wouldn't say I've fully forgiven either my mom or Liz, I couldn't stay angry after the baby bomb. That doesn't mean I know how to get past what happened. In each conversation, it feels like there's a Zoey-shaped barrier between us. But Liz is trying, so when she suggested these *family dinners* via Zoom, I agreed, even though I have total Zoom fatigue.

"How clean is your apartment?" Liz asks by way of greeting.

"Quite," I say with chagrin.

She frowns. "I'm sorry, Cee."

"I'm fine," I say. "Stand up. I want to see the bump."

The smallest of bumps is visible under Liz's shirt, and the sight is so unexpected, a tremor runs through me. Her normal preppy look has been replaced by jeans and a summer sweater. She looks happy. Motherly. I wish our détente on the Zoey situation could be a full-on treaty, but we've been waging the war for seventeen years, and there's no resolution. Liz will not step away from Zoey and our dad, and I refuse to capitulate.

My mom comes into view and waves with the wine she's holding. A whole bottle, for herself.

"Thirsty, Mom?" I ask.

"I sold a one-point-eight-million-dollar home today. I deserve some wine."

"Oh my god!" Liz says, pulling Mom into a hug. It's endearing to watch, but I also wish I could hug her too. That my toast didn't have to be to a screen.

"Congratulations," I say.

"Thank you, girls. Now"—she opens up the takeout bag—"I brought the naan for us. Do you have yours?"

Naan fixes everything. That's been a Reid women mantra since my first heartbreak back in high school. I hold up my slice. "Naan is accounted for."

Liz's eyes meet mine. "How are you? And do not say fine."

"I'm coping." I pick at my masala. "I miss her."

It's the most I've said on the topic of Evie to anyone. Even to myself, if I'm honest. I don't want to look at it too closely because there's too much to unpack. Too much that squarely falls on me. I do miss her. But Evie was clear. There wasn't a test hidden in her breakup monologue. She didn't simply need to know I loved her and needed her. I hurt her.

"Do you think—"

I shake my head at Liz's inquiry. "She wanted to end it for a while. It's like when you play hard to get because once they have you, they don't want you? Well, she finally had me, and she didn't like me."

"She said that?" Liz asks quietly.

I shrug. "Essentially."

"What a bitch."

I shoot a look at my mother, who is shaking her head with pursed lips. "Mom."

"What?" She takes a sip of her wine. "There's a time for lying, and that was it. She could've been nicer about it."

"Evie would never lie about something like that. She would think that it would stunt my emotional growth." Even saying those words makes my heart hurt. I miss her psychologist voice and her prying and her digging.

Anna snorts. "I think your growth was stunted long ago."

"Mom!" both Liz and I exclaim at the same time.

"Oh, eat your naan. You'll feel better."

I take an exaggerated bite, and yes, I do feel better. Carbs are magical. "How are you feeling, Liz? Still sick?"

She pauses with a forkful of rice halfway to her mouth. "Clearly not if I'm eating Indian food in the middle of the day. The doctor said it's normal this close to the end of the first trimester to start to feel better. Stop changing the subject."

I roll my eyes. "There's nothing to talk about. We broke up. End of story."

"But you love her." The rest of her thought—*and you never love anyone*—hangs in the silence between us.

It's such a Liz thing to say. Even after everything that happened with Julian, she's still a hopeless romantic. If you love someone, let them go. If they come back, they're yours. How many times has she spouted those lines? And Julian always comes back. Even now.

But Evie isn't coming back.

"And Evie thinks I can't truly love someone until I forgive Dad. We're at an impasse." I clamp my mouth shut. I didn't want to get into the details, but Liz's prodding makes me want to prove that I'm right. That my relationship is forever and always doomed.

"You know, honey," Mom hedges. She rarely hedges, but then I've never blown up at my entire family before and then left the state. "Forgiveness doesn't make you weak."

My sister nods encouragingly. "It doesn't mean you have to suddenly have Sunday dinners with Dad."

"It might make you feel lighter." Mom looks down at her hands, her left thumb going to her ring finger unconsciously. It's been one of her tells for years. "Carrying all that weight around, it's too much for anyone."

I turn my attention to my sister, annoyed at this tag-team effort that's seventeen years too late. "Are you going to forgive Julian?"

"I forgave Julian a long time ago, Cee," she says. "That's sort of the point."

"Will you take him back?" *Again* goes unsaid but it's clear we all heard it.

At this point, I honestly don't even know what makes more sense or what I want her to do or even what she will do. Liz and Julian are Liz and Julian. They do things like this, and somehow it works out in the end. And not in an icky way where you wish they would get a divorce, but in a fully committed, sickeningly sweet way that makes you believe in love. Now there's the baby. But a baby is no reason to stay in a failing marriage.

"I don't know," she says. Her hand drops from view, and I know she has it pressed to her bump. "I don't think I'll know until, well, until I know. We haven't seen each other since before... and he was with someone when I called."

I shift in my seat, pulling my leg up under me. I wonder if Liz's "before" is Spencer or the baby or Julian's cheating. But all I say is "Someone?"

"Sheila. Definitely Sheila. But I can't be mad at him for that, can I? I mean, I slept with Spencer and had no intention of..." She pauses and chews at her bottom lip, her eyes going from me to Mom and back. "How did you know, Mom?"

Our mother looks over at her, surprise etched into her features. "About your father?"

"Yeah," Liz says, taking a sip of water. "The other night you said you *had* to divorce him."

Mom plays with the food on her plate, her eyes unfocused. "I might have been able to forgive him the affair, but I couldn't raise the child that came out of it. And he was always going to keep her. I mean, that woman gave him no choice, but even if she had, your father would've used every legal connection he had to get custody of Zoey. I couldn't look at him without pain. There was no hope or love mixed in with it.

"One day, he walked into the house after work, and I remember I was cooking spaghetti and meatballs in bulk for one of your team dinners, and he came into the kitchen, and our eyes met, and something clicked. I knew our marriage was over. The next morning, I asked him for a divorce." She sighs and finally looks up at the both of us. "All that is to say, when you see Julian tomorrow, I suspect that you'll know the way forward."

Liz nods and picks up another piece of naan.

"Either way, we all have your back—me, Mom, Zoey, and Dad."

The names are awkward in my mouth, but I try because she's my sister, and she needs to know that she isn't alone in this. Her village will include all of us, no matter what.

"I know." Liz bites her lip and looks at me with wide, guileless eyes. I'm not going to like whatever she says next. "Speaking of Dad and Zoey, I'm, uh, having dinner with them next week. Meeting Zoey's new beau for the first time and Dad's girlfriend. Any chance you might feel like coming back to New Jersey for a few days?"

"I highly doubt Zoey wants me intruding on her last days with all of you," I say sharply. How could she after all I said? Plus, there is no way I'm going to that dinner. I can't put on a show like Patrick Reid has three loving daughters for his girlfriend. I can't act like I didn't say mean things about him and Zoey, basically to their faces, or that my resentment didn't end the one relationship I had in over a decade that mattered. I can't pretend. It's too much to ask.

"That's not an answer," Liz prods.

Why can't my sister ever leave well enough alone? "I can't keep flying across the country every few weeks, Liz."

"Oh, come on. I'll pay for your ticket."

"Liz, no, I can't."

"Why?"

It's the question I've been asking myself since Evie broke up with me. Why can't I move past it all? Everyone else has. But how do you brush away all those years of pain and hurt? How do you sit down to dinner with the physical embodiment of the worst moment of your life? When any innocence you had left vanished forever? The answer is simple. You do. People do it every day. Zoey talks to her mom. My mom helped my dad. But I don't know how to get there. How to even want that.

I was happy this summer with Evie. Happy going all in. It was exhilarating and terrifying. I felt walls coming down. But that's all gone now, and I'm vulnerable and unprotected, exactly what I spent all these years avoiding.

Liz grimaces at my lack of a response but acquiesces. "Think about it, okay?"

I imagine that I'll be doing little else for the next three days and much longer than that. The only wall I have left is my stronghold. If I let it down, I'll be defenseless. If I let it down, who will I even be?

Chapter 49

Liz

"You can't push her like that, honey," my mother says. Her tone holds little chastisement, but I still feel it across the line. "You know how your sister is."

I shift the phone to my other ear. "Stubborn as a mule?"

I'm reorganizing the stack of books and magazines on the coffee table for the third time this morning. Coffee-table books were never my thing, but this table begged for one. The copy of *Humans of New York* my mom gave me will have to suffice.

"You can't undo seventeen years of anger with one dinner," Mom continues, her tone even. She never takes sides. Somehow, she always toes the line. "Or even one summer."

I sigh, a bit dramatically, because I can and because Cecilia. I pick up the latest edition of *Talented* that Zoey left behind. "But she doesn't even try, Mom."

"She is trying. She never would've included your father and sister in a conversation about family before."

True. But I can't see a future where we can all come together without awkward silences and death stares, where I don't have to watch my words in order not to offend my older sister or hurt my younger one. "Is it wrong that I don't want my daughter growing up with this needless drama? You and Dad are friends, Mom! Finding that out, it's like this whole new world opened up before me, and it seems infinitely easier."

My mom sighs. "I am sorry I never told you. It seemed, well, I didn't want to confuse your feelings at first, and then there never seemed a right time, and then when she was old enough, Zoey didn't want you to like her because I did. She wanted your relationship to be organic sisterhood. I did try to show you the relationship, but perhaps you thought I was being polite."

She pauses, and I can imagine her sitting at the breakfast nook, sipping a late-morning coffee, wringing her hands as she tries to find the right words that won't betray either of her daughters.

"It's not wrong to wish away the drama, Liz, but she's allowed her feelings too."

Toe, meet line. "I know. Anyway, I have to go, Mom. Jules will be here in a few minutes."

"Right. Good luck, honey."

I'm not sure luck is what I need, but I'll take it. As soon as the call disconnects, my phone buzzes. I swear if Julian is running late, I'll kill him. But it's not Julian. No, the name on the screen sends a jolt of longing through me. Spencer. We haven't spoken since that last time at Barnes & Noble. He's respectful like that. I asked for space, and he gave it. I click to open the text. *Hope the morning sickness has passed.* Another one pops up. *I miss you.* And then a third. *I needed to say it.*

Today, of all days. There's no rhyme or reason to it. It's a random Monday, but he's thinking about me. I press my eyes shut as pressure builds in my head. How do I answer? The truth? I miss him. I yearn for him. I dream about him. Silence? Ignorance? My fingers hover over the keys. I can't text Spencer while Julian is on his way here. It's unfair to both of them. I pocket my phone. Silence will have to do for now.

The doorbell rings, and I jump at the sound. I sit for an extra moment, composing myself, praying that when I see him I'll have my answer. Both choices are a risk. Going back to him doesn't fix our marriage. It doesn't erase Sheila or Spencer or the new knowledge we have about the holes in our picture-perfect story. Leaving him presents a hard road. Being a single mom never crossed my mind, and I can't imagine it's remotely easy. Even with family and a co-parent, those nights where the baby doesn't sleep will be long and lonely.

I cross the short space to the door and count to five. It'll be fine. Either way. My heart will know the way. It always has before. I open the door, and he's there. I blink, but he looks the same as ever in a polo shirt, khaki shorts, and boat shoes. His hair is slightly too long, but his expression is bright and his smile big. Did this summer not happen to him?

"Babe!" He pulls me into a hug before I can stop him.

His scent surrounds me, and my body relaxes into the familiar and the known. We fit. We've always fit. I hold on to him, afraid to let go. Afraid to look into his eyes and know a different truth. Because now that he's standing in front of me, I'm not ready. I'm not sure I will ever be ready for this moment.

He pulls back, and his blue eyes lock on mine. He smiles again, and then his lips are on mine. I'm too shocked to pull away. My lips part, and the tiniest flare of something goes through me. This kiss is not quick or congratulatory. It's wanting and longing and territorial. I let him deepen the kiss, and I can't lie. I feel it. His tongue dances with mine, and his fingers tangle in my hair, and he does all the things I like, but the kindling doesn't catch. My desire washes away, and another kiss that almost always tastes like coffee comes to mind. I picture Spencer's strong hands soft on my body, and I can't banish them. Julian is kissing me, but I'm with Spencer.

I pull back too quickly, putting my hands out between us to ward off any further attempts at kissing. "Jules."

"Sorry." He at least has the gumption to look ashamed. "It's just... We're having a baby, and I've missed you."

I swallow the fact that he's come from vacation with another woman. Julian only sees the story he wants to see, and for him, it doesn't matter that he was probably dick deep in someone else a few days ago because he's here now, and all is right in his world. *How did I ever mistake this obliviousness for romance?*

He reaches for my hand, and it feels heavy in mine, as if we're no longer holding each other up, but he's weighing me down.

"This summer has been the worst, Liz. I'm glad it's over."

Something unfurls inside me. A weight drops, and the fogs clears. My heart aches and soars in equal parts. And between one blink and the next, I know.

"I want a divorce."

Julian's jaw goes slack, and he steps away from me. My words blindsided him, though they shouldn't have. Maybe if there wasn't a baby or if he didn't build this fake rom-com in his head where that fact magically put us back together or if he spent a moment of this summer considering that I might not come home, he would've been at least partially prepared for those four words. But that's not Julian.

"But we're having a baby," he says pointedly.

I press my hands to my stomach. "We don't have to be married to have a baby together."

His expression goes from confused to annoyed in an instant. His eyes darken, and lines crinkle his forehead. "I won't let you keep this baby from me."

"That's not what I want," I say calmly. "This is our baby. We can co-parent or something. But we... I can't do this anymore."

"Do what?" he asks, his voice rising. "Be married to me? Love me?"

"You don't want to be married to me, Jules." I consider taking a step toward him, but his expression is hard. Instead, I walk into the living room and sit in the armchair. Julian follows but doesn't sit. He stands behind the couch. In a minute, he'll be pacing. "You think you do. You always have, and you always come back. But you also always leave."

"And you never let me forget it."

Is that true? I've spent the last five years since the wedding purposely not making him feel that way. The ring sealed the deal and the drama of our past with it. But maybe I haven't done as good a job as I thought.

"You just came from vacation with another woman," I say, annoyance tinging my words. "Do you honestly want me to believe you haven't been fucking Sheila this whole time?"

He stiffens at the accusation but doesn't deny it. He doesn't even try. "As if you didn't sleep with anyone else this summer."

I wonder for a second how he knows. I kept Spencer as close to the vest as possible without making him feel like a secret, and I didn't tell anyone we had sex except Zoey. And yet, Julian is looking at me smugly, as if he's certain.

"You weren't exactly subtle about it either," he says. "My friends saw you down the shore all over another guy."

Sorry is about to come out of my mouth, but I swallow it down. I have nothing to be sorry for. "And did you tell them we were separated because you decided to have an emotional affair?"

"Seriously?" he asks, his eyes flaring.

"You always think there's something better out there. Better than me—your wife, your muse." My voice cracks toward the end because it's true. Julian is always searching for something, and he always will be. "I won't spend my life picking up the pieces and making excuses and wondering who the next Sheila will be. I deserve more than half your heart."

His expression changes to one of pensiveness. He crosses his arms, not liking whatever answer he's come up with in his mind. "Is this about *him*?"

An image of Spencer splayed out on a beach towel passes through my mind. I could love him, but this isn't about him. "No, this is about our daughter. I want you to be a part of her life, Jules. I want us to find a way to be friends and raise her together, but..."

"But what?"

I stand and fix him with a stare so intense he straightens from leaning on the back of the couch. "But if you hurt her by disappearing like you've done to me our entire relationship, that's it. No second chances."

"I would never do that to our daughter."

Maybe he won't. Probably he will.

"We'll see." I walk into the kitchen without looking back at him. The sonogram photos are held to the fridge with a Cape May magnet. I pull the last two off—my least favorite, if I'm being honest—and hand them to Julian. "Take these. My next appointment is in two weeks. It's an important one. Will you come with me?"

He blinks back tears, and his hands tremble against the grainy images. "Yes, of course." He looks up at me, his face pale, his eyes glassy. "Did you tell Jane?"

I shake my head. "I thought you would want to do that."

"Can we tell her together?" His face has settled into resignation, and tears slide down his cheeks. Reality has finally reached Julian. "The good and the bad?"

"Yes, we can."

He wipes away the tears. "How do I do this without you?"

I touch his face, the way I have a million times before. It has never felt so much like a goodbye. "You'll figure it out, Jules. And I think you'll be happier for it."

Chapter 50
Cecilia

This seemed like a better idea when I was back at my house. Standing outside Evie's front door now, I want to vomit. I shift the box in my arms, glancing down at the collection of items I found scattered across my house. Each one breaks my heart. This sad collection of insignificant things is the only proof that we ever existed. That and the hole in my chest I don't know how to patch. Evie's words cracked me open with their honesty, and Liz and my mom's intervention only broadened the fissure. Forgiveness doesn't make me weak. Neither does apologizing.

I knock, hoping she's home and equally praying she's out or has company or sends me away. I would send me away. There's a shuffling behind the door, and then Evie stands there. She's wearing cheerleading shorts and a ribbed tank top. Her skin shines with a fresh tan, and her hair flows in auburn curls down her back. And that smile. I'm not sure I've ever seen her smile like that. It fades as soon as she looks up and finds me standing at her door.

She shifts the phone pressed to her ear. "Layla, I'll call you back."

"Hi," I say after she hangs up. She hasn't invited me in or said anything. Her eyes bore into me. Her expression isn't angry or sad or expectant. It's indifferent. And that is worse. How can she be indifferent to me already?

"What are you doing here?" she asks.

I hold the box out. "I thought you might want your stuff back."

She takes the box, her eyes skimming the contents. After a moment, during which I literally want to die, she pulls the door open and steps back. "Thanks. I missed these slippers."

"I figured." We stand in the vestibule. It's clear she's not going to invite me all the way in, only enough to be polite. Still, I'm grateful. "How are you?"

She grimaces and holds up a hand. "Let's not do this, Cee."

My name in her mouth is like an uppercut. I step back and take a big breath. Her scent invades my nostrils, attacking the gaping wound in my chest. I'm too raw for this, but it's now or never. I can tell that by Evie's rigid posture if not by her words alone.

"I have something to say. Then I'll go."

She nods and drops the box at her feet. "As long as it's not a speech about why we should get back together."

I shake my head. "I think you made yourself clear on that matter."

She almost smiles but pulls it back and crosses her arms. "Okay, then."

"You were right," I say. "About everything. What I did to Liz and Zoey was wrong, and how I treated you was unforgivable. I... I forgot what it was like to really be with someone. To be open and trusting. To depend on another person and have them need you back. You were this amazing thing in my life, Evie, and I didn't appreciate you. I'm not sure I knew how. And that's on me."

She steps forward, her gaze softening at my words, and reaches out a hand.

I take the olive branch, linking our fingers. "I'm so sorry. I know that doesn't matter now, but I had to say it."

"It matters, Cee," Evie says softly.

I let our hands fall apart and look up into her eyes, which are wet with tears. "Thank you for forcing me to face my choices. Because all of this, the last seventeen years of my life, has been a choice. And this summer made me see that maybe I'm choosing wrong. I have a lot to work through, and I'm honestly not sure where to start, but I'm going to do it." I pull in a breath and step back toward the door. "I wish it hadn't cost me you."

She doesn't say anything as I pull open her door and leave. She doesn't follow me into the hallway and jump into my arms. That's not my story. It's never been my story. But I hold my head high as tears streak my cheeks. My heart is heavy with this loss. I'm going to feel it for a long time. But my soul... My soul is a little bit lighter.

Chapter 51
Zoey

I adjust Max's tie for the third time. Dad and his girlfriend, Robin, are running late. Professors, seriously.

Max swats at my hand. "It's straight, Zee. Geez. Why are you so nervous?"

"You're meeting my dad."

"Yes," he says, twirling a piece of my hair around his finger. "Not a big deal."

When Dad suggested that I bring Max to this dinner to get all the introductions out of the way at once, it seemed a reasonable idea. He wants eyes on Max before I leave, considering he won't be around to chaperone. As if I didn't spend the last year practically living with Andrew. But get an older boyfriend with his own apartment, and suddenly there are rules.

I pull Max in by his tie and kiss him. My entire body jumps to life. The decision to wait to sleep together was a smart one. I know that in my mind, but with him standing there all dressed up, I wish we were back at his apartment, with me undoing his shirt button by button while his hand slowly unzips my dress and his fingers skim down my spine, making my toes curl.

"Whoa." Max stares at me in amusement. "What dirty thing was I just doing in your head?"

I blink away the fantasy. He's too good at reading me much too soon. Maybe it doesn't have to be a fantasy. We have all night and all weekend and so much more time. He smiles down at me, his fingers again playing with an errant curl. A pulse runs through me, and my heart speeds up. I lean into his hand, watching him watch me.

"I love you," I say and mean it. Mean it in a way I didn't think possible after this summer.

The way he kisses me then is far too indecent for this restaurant, especially while we're waiting for my dad, but I don't care. I love Max. I don't know when it happened. Maybe in this instant. That finger on my hair, those eyes reading into my soul. Maybe it was when he said I wasn't a fling or when we spent the whole night making out and watching that stupid show and talking until three in the morning before I passed out on his bed fully clothed. Maybe it was when I woke up in his arms that next morning. The *when* doesn't matter, really, only that we're here.

"Good," he says. "Because I love you too."

I pull him back in by the tie for another round before a too-familiar throat clearing sounds behind me. *Crap.* I turn around quickly, keeping a hand in Max's. "Hey, Dad."

He eyes me and Max warily, but he only holds out his hand. "I'm Patrick, Zoey's father. I hope you're Max."

Max adjusts his tie and takes Dad's hand, a smile breaking through the tension on his face. No big deal. What a liar he is. "Nice to meet you, sir."

I focus on the woman standing next to Dad. She's petite and brunette and beautiful. Behind her glasses, funky square rims in a flaming red, her blue eyes sparkle.

"Zoey," Robin says, breaking the standoff between the men. "It's nice to finally meet you. Your dad talks about you all the time."

I nod. "It's nice to know you exist."

"Shall we?" Dad asks hurriedly and takes Robin's hand. "I'm sure we're already dreadfully late for our reservation."

Robin blushes. "I know, I know. But I discovered..." She trails off at the amused look on Dad's face. "Right, dinner."

I hold in a laugh, but a huge smile breaks through. They're two peas in a pod.

We're nearly through with dinner when Dad turns to me with a tentative smile. "We have some news."

My eyes narrow. *News?* There's no engagement ring on her finger. "Okay?"

He takes Robin's hand, and I in turn take Max's, my pulse kicking up a beat. "Robin's going to be moving in with us."

I blink, the news sinking in. Dad has a girlfriend, and she's moving in. *Whoa.* I always wondered when that might happen until I concluded it never would. But here we are. And Robin is lovely. She's vibrant and intelligent and everything Dad needs. Dad's glowing, and for the first time, perhaps ever, I see him as the world sees him, as another person and not only a dad. He's so in love. The glint in his eye and the way he says Robin's name—how did I never notice a change?

"Dad," I say, sliding my hand into his, "I'm happy for you."

He squeezes my hand. "You're really okay with someone moving in?"

I shrug. "I've had you to myself for seventeen years. It's time I shared."

"Well, I'm glad you feel that way because it's not only Robin."

Robin has kids, but they are grown and married, if I understand correctly, and there's certainly no room in the townhouse for any of them.

"Oh, stop it, Pat. You're freaking her out," Robin says, and I can only assume I look concerned. "I have two grumpy old cats and a kitten."

"Lenny is going to be so jealous," I say with a grin.

Pets. Real pets.

"I don't know," Dad says. "I think he'll rather enjoy the company and the cat food."

Max and Robin stare at us, completely lost. I laugh out loud, and a few heads turn our way. How do you explain that you named the squirrel that lives on your balcony?

"Lenny is a squirrel." Dad dabs at his eyes with his napkin.

"Who I feed because I'm pet deprived," I say with a grin.

"Well," Robin says, a smile warming her face, "pet deprived you are no more."

Someone to take care of Dad and a kitten. The night has taken a surprising turn.

Across the restaurant, I see Liz making her way toward us. She looks fabulous in a wrap dress that hides her growing bump. We decided to have Liz come for dessert only, so that I could meet Robin before the whole family descended. And after Dad's news, I understand why. I catch my sister's eyes as she sits down, asking an unspoken question—Cecilia? She gives a slight shake of her head before taking a sip of water.

It's not unexpected, and I refuse to let it ruin this night. Good things are happening. It's Cecilia's loss. It's always been Cecilia's loss.

"How are you feeling these days?" Max asks Liz, handing her the dessert menu.

"Kind of like a hobbit."

"Swollen feet?" Robin asks.

"Eating seven times a day," Liz says with a laugh. "Breakfast, second breakfast, elevenses..." She trails off, and her eyes focus on the door, her mouth slightly ajar in shock.

I follow her gaze, as does the rest of the table. Across from me, Dad stiffens, and Robin reaches for his hand. Max takes mine, and Liz pulls me into her. Standing by the hostess stand is Cecilia. She notices us in the crowded restaurant and offers a tight smile before making her way over. She stops at the head of the table. Tears well behind my eyes, and I let them come.

"Is there room for one more?" Cecilia asks, her voice tentative and shy and a little scared.

"Of course, dear." Dad stands and offers her his chair before flagging down the waitress. I know he wants to hug her, but he won't. Small steps. Against the wood, his hands shake. "Did you just get in?"

Cecilia sits down and takes a sip of the water the waitress swiftly brought over when she saw a new person arrive at our table. "No, I arrived yesterday. I would've been here sooner, but I got caught up making an offer on a cute little condo over in Asbury."

"You're moving back?" Liz asks incredulously.

"Yes." Cecilia fixes her gaze on me. "I thought it was about time I spent some quality time with my sisters."

Epilogue
Zoey
Late February

I grab for my phone, wanting nothing more than to stop the incessant buzzing, but quickly pick up when I see the caller ID. "Jules?"

"It's time," Julian says, his voice harried.

"What?" I roll over, my arm slamming into Max, who is still passed out. "Now?"

"Well, last night technically. Her water broke around two. But the doctor says it's almost time to try pushing again."

Pushing *again*. Which means there's already been pushing and no one called me. "You are only calling me now?"

"It takes forever for these things to happen," Julian says calmly, something he knows because his sister had babies. "And we knew you were in town."

I'm not sure halfway across the state means in town, but then there's only so far away you can be in New Jersey. And it is seven in the morning on a Saturday, so we should be able to make it to Parsippany in about forty minutes. Unless... I jump out of bed and pull back the curtains. No snow. *Thank god.*

Max groans as the light seeps into the room, and then he flops over.

"Can you rally the troops and get your butt over here, godmother?" Julian asks, a smile evident in his tone. I wonder briefly how much coffee he's already had.

"Yes, of course. Tell Liz I love her and to keep that baby in there until I arrive. I have dibs on seeing her first."

"You're going to have to fight the grandparents on that one," he says, laughing. "But I will tell her your feelings on the matter."

"Or"—I giggle because I must still be half asleep or completely wired—"maybe don't unless you want to get smacked."

Max sits up behind me and leans his head on my shoulder. "Is it go time?"

I kiss his cheek. "It's go time."

Less than an hour later—Max gunned it as soon as we hit the highway—we're sitting in the hospital waiting room. No one else has arrived yet. I close my eyes, calming down for the first time since my phone rang.

"Hey, guys."

I turn at the familiar voice. "Hey, Spence." I stand and give him a half hug around the coffees he holds. "Guess there's no news if you're getting coffee?"

"The epidural slowed labor, but they gave her some meds to start it again. We're going to try in a few more minutes. They'll help her, if needed."

That sounds *painful*.

"Well, I better get this to Julian before he falls asleep again. Liz is going to murder him if that happens."

I laugh. "Yes, I think that would be frowned upon."

"Nothing a woman does during labor is frowned upon," Spencer whispers, leaning in close to me.

It's been an interesting few months, to say the least. Spencer and Liz couldn't quit each other, and a month after they broke up, they were back together. He hasn't left her side since. Spencer and Julian entered into a tense truce. Though things have lightened lately as Liz and Spencer moved into a house a few towns over from Princeton and Julian met a woman—not Sheila—who he seems to be smitten with. Liz and Julian transitioned to soon-to-be co-parents fairly easily. They focus on Baby Paige and what will be best for her instead of the frustrations that come with separating their lives.

Anna arrives next with Cecilia in tow, followed by Dad and Robin then Jane and Julian's parents. A few minutes later, Spencer's ex-wife enters, Ryan clinging to her hand.

I walk over to them and extend my hand to Ryan, who has become quite the fixture in my life. "Hey, buddy. Want to come sit with me and Max?"

"Max is here?" he asks excitedly.

"You bet I am, little man," Max says, coming up behind me. Without even a wave to his mom, Ryan follows Max to a row of chairs against the wall, talking a mile a minute.

"Hey, sis," Cecilia says before pulling me into a hug. She's dressed for work, and I wonder if she and Anna came together from their new office for Reid Real Estate.

Things between Cecilia and me aren't perfect, but she is trying, and that's enough for now. We talk most days, even if only a quick text, and she even came to visit me at Bellewood for family weekend with Dad. They took separate cars, but we all shared a meal, and no one screamed or cried. And for the first time ever, we had a Reid Family Christmas. The townhouse had never been so full. It was a magical night, made even more magical when Dad asked Robin to marry him.

"How's the remodel going?" I ask. "Finally settle on a backsplash design?"

Cecilia grins. "Yes, but now I have to pick out flooring."

I laugh. After a few months in her standard condo, Cecilia decided to remodel—well, nearly everything—but started with the kitchen. Except she's loath to make any decision without considering ten options first. "It'll all be done in a few years then?"

She starts to retort but stops when hurried footsteps sound behind us. I glance back to find Julian. Excitement bubbles inside me as I ask, "She's here?"

Everyone stops talking at my excited words. Julian nods and smiles at the crowd. "She's here—Paige Anna Madden, seven pounds, six ounces, twenty inches. Liz is asking for you, Zoey. Cee, you too."

We follow Julian through the ward doors and down the hall, stopping outside room 612.

"You ready, Aunties?"

Liz sits on her bed, sweaty and tired, but radiant. Baby Paige is nestled against her chest. Spencer sits on the edge of the bed, staring lovingly at the both of them. Paige's hand is wrapped around his pointer finger.

"Hi, Mama," I say, sitting down across from Spencer.

Cecilia stands beside me and grabs Liz's free hand. "How are you?"

"We're good. Tired, but good." She shifts the baby so that she's snuggled in her arms. A sweet, perfect scrunched-up bundle of cuteness. "Someone wants to meet her aunts."

I reach out a tentative hand, letting Paige wrap her tiny fingers around my pinky. "Hello, Paige. I'm your Aunt Zoey, and this is your Aunt Cecilia." I reach for Cecilia's hand and squeeze it tight. My world feels whole in a way it hasn't for my whole life, and I let the tears come. Happy tears. Earned tears. Despite everything, we made it here. Together. "We're going to have the most amazing adventures together, baby girl. Just you wait."

Acknowledgments

It's funny to be writing this because for so long I didn't think this book would ever see the light of day. *The First Love Myth* is the book I wrote during the pandemic. This book and these characters went through a lot. So much so that, at times, the thought of revisiting it made me squirm. But I knew the story of the Reid sisters was an important one. And one I wanted to tell. So as my dedication says, thank you to my readers, who gave me the courage to submit this to Red Adept Publishing, and thank you to Lynn McNamee for embracing the novel. I truly enjoy being part of the Red Adept family.

So many people helped with this book over the four years since I first wrote it. A special thanks to beta readers Robin, Elena, Shannon, Janet, and Diane. A big thank you to Erica Lucke Dean, who keeps me honest and listens to all my writing woes at all hours of the day. *The First Love Myth* wouldn't be where it is without my RAP editors, Jessica and Darlene.

I'd like to give a special shout-out to my best friend, Katie. You're the inspiration for all the besties in this book. And finally to my family—Tim, Hailey, and Charlie—thank you for continuing on this journey with me and for being my biggest fans. I couldn't do any of it without your love and support. I love you more.

About the Author

Casey Dembowski loves to write stories that focus on the intricacies of relationships–whether romantic, familial, or platonic. Her novels focus on the inner workings of women and how everything in their lives leads them to exactly where they are, whether they like it or not.

The first story Casey remembers writing was in the second grade, though it wasn't until she turned twelve that she started carrying a battered composition notebook everywhere she went. Since then, there hasn't been a time when she isn't writing.

Casey lives in New Jersey with her family. She has an MFA in Fiction from Adelphi University, and currently works in corporate marketing communications. In her (limited) spare time, she enjoys reading, baking, and watching her favorite television shows on repeat.

Read more at https://caseydembowski.com/.

About the Publisher

Dear Reader,

We hope you enjoyed this book. Please consider leaving a review on your favorite book site.

Visit https://RedAdeptPublishing.com to see our entire catalogue.

Check out our app for short stories, articles, and interviews. You'll also be notified of future releases and special sales.

Made in the USA
Middletown, DE
27 October 2024

62788120R20167